The Serial Killer's Son

Charlotte Stevenson

BLOODHOUND
— BOOKS —

www.bloodhoundbooks.com

Print ISBN: 978-1-916978-06-5

To Allen, Michael, Hannah, and Daniel.
I love you all more than I can possibly say

"If you don't heal what hurt you, you'll bleed on people who didn't cut you."
— Anonymous

Prologue

Before

I roll over in bed and the faint smell of stale urine escapes from under my sleeping bag. I haven't had any accidents for a few weeks, but it still lingers. Father took my bed covers for good after the last time they got wet, even though I'm the one who always washed them. I have a sleeping bag now. It's okay I suppose, I'm still almost warm enough.

I miss my covers every day. My favourite memory of Mummy is her sitting on my bed and softly singing or reading stories. I close my eyes tightly and try to picture her but she's only an outline now, a disjointed shape with no colours. Soon she'll disappear from my head altogether. Like she did in real life.

It's not night-time and I'm not trying to fall asleep. It's the weekend, and I have to stay in my room at the weekends. In lots of ways that's good. It's safe in here but there's nothing to do. I shouldn't complain. I have a bed, and Father says that's all I need. He won't have me turning into a spoilt brat.

I close my eyes again and take myself away to my imaginary room. Father doesn't know about this room, and I don't have to tell him. It lives inside me, and I have decorated it just as I like.

The walls are clean. There is no damp, peeling wallpaper and the walls are painted a beautiful sky blue. Instead of an overflowing bin in the corner, there is a huge wooden toy box. It is teeming with dinosaurs, dolls, cars, and games. The curtains cover the whole window and beside my bed is a proper bookshelf crammed with books. Not just my schoolbooks, but storybooks. Books about dragons and knights or princesses waiting to be rescued. The images blur and begin to distort as heat and pressure build behind my eyes. I let the images of the room disappear and wipe my face on my grimy sleeve.

Weekdays are my favourite. I get to go to school. Father says I have to be normal at school. I'm not sure what he means, but I haven't gotten in trouble with him about it so far.

I flinch as I hear the front door open and close and my father's heavy footsteps bouncing up the stairs. The noise stops suddenly outside my door and an uneasy feeling creeps over me. I suppress a shiver and keep my wobbly legs as still as possible, listening intently. The floorboards creak outside the door, but he doesn't shout through it or come barging in like he usually would. Something is different.

I can't speak first; he doesn't allow that. I think I might throw up. I hear another small squeak as Father shifts his weight. Terror seals my throat as the thought that he may not be alone occurs to me. That can't be it. It's only been three weeks since he hurt that poor lady with the black hair. Usually, it's months. I know I did well last time, he told me so. Dread gnaws at my stomach as I wait powerlessly.

The door scrapes across the threadbare carpet as Father finally opens it and walks into the room. He is dressed for work and has a carrier bag in his hand. The white, plastic handles are scrunched up tightly in his fist. I can't see what's inside. I look from the bag to his face, trying not to flinch.

He runs his empty hand through his hair and strokes his

chin as I watch him curiously. I don't know what the look on his face is. He looks around the room before walking uncertainly to the foot of my bed and placing the bag down gently. His closeness and weird behaviour make the hairs on the back of my neck stand on end. The plastic crackles and the top of the bag opens slightly. I don't dare look at what's inside.

"There." His voice is quiet and croaky as he gestures toward the bag before abruptly turning away and leaving the room. I hear his footsteps hammer down the stairs and the front door slam loudly.

I stare at the bag for a while, hoping it will magically open and reveal its contents. I bounce on my bottom a bit and the battered mattress squeaks beneath me. The bag wobbles but remains stubbornly closed. I sit quietly for a few more minutes, contemplating my next move. I know this is silly. Plus, I have to open it before he gets back. Whatever it is, he wants me to have it. He'll be furious if I leave it there unopened. It's this thought that makes me do it. I slowly get to my knees and lean forwards, resting one hand on the bed and reaching out with the other toward the handles of the bag. I pull one of the handles and wiggle my hand inside to loosen the scrunched-up plastic. My stomach flutters as I peer uncertainly into the top of the bag.

I hadn't formed any options in my mind about what might be in there. But, if I had, it certainly wouldn't be what I am looking at now. I jump up and grab the bottom of the bag, tipping the contents out onto my bed and marvelling in turn at each one. A happiness that I haven't felt in a long time grows inside me and I feel dizzy with excitement.

Father has brought me gifts. Thoughtful gifts. For me.

I pick up the notebook and skim through the pages. The pages are clean and crisp and brand new. To accompany the book, there is a new packet of felt-tip pens and a couple of sketching pencils. I can't wait to use them.

My hands tremble as I reach for the final gift Father has given me. It's a storybook. The gold lettering shimmers against the beautiful blue hardcover. I stroke the letters and read the words aloud.

"*Favourite Fairy Tales.*"

I handle the book with great care. I don't want to bend or crease any of the pages. I flick through the titles of the stories and gorgeous illustrations as tears well in my eyes. I breathe in the comforting smell of the pages. I can't remember a time when I felt this happy. Surely Father must care for me if he's given me these amazing gifts. I am shaking, but not with fear or worry. I want to cry, but not with pain or sadness. Perhaps everything will change. Maybe Father wants to be good and kind now, maybe he won't do any of those terrible, horrible things anymore. Maybe he's had enough of killing people. We could be a proper family.

I snuggle down into my sleeping bag and begin to read. Losing myself in a world of magic, wonder and hope.

Part One

Chapter One

"Sir, I'm afraid I have some bad news." May looks almost afraid standing in the doorway, twisting her fingers nervously.

"Come and sit down, May, please." I point to the other chair at my desk and try to give a welcoming smile. I realise my knees have started to bounce. As I adjust my position, the leather chair beneath me emits a squeak, revealing my nervousness. My hands start to tremble, and I clasp them together tightly and compose myself. May sits but continues to fidget. "May, please, what is it?" I tilt my head and try another smile. I know that irritation is a completely inappropriate reaction to this situation, but that's how I feel. Outwardly, I try to appear caring, curious, and concerned.

She takes a deep breath and looks down at the table.

"Sir, your brother has died." We sit for a moment in silence. Neither of us moves. "I'm so terribly sorry."

I look across at her. My face feels cold, and I instantly feel stiff and unable to move a single muscle. I think I must stay rigid for too long as the expression on her face tells me that she is waiting for me to do something. I notice that May has tears in her eyes, despite having never met Miles. She is watching me inquisitively and I get the overwhelming feeling that I am disappointing her.

"Is someone here?" My body suddenly springs to life and my stomach drops at the thought of having to deal with an actual person turning up unannounced.

She shakes her head, tears still threatening to spill down her cheeks. "No, your brother's father-in-law called. I did what you always tell me to do. I'd already told him you weren't here and offered to take a message before he told me. I felt awful."

She shouldn't feel awful. I couldn't have taken that call. My stomach starts to churn, and I am gripping my hands together so tightly that my fingers feel numb.

"Thank you for letting me know, May. I'm sure that was a difficult call to take. Please make yourself a cup of tea and take some time if you need it." The words come out in a flurry and despite feeling light-headed, I stand and gesture towards the door quickly, before hiding my quaking hands behind my back.

"Sir, are you not...? Can I...?"

I look across at her. She is observing me curiously. My heart is racing, and a sharp pain is escalating in my chest, but I need to say something. I count to ten and breathe deeply, exactly as Dr Pathirana taught me all those years ago. The breathing wins, thankfully.

She is looking down at the table again. I study her reflection on the polished wooden surface.

"I'll be fine, May," I manage. May has worked here for almost a year now and I know that she is kind-hearted. I am doing my best, but I wish she would stop talking and leave. She doesn't do either.

"Sorry, Sir. It's just... I want you to be okay."

I give her an apologetic look and say nothing.

I silence the runaway train of thoughts hurtling around my head. I don't want May to know I feel anxious sometimes, it's important to me that she sees me as together. I tilt my head and look May in the eye. I use every ounce of concentration and strength I have to shift my face to how I want it to look.

"Thank you, May, I think I just need a moment." I worry that my words sound rushed and insincere. But she nods and I see relief spread across her face. My body starts to slow down, and I feel the panic ebbing away. May stands up slowly and smooths her dress unnecessarily. The silence is painful.

"Okay, Mr Barclay. Please let me know if I can help with anything. I mean it. Anything." She averts her eyes and turns to leave.

"May," I call after her. I didn't know I was going to do that, and I don't know what I am going to say.

"Yes? I mean, yes, sir?"

I find some words and put them together.

"Thank you for being so kind. But I can deal with everything. I'd just like us to carry on as normal, please." She nods politely and closes the heavy door with barely a click. I am beyond relieved to be alone again. I sink back into my chair, close my eyes, and shut out the world.

May is the receptionist here and also my personal assistant. I am lucky to have lots of money and I have invested it wisely. I didn't earn the money, I inherited it from my adoptive parents. She keeps track of any meetings I have with investors or my accountant and answers the telephone. I like to think of what I do as a job, but I suppose it isn't really. It remains unsaid. The arrangement suits us both.

I sit and tap my fingers on the edge of the desk. Miles is

dead. I try and let it sink in. It doesn't. I'm not sure what to do. I have an overwhelming feeling of coldness and my body feels unnaturally heavy.

I think Miles and I were close; I know that other people would certainly describe us as close. Especially people who knew us as children. This will be a huge shock to his family, I am sure. His wife. His children. They will be devastated. My skin tingles.

I realise I didn't ask May if she knew what happened. I'd like to know, but I don't want to start up another conversation with her about it. Even the thought of it makes me nauseated. It must have been something sudden, an accident most likely. That surprises me though, he was always so careful. Perhaps a secret illness, but I don't think he would have kept that from Susannah.

I consider calling Susannah right away, but quickly change my mind. She will have plenty of people supporting her, and I don't want to say the wrong thing and make her feel worse.

I finish my day and retire to my bedroom.

My workplace and my home are one. The ground floor at the front of the house is for work and the remainder of the house is mine. A large family, or two, could live very comfortably here, with rooms to spare.

My bedroom is smaller than most rooms here and devoid of the grandeur and echoey high ceilings throughout the rest of the house. I don't enjoy going outside and most days I am perfectly happy to stay right here.

My heart sinks as I think of all the things that have to happen next. The heartfelt condolences: I don't wish to receive any. The funeral: I don't wish to be comforted or feel obligated to comfort someone else. And I don't want to tell anyone these things.

Miles is dead.

I know it is true, but it doesn't feel real.

The correct response to the death of a family member is tears and sadness. People don't stop to think about what's happening on the inside. I rarely cry, but if I don't show that to everyone, then they will think I am some kind of monster.

Chapter Two

I call George. His deep, slow voice soothes me, and I instantly feel more grounded. George has been working for me for the last twelve months and I can honestly say it's the most at ease with another person that I have ever felt. He drives me anywhere I need to go and takes care of any errands. Our relationship works.

I spend a lot of time wondering about George and I sense he has a history. I have never met anyone with a story worse than mine. I'm not being dramatic, it's just a fact. It's not that I hope he has a terrible past, but rather that I think the damaged can somehow sense each other, even seek each other out. I have never questioned him about it. I would like to and perhaps one day I will find the courage. George has a strong work ethic and I doubt he would ever reveal anything voluntarily.

"Hello, George."

"Good evening, sir." I picture George on the other end of the telephone. I imagine him sitting in a large leather chair. His tall, strong body filling most of it. I think of his stern but kind face.

At fifty-eight, George is almost twenty years older than me, and he has a strong, military air about him. Outwardly, we could not be more different. My appearance screams privilege and perfectionism. I wear the upper-middle-class uniform. I am never seen without a shirt and tie, and everything is tailored. I don't know if I like it, but it has become comfortable over the years. The outside of me is accepted by everyone I meet. At thirty-eight, I still have bright blond hair and there is never a hair out of place. Alongside my lean frame, it makes me look younger than my years. I don't mind this at all.

There is no need for pleasantries with George. It is comfortable and easy. We can just be.

"George, I assume you heard the news about my brother?"

"I did, sir, what can I do for you?"

I give George instructions regarding flowers, clothes and other things that need to be organised for the funeral. He listens intently, as always.

"I would like you to drive me there, George." It's more than that. I need him to drive me there, but I don't say that.

"Of course, sir. Anything else I can do?"

"I'm not sure yet. I'll be calling Miles's wife, Susannah, shortly. If there is anything else, I will let you know." I don't expect Susannah to ask for anything.

"Yes, sir."

"Goodbye, George." I almost hang up but instead, I add, "And thank you. I appreciate it."

"Not a problem, sir. I'm here whenever you need me."

I want to say something else but now is not the time.

"Goodnight, George."

"Goodnight, sir."

I end the call but keep the phone in my hand. If I put it down, I don't think I'll pick it up again this evening. My head is foggy and slow but busy at the same time. I'd rather do anything than call Susannah right now. She'll be an emotional wreck, and rightly so.

I should have called Susannah as soon as I found out. I've already pushed it to the limit of acceptability by waiting this long. I'd rather not put the spotlight on myself unnecessarily, by behaving inappropriately. I dial Susannah's number, my heart thumping along with the ringing from the handset. I pray hopelessly that she won't answer. Instead, she answers after the first ring. Her voice is croaky and terribly sad.

"Hello."

I wait for a second and compose myself. Familiar anxiety is rising inside me, but I need to get through this. I've spent a lot of time working out what I'm supposed to say and how to behave in almost any situation. I've developed a way to make it look easy, but inside I find it so incredibly hard.

"Hi, Susannah, it's Montague. I'm very sorry for calling so late. I didn't want to bother you right away." I'm relieved with how that sounded.

"Oh, Monty." Then she wails. I was expecting her to cry, but it continues for the most extraordinary amount of time. I wince and move the phone away from my ear. An unwelcome lump forms in my throat and I feel like I'm intruding by listening. The odd word tries to come through the tears and sniffing, but nothing that makes any sense. My heart sinks. I feel horrible. Horrible and useless. She deserves a better outlet for her grief.

At least this is not happening in person, and I make a note to mentally prepare myself for this on the day of the funeral. Once she stops crying, she calms quickly. I say nothing and she begins to talk. I do my best to make all the right noises in all the right places. My head is pulsing so loudly, that I'm surprised she can't hear it.

Susannah tells me that Miles died from a catastrophic stroke, he didn't make it anywhere near an ambulance or hospital. He dropped down dead. Just like that. Miles was a good man, a family man. His death will leave an enormous hole in their family.

"There was nothing wrong with him," she tells me. I hold back from telling her that evidently wasn't true. It's completely unhelpful and not what I should be thinking.

As she talks, I wonder whether Miles had felt anything in the weeks and months preceding his death. Perhaps he just kept it to himself. I don't say that either, she doesn't need to hear these things.

Instead, I say, "I know, it must be such a shock. He was so fit, always running. I can't believe it." I always told him that all that running was bad for him. He did far too much. As though he was running away from something. I suspect he was stressed, and I know he liked a drink to unwind every night.

I let her talk and unburden herself. She's fragile. I find the right moment and offer money for the funeral. Miles was just as wealthy as me. We inherited the estate equally when Henry and Lois died. I wasn't expecting it at all. He'd been their son for ten more years than me and he was their blood. But even in their death, they showed me, as they always had, that they considered me their son. Miles wasn't upset either. I thought he had every right to be. But they were all genuinely good people.

I know Susannah will have inherited all of Miles's money. She is alone now, but has the boys to look after. I am all alone and have enough money to last me until my dying day, and nobody to leave it to. At first, she politely refuses.

"No, Monty, I couldn't. I can pay for everything."

"Susannah, I want to. Please." I don't add a reason, I don't want her to feel sadder and more scared about the future than she already does. She politely refuses once more before gratefully accepting.

"Will you speak, Monty?" I was afraid of this. It's good of Susannah to ask, but the simple truth is I don't want to. There are lots of reasons and I don't want to think of them or explain them to another person.

"Susannah, you know I would love to." I pause, hoping she'll interject. She doesn't, there is silence. "But I would simply find it too hard, and I'd worry I wouldn't do Miles justice. I hope you understand." She begins to cry again between words, but I can hear her agreement somewhere in there.

"Of course, I understand. I'm exactly the same, I'd never get through it without crying. I'll ask the minister to speak for all of us."

Minister? I didn't know Miles was religious.

"That sounds like a lovely idea." Whilst I'm not sure why we have a minister, I do think someone else should speak. It takes the pressure off. My mind drifts off as Susannah tells me the details of the funeral.

Miles was too young to have a stroke. He and I are – I mean were – the same age. Everyone assumed we were twins when we were boys, but not as adults. Surprisingly, I have aged rather well. He always looked exhausted.

Henry and Lois were not open about my adoption outside of the family. We moved shortly after I arrived, and there were never any questions. Henry and Lois tried their very best. Telling me there was nothing wrong with me. I'm not what anyone would call normal or usual. I am a product of the environment I was raised in. Both environments. I think of it as evolution on a small scale. Necessary and unavoidable.

I wind down the conversation with Susannah and wish her goodnight. I consider her future. Time, many believe, is a great healer when it comes to grief. I don't agree at all. I think it's something else entirely. I don't think we heal; I think we forget. I think our brains learn how to function and pack away anything unhelpful in boxes in our brains. We forget how we felt, we forget people or things that once meant something to us. I can understand how that could be mistaken for healing.

But sometimes, those boxes tumble down.

Chapter Three

Today is the funeral. My stomach is churning at the prospect of it all. I have carefully chosen my clothes and I have bought beautiful flowers. I examine my expression in the mirror. I want to present myself as the caring, grieving brother, but I do not want to appear overly self-serving. I want to stay hidden and that can only be achieved by appearing completely unremarkable. I am content with what I see. Inside is a different story entirely.

I settle into the car seat and breathe in the heady aroma of the leather. George sets off down the sweeping driveway, flanked by centuries-old trees. It's a long drive to the crematorium and George has chosen music that he knows will calm me. I love Bach. Despite most of my outward self being an invention of necessity, my love of classical music is true. I've absolutely no idea where it came from. Certainly not from my blood. I watch my knuckles go white as George pulls the car onto the road and away from the safety of home.

"Sir, shall I come in with you or wait outside?" George has become an increasingly important part of my life; he has shown me loyalty and kindness and he makes me feel grounded and safe. I have never told him this. I like having him close to me, and I'd like to think that my presence pleases him, too.

"Come with me please, George." I need someone there with me today, and there is no one else.

"No problem, sir." There's something in the air, something unsaid.

"George?" I ask tentatively. I don't want to scare him away.

"Yes, sir?"

"Has anyone that you care about died?" His eyes flicker to me briefly in the rear-view mirror. I can see that the question was unexpected. He chooses his words carefully, as I always do. I can see the inner workings of his thoughts as he turns them into a sentence before he speaks. It's intriguing to watch. I've perfected the art of this over the years, it doesn't show on my face anymore.

"Both my mother and father are dead." He pauses briefly before continuing. "They've been gone a long time." There's something about his answer that bothers me. He looks uncomfortable and doesn't offer up any further words.

"I'm sorry to hear that, George." I consider telling him that my parents are also dead.

"Thank you, sir." He avoids my eyes. Every day I see something new in him that I recognise. I want him to know he's not alone. I take a risk.

"How do you think I am feeling today, George?" I know this is not a kind thing to ask. I am making him uncomfortable, and I am doing it on purpose. I want him to know more of me, I want to know more of him, and I want to tell him that I think we could be something to each other.

"I don't know, sir." He swallows hard, and the strong muscles in his neck pulse. He answers me out of politeness and obligation. "How are you feeling?"

I don't want to answer that.

"I'm sorry if my questions are making you uncomfortable, George." He flushes slightly before shaking his head but doesn't say anything. "Let's put it another way. When someone close to us dies, father, brother, etcetera. Do you think we should feel sad?"

He answers more quickly than I had expected. "Yes, I think we should feel sad."

I'm not surprised by his answer. I don't think I am mistaken about what I see in George, but for some reason, he doesn't trust me. I look up with surprise when he continues to speak. George never offers up unnecessary words.

"Sorry, sir, what I mean is..." He tails off. I stay silent, leaving the space open for him. He wants to speak. "Yes, I think we should feel sad. But maybe some people don't. And maybe that's okay."

That was hard for him to say. But he said it anyway. Something is back in the air again, and I am relieved.

"Thank you, George." He smiles at me. "I'm never quite sure whether how I am feeling is right. It's exhausting." I can tell George is done talking. I lighten the mood. "Sorry about that, George. I don't often meet anyone who understands anything about how I see the world."

George seems a little embarrassed by my comment and smiles uncomfortably.

"Yes, sir."

I consider telling him he can call me Montague or even Monty from now on, but I think that would be the wrong choice for both of us. I look out of the window as we begin to slow down. We are approaching the crematorium. I am taken aback to find we have been travelling for over two hours. I don't know where the time has disappeared to.

"George, thank you for a lovely car journey." I wish I hadn't said lovely, given the circumstances, but that's how it felt.

"No problem, sir."

I take a moment and prepare myself before getting out of the car. The biting air hits me like a slap in the face. I pull my coat around me and hug my body tightly. The morning is appropriately bleak. Dark, ominous clouds threaten rain. I don't want to be here. I take a deep breath and hide inside myself.

"George, I must warn you, Miles's family will be extremely emotional. There will be a lot of tears." George nods and we walk towards the dark crowd of people standing outside the bleak, red-brick building.

My adoptive mother had wanted many children. Everything about her was motherly and warm. She exuded care and kindness. Sadly, that wasn't to be. Miles's birth had been a traumatic one and left her unable to carry another child. I never heard her complain about it once, even though I knew how it ate her up inside.

We only ever spoke about my arrival once. They told me that they had heard my story and actively sought out adopting me. I don't know if that is true, and I can't imagine what possessed them to want to take in such a damaged child. I didn't ask and I tried not to think about it. I feared what the answer might be.

I stayed with a few families before Henry and Lois adopted me. My memory is littered with holes during that time, but I remember very clearly arriving in my new home. I was so grateful for the warmth and kindness of my new parents and my brother. I thought some of their goodness would rub off on me, that it would balance out the rest of my childhood somehow. I felt I owed it to them to show that they had done a good job and that they had saved me. I couldn't face telling them that my past still lived within me. What if that meant they sent me away? So, I adapted. They loved me. And the negative parts of me began to shrink.

It's easier than you think to be two people. You feed the one you want to thrive. You starve the dangerous one.

Chapter Four

I can blur things when I need to. Think of it as turning down the volume on the TV.

I shake hands, I hug people, and I accept and give condolences. We haven't even got to the ceremony yet and my head is pounding.

I want to go home, where everything is safe and known, and wash this hideous day off me. I tuck in behind Susannah as we walk through the crowd. The widow is the person everyone wants to see. Most people here are not broken by Miles's death, it will not devastate their lives. I avoid attention as much as possible and I get little more than a nod until the service starts.

I tune out for most of the service. I can't concentrate properly but I know that's perfectly normal after a death. I look around, silencing my thoughts and focusing on the details of the room for the first time. Despite almost every seat being occupied, the room feels sparse and unwelcoming, and the scent of lilies is overpowering. I close in on people's faces, observing. People cry and bow their heads as they are expected to. I watch.

Finally, the curtains close and the coffin goes off to burn. I'd like to be cremated when I die. I thought a lot about this as a child. Not just about the end of life, but about the end of a physical body. It's true what they say, a person truly does leave their body. I don't know where the important elements of a person go, but there is a moment when the body becomes no different to any other inanimate object. I have seen it.

I have always thought that people choose to bury bodies because it makes them feel more comfortable. That it's more like putting a person to sleep and setting them on fire is somehow brutal and inhumane.

When the service is over, everyone is instructed to file out in an orderly manner.

I tap George on the arm. "Let's go. Quickly."

Everyone will be leaving for the wake shortly and I've already told Susannah that I won't be attending. I feel completely disorientated and I can't even remember how to get out of here. There is a wall of people and no way past without making a scene. I tuck in behind a man in front of me, almost pressing my nose against his musty wool coat. George puts his hand on my shoulder to steady me.

As soon as possible, George and I peel off from the crowd. Nobody notices us. It has started to rain, and everyone is huddled together by the entrance. A swarm of black coats and umbrellas. George opens the door to the car, and I almost fall inside with relief. He gets in quickly, starts the car, and begins to drive away without being asked. I breathe in big gulps of air and close my eyes.

"Anything you need, sir?" George is concerned but he knows I don't like to be asked how I am.

"No thank you, George." My voice is barely a whisper. I try to smile, but it feels weak and unsure.

"Just let me know if there is, sir." He leaves it there and I am grateful.

We drive in silence. Sometimes I look out of the window

and sometimes I close my eyes. Neither help. I want to talk to George, but I'm scared of what I might say, of what he might think of me. What if I am wrong and he doesn't want to listen?

I take out my mobile phone with shaking hands and make a telephone call. A call I was hoping I wouldn't have to make again. Before I talk to George there's someone else I need to speak to first.

Chapter Five

Before

Mummy tucks me tightly into bed and perches close to me. She runs her fingers through my wispy blond curls. I love it when she does that, but recently, her hands have become bony and cold. Her wrists are so thin it looks like her hands might break clean off. She looks down at me with love swimming in her pale blue eyes. There is a nasty, crusty cut on her forehead that is framed by a multicoloured bruise. It looks horribly sore, and some of her hair is missing just above it. I don't ask her about it, it will make her cry.

She starts reading to me. Tonight, it is *Jack and the Beanstalk*. It's one of my favourites. Now I'm five, we are allowed to read bigger stories. Still only one each night, but it means she gets to stay here longer. We aren't allowed any other time alone together, and even at story time, my bedroom door has to stay open.

As always, the story ends far too soon. Mummy lies down next to me and plants lots of tiny kisses all over my cheeks. Her lips are bone-dry, but it's still the most magical feeling ever. She leans into my ear and instead of wishing me goodnight. She whispers quickly and urgently.

"I am going to come back later tonight. *Don't* make a sound. Let me pick you up and carry you away. We are going to get out of here."

She leans away from me and a tear drips from her wet eyes onto my face. She nods slowly and wipes the tear away gently with her thumb. Fear and excitement crawl over me, and my throat squeezes shut.

Mummy leaves quickly. If she stays here too long, he'll get angry, and that means at least one of us will get a beating.

I lie still as I always do. Trying to control my wild breathing. This is going to be my last night here. Mummy and I are going to be free. We can read stories for as long as we like and spend every day together. My heart could leap out of my chest at this wonderful thought.

I don't dare sleep, but I close my eyes and pretend to be fast asleep in case he comes in. I lie like this for hours, imagining our wonderful new life together.

Eventually, I hear Father go to bed. Mummy doesn't have a bedroom, she sleeps downstairs, but I don't know exactly where. I'm not allowed out of my room at night-time and she's always awake before me. I don't hear Mummy coming up the stairs. The first thing I hear is her small footsteps outside my room. She is as quiet as a mouse. My whole body is tingling, and my bladder is full, but I lie still as a statue, just as Mummy told me to. I peek at the door through one eye, and I see the handle slowly twisting. I hold my breath and don't dare even blink.

She's here. We are finally leaving.

My lungs burn, waiting for her to appear in the doorway. I scan my sparse, uncared-for room. The shaft of light from the gap in the ill-fitting curtains illuminating the floor in front of the door. I will her to open the door and save me from this nightmare, but instead, I hear a sudden, thunderous crack against the door. The door shudders against the force but remains closed.

I hear Father bellowing first, and then Mummy screams back. Guttural and animal-like. She emits blood-curdling shrieks that chill me to the bone. I have never even heard her raise her voice before. I pull my thin blanket over my head and pray. The cacophony of screeching escalates further and is interspersed with more deafening bangs against my door. I hear the wood splinter and peer out briefly. The door is still intact on this side.

All the noise ceases in an instant. Everything is eerily quiet. I close one hand over my mouth and another over my chest, trying to hold in the noises my body is making against my will.

I hear Father sniff loudly outside my door and then he yells.

"Don't you fucking dare come out."

My whole body is rigid with horror and my bladder gives up on me.

He heaves a sigh, and I hear him drag something down the stairs carelessly. It sounds heavy, and I hear a dull thud as it hits each stair before a loud slam as he bangs the kitchen door.

I lie in my soaking sheets and try to find the smell of Mummy on my pillow.

Chapter Six

"Good morning, Mr Barclay." It's been many years since I set foot in this office, so I don't know why I am surprised to find that Dr Pathirana has a new receptionist. She is very smiley, too smiley in fact.

"Good morning..." I look at the nametag pinned to her crisp, white shirt, "...Elizabeth." She doesn't look like an Elizabeth at all. I'd like to tell Dr Pathirana that it's inappropriate for her receptionist to be so smiley, nobody is here because they are happy. But that would be absurd of me. Elizabeth gestures to the beautiful white leather chairs and I sit. This may be the most comfortable chair I have ever sat in. I know I won't be waiting long; as with many things in life, you get what you pay for. The room strikes the perfect balance between professionalism and elegance. It is spotless and airy, with expensive, understated art on the walls.

I hear the doctor's soothing voice calling my name and I'm relieved to see she has changed very little; she looks much younger than she must be. Her jet-black hair is pulled back from her face in an effortless low ponytail that falls over her left shoulder. Her face is almost implausibly smooth and radiant. I joke to myself that not having to listen to me might have taken years off.

I'm delighted when Dr Pathirana gestures to an identical chair to the one I have just vacated. It is at odds with the rest of the room, which is peppered with various nods to Dr Pathirana's Sri Lankan heritage. We sit and I instantly feel relaxed. I've done a lot of hard work in this room over the years, initially against my will. But there is a serenity in here and I trust Dr Pathirana with my thoughts more than I trust anyone else.

"I was surprised to hear from you, Monty." She smiles, she means it in the best possible way. "It's been a long time, and I would never have imagined you'd come here without... encouragement." She smiles again, and I notice that her teeth are whiter and straighter than the last time we met. This woman has seen the worst of me and has heard me say unspeakable things. She treats me with respect, and as such, she has earned mine.

"Thank you for seeing me at such short notice, Doctor."

"You are very welcome, Monty. As I said many years ago, I am always here if you need me and, if I am honest, I am a little intrigued." Dr Pathirana is the most sought-after psychiatrist in the city. Her waiting list is months, if not years long. But I am the kind of patient that most psychiatrists will only ever read about in books. I know that if I call, she will answer.

Also, it doesn't hurt that I have money. Dr Pathirana is a good woman, but if money didn't matter, she wouldn't be in this luxurious office, charging hundreds of pounds per hour.

"Intrigued? As to why I am here?" I can certainly understand that.

"Well, yes, that. But also..." she stops and leans forward in her chair. "I got so used to hearing what you were up to. We spoke almost every week for many, many years." She looks pensive, clearly thinking of something in particular from the past. "I guess I'm intrigued to know what you've been doing. What have you been occupying yourself with all these years?"

I made a clean break from my sessions with Dr Pathirana over five years ago. I'd considered myself to be as fixed as I was ever going to be. Nobody had been making me come and see her for a long time and, although I would never have admitted it to her, I was becoming dependent on my time here. I didn't want to depend on her forever, and I have found other ways to cope.

"I'm good, thank you. I don't think I need to be here as such. There's been a bit of a change in my life, and I just wanted to talk it through with someone I trusted. Someone who knows me."

She nods and waves her elegant hands toward me, encouraging me to continue. I catch a trace of vanilla-scented perfume from her wrists. The familiarity of it soothes me and I instantly find that my words come easier.

"I'm here because I think I am making a friend." She looks up suddenly. Clearly, she is surprised, and I suppose she is right to be. On reflection, it seems like a ridiculous reason to come to see a psychiatrist.

"Go on, Monty. I'm listening." She relaxes back into her chair, and I mirror her.

"I think I've met someone who feels like a kindred spirit. I can't quite explain it." Dr Pathirana doesn't react, so I continue. "I feel really happy about it but there's something niggling at me, something that concerns me. I thought it best to talk it through and make sure I'm not doing anything... unwise." I can't think of a better word. Nobody else in the world would understand why I have concerns about having a friend. Everyone has friends.

She knows the answer, I'm sure, but asks me anyway. "Do you have other friends?"

"No, I don't. At least not what I think a friend should be. I have colleagues and acquaintances, people who work for me. In fact, this potential friend works for me. I have professional relationships, but not friendships."

"So, what is worrying you?"

"I don't think there is anything wrong with me as a person living as I do now. I just don't think I've met anyone who would be a genuine friend. Whether I'm someone who can even have friends."

She leans forwards again and fixes me with a look full of empathy.

"I don't feel things the same as other people. It worries me. A lot. I've always thought I'm lucky to have a life of any kind. And given... everything, maybe I'm better keeping away from everyone." Even to me, these words sound sad. They are the truth, but it still hurts.

She nods. "Monty, I have been a psychiatrist for decades and I have never come close to meeting anyone who has been through half the trauma that you have. The fact that you have survived it and are sitting in front of me answering these questions is nothing short of a miracle." The kind words hit me hard in the chest. My cheeks flush and I unconsciously look down at my feet. I appreciate what she is saying, but it's not how I think about myself. "You shouldn't be afraid; you should be proud."

I'm grateful for her reassurance, but I'm not sure she fully understands my concerns. That's not surprising, as I'm not articulating them very well at all. I try to explain myself further.

"I think I've met someone a bit like me. If that's true, I wonder what has happened to him. Or, what if he's naturally like that? I'm worried that might be a problem for me. Does that make sense?"

"Yes, Monty. It does." I can see she's thinking about what I have just said.

"I would like to have someone in my life who I could maybe be more natural with. Someone who might understand and not think I'm peculiar." It's all tumbling out now. My palms feel clammy, and I have an overwhelming urge to cry. My words are too fast and I'm saying them before I've had a chance to check them. "I have become so good at playing a part, at being the perfect gentleman. But pretending every day is exhausting. It's starting to eat away at me." I look down at my hands. They feel stuck together with sweat and my knuckles are deathly white. The skin is so tight, that it looks as though it might split open. "If I had someone, even just one person who I could be my actual self with, I think that would be good." I can feel the emotion rising in my throat, and I clear it to avoid my voice cracking. "But my big concern is that it might in fact be bad." She is writing, I don't mind that, it makes me feel less scrutinised.

She stops for a moment and meets my eye.

"I understand, Monty. As much as I can, anyway. It must be so hard for you." She is right. It is hard for me, and I appreciate her acknowledging me.

She continues. "I wonder whether the best way is to try a gentle approach with this friend?" I realise I am holding my breath and I exhale slowly. I am relieved to hear that she isn't instantly dismissive of the idea. "Perhaps reveal a small part of yourself, something you are more comfortable sharing and see how they react. Then take it from there."

She's telling me to do what I have already done. I'm equal parts relieved and disappointed for not trusting my judgement. I nod and tell her about the conversation with George at Miles's funeral. I see a flash of something across her face. She composes herself quickly, but not quickly enough.

"You didn't mention that your brother had died." She leaves it hanging there. Not a question as such. More of an accusation. At least that's how it feels. Is she judging me? My brother has just died, and I didn't care enough to mention it until now. I say nothing but I look straight into her eyes, hoping to catch some of her thoughts. Although she knows precisely what I've been through, I know she's still taken aback by me sometimes. I feel obliged to explain myself.

"Doctor, he wasn't my real brother. I've found his death difficult, certainly, but..." I trail off. I'm not sure how to finish the sentence. Especially as it's not how I actually feel.

She moves to the edge of her chair and reaches out her hand.

"Monty, please don't worry. It's important that I don't censor my natural reactions. They are organic and a part of our relationship. I don't judge you, Monty, but I do have my own feelings and reactions to the things that you say."

Her direct words soothe and ground me. She is right. Of course, she is. We sit in silence for a moment.

"I think George understood how I felt. About Miles." I realise now that I should have told her about Miles first. I consider trying to tell her that I find it easier to try and forget that Miles has died. But I don't think that will help.

"Then maybe talk with him some more, see how you both feel?" I nod and she continues. "But, despite my encouragement, I must admit that, like you, I do have reservations. You have done so incredibly well. You don't want to build a relationship that fuels any kind of negativity." Now she has hit the nail on the head. "Remember all of the poisonous thoughts that were consuming you as a younger man. Any relationship you build needs to be good for you."

"I think he may help though," I reassure her. "And if he doesn't, I'll step back. I've managed all this time without a friend, and I have other things in life to keep me occupied."

She smiles. "I'm so glad to hear that, Monty. I've always

thought your recovery was so exceptional, you don't want to jeopardise that."

We have twenty minutes left but I feel like I am done for today. I've decided that I am going to invite George to stay after work for a drink. I hope it goes well, but if it doesn't, then I'll move on.

I stand up to leave, but Dr Pathirana continues. "Do you think you could ever contemplate a romantic partner?"

It's not something we have ever discussed. I don't say anything, but I do sit back down. "Why do you assume that I haven't?"

She's a little lost for words. "Sorry, Monty..." She recovers quickly. "It's just you were so concerned about making a friend and you've never mentioned romantic relationships before. Please don't take offence, that was not my intention."

"Of course." I know there is no malice in her question. It is a completely reasonable assumption.

"I'm sorry, I should have asked that more professionally."

"Actually, Doctor, I have a girlfriend. Her name is Penny." I smile and she hides her surprise wonderfully. I can tell she suspects I am lying, but after her faux pas, I don't think she will challenge me.

"That's wonderful, Monty. Can you tell me about your relationship?" She takes notes as I talk. I keep it light, avoiding anything too personal. I know that she has many more questions and eventually, she asks one.

"Does she *know* about you?"

It's certainly one of the questions I was expecting, and I wonder how best to answer it without inviting any questions that will make me uncomfortable.

I settle on, "In a way. Certainly, as much as I can allow her to."

She nods as she writes, and I think we are both relieved when the clock hits the hour.

"I think you should attend every week until we see how this friendship goes. You know I don't say this to any other clients, but please call me any time. Day or night. I am always here for you, Monty. You're taking some fantastic new steps, but you are right to be cautious. I truly hope it goes well, but if not, please do call me before..." She doesn't finish. I'm not sure she knows what the right words would be.

"Of course, thank you, Doctor. Your support, as always, means a lot to me. I'd be happy to come every week."

We shake hands and I return to the waiting room. The brightness startles me momentarily. I nod politely to Elizabeth on my way out. She is still smiling.

George is waiting outside. Leaning against the car with his hands in his trouser pockets.

"Have you been here the whole time, George?"

"Yes, I thought it best, sir. Straight home?"

"Yes, George, thank you. But there is something I'd like to talk to you about." I'm worried that if I don't ask now then I'll continue to put it off. Dr Pathirana's validation is important, and I am concerned it will wear off if I don't do something immediately. "Could we possibly have a drink after work today, 6pm, in the lounge?"

He answers without hesitation. "Of course, sir." He doesn't ask any questions and we travel in easy silence for the journey home. I'm grateful for the time to think and decompress after my session with the doctor.

I enjoyed it. I think. Not leading with the news about Miles was a mistake and a part of my mind is still struggling with the look on Dr Pathirana's face. I've had to pack a lot away recently and it's weighing down on me.

I think about what I told Dr Pathirana about Penny. It's

probably the first direct lie I have ever told her. Perhaps I shouldn't have mentioned Penny at all. I am sure Dr Pathirana noticed that I was being deceptive.

I have indeed found a way to cope with my life in my years away from Dr Pathirana.

A way that she would not understand.

It is my biggest secret, a secret that must stay hidden forever.

Chapter Seven

I take a hot shower before George arrives. I need to relax and refocus. I gradually turn the water temperature up until I can hardly bear it. Steam fills the bathroom, and before long I feel light-headed. Seeing Dr Pathirana hasn't upset me, but I do find her sessions extremely hard work. I feel drained.

I'm tempted to cancel George. I don't feel at my best, and I worry I won't come across very well. But I don't. I will keep my word.

I make my way to the lounge shortly before 6pm. I relax into one of the wingback chairs spaced evenly around the coffee table. I feel so small in this room. I consider putting on some music to fill the vast, empty space when there is a small, almost inaudible knock at the door. It's May with the tea and coffee I have asked her to bring for us.

May peeks her head around the door rather than entering. "Hello, sir, where would you like it?"

"On the table please, May." She seems a little shaky but makes it to the table with the tray without spilling. She is chewing at her bottom lip and her eyes keep flitting back to the door.

"Shall I stay and pour for you, sir?"

I smile at her. It's obvious that she wants to leave. "Thank you, May. You should get yourself home now."

"Thank you, sir."

She exits the room quickly and pulls the door behind her. I think I hear her heave a sigh of relief. Miles's death has clearly stayed with her. I must remember to talk to her about it, I don't want her to feel uncomfortable around me.

I had contemplated serving champagne for George; it's the only alcohol that I drink. I don't enjoy the feeling alcohol gives me, but I do enjoy a small glass of champagne. Most of all, I enjoy the reaction of others when I serve it to them. They always seem so happy. But alcohol didn't feel right for this occasion somehow.

I'm not sure what this meeting is going to be, but I am sure I'd rather we were both sober. My heart is racing with a combination of mostly apprehension and some excitement. I push my shoulders down and breathe deeply and slowly in an attempt to release the building tension. It is exactly 6pm, and I know that George will arrive within the next sixty seconds. As expected, I hear George's assured knock on the door almost immediately.

"Come in, George." I gesture to the tray and seats at the table. He is far too polite to sit without an invitation. He chooses the chair opposite me and his head almost reaches the top of the high-backed chair. He looks pleased to be here and that makes me feel good.

"Good evening, sir." He smiles and clasps his strong hands in his lap.

"Good evening, George." I return his smile and he leans over to pour drinks for us both. I watch as he lifts the pot carefully, and a contented feeling washes over me. He makes my coffee perfectly. He places my cup in front of me and I inhale the rich, delicious aroma.

"George, I hope you don't mind me inviting you for a drink?"

"Of course not, sir."

"It's not part of your job to be here, don't feel obliged." My mouth is dry and I'm aware that I'm in danger of rambling.

George nods. "I understand, sir."

"Can I ask you something, George?"

He nods again. His face is warm and welcoming.

"You've been working here for a year now. I enjoy the time we spend together." I know that my words are far too formal. I wish I knew how to be more relaxed in conversation, I must try harder. I pause but he doesn't speak. I want to encourage a natural flow of conversation, but I don't know how to do it. I suspect he won't talk unless asked a direct question. "Do you have any friends, George?"

There is only a slight movement on his face, and he looks up and to the left briefly. If there is any significant emotional response to my question, positive or negative, I can't detect it. He answers quickly.

"Not as such, sir." I raise my eyebrows and gesture for him to elaborate. "Uh... I have people I work with. I guess I have people I see outside of work sometimes." He stops and thinks for a moment, raising his eyes again. "But, in all honesty, I like my own company. It's just... the way I am."

"It's the way I am, too," I say. "Often, I find other people rather tiring and, well... different from me. Does that make sense?"

"Absolutely, sir."

There's a sense of hierarchy in our working relationship that I suspect is preventing George from elaborating. I hope that may ease over time and I'd like to do something to break it down more quickly. I want us to be closer, but I worry about what will happen if this doesn't work out the way I hope it will.

"George, may I be completely honest with you?" So formal again. This isn't how friends speak to each other.

"Yes, sir. Anytime."

"You know I have a doctor who I talk to sometimes?"

"Yes, sir, but..."

He answers hurriedly and busies himself by reaching for his coffee. He is avoiding eye contact and is clearly flustered by the prospect of me revealing something too personal. He retreats into the chair and crosses his legs, resting the cup on his knee.

I look him in the eye. An attempt to put him at ease. "Please, let me finish. She is the only person in the world who I am honest with. But... her reactions bother me sometimes. She helps me, but she doesn't understand me and doesn't see the world the same way I do. Can you understand what that might be like?"

"I... I'm not sure, sir." His voice is higher, and I notice a slight flush come across his ears and the sides of his face.

I can see he'd like me to stop this line of conversation. I try one last question.

"Do you ever worry about the reaction you get from people just for being yourself? Just for saying how you feel."

He takes a sip of his coffee, closes his eyes, and exhales. I can feel the emotion radiating from him, but it is painfully obvious that he is not ready to talk yet. I continue.

"What if it didn't have to be that way? What if you and I could be honest with each other? What if, even in a very small way, we could live as ourselves, our real selves, even if just for a fraction of each day?" He is looking at the table now and I catch his eyes wince as though in pain. I feel my cheeks colour and I suddenly wish I could take back everything I have just said. My questions are too intimate, and I feel foolish. I stop talking, and he seems relieved. I suspect I have pushed this too far.

"I'm sorry, George, I don't want to upset you."

He looks up, his expression is one of concern. "I'm not upset, sir. It's just, I'm worried that..."

I know why he is worried. He's worried that his job is under threat. "Don't worry about anything, George. Let's just go back to the way things were."

He looks unsure and opens his mouth as though to speak. No words emerge but he nods in agreement. The atmosphere is somewhat tense and I'm furious with myself for pushing things too far. I should have been content with enjoying George's company. I've ruined our understanding by looking for something that I can't have. I stand and he mirrors me.

"Good evening, George."

"Good evening, sir." He walks purposefully towards the door and closes it behind him. I stand with my back to the door and close my eyes. I turn and reach out my hand to open the door, but change my mind. I sit back down and contemplate our evening. I think George wants to take our relationship further, but he is not ready. I have to respect that. I have to wait.

Chapter Eight

I wake unexpectedly. My heart jumps and panic surges through me. It takes me a second to realise what I am hearing. At first, I think it is screaming. Terror and confusion swell inside me. The ear-splitting shriek continues but I don't dare move.

Suddenly, I understand. It is the alarm. There's a breach in the house. I sigh with relief and the adrenaline surging through my body begins to slow. I knew this would happen one day. I get myself together and walk downstairs.

I'm not afraid anymore. I suppose I should be. I don't know exactly what I'm going to find.

I stop at the alarm system and, as expected, the panel informs me that the breach has been triggered in the basement. I reset everything and continue down the many steep stairs. The basement door is closed, and everything is dark and gloomy. I turn the lights on in the corridor, and the sudden contrast assaults my eyes. I take a moment to adjust. When I feel ready, I speak loudly and very clearly towards the door.

"I am coming in. Do not do anything stupid." I unlock the door and open it slowly. An unclean smell emanates from the room. The light from the corridor seeps into the room, but all I can see are vague, blurry outlines. I reach my arm into the room and click on the light. The room is not as I left it. It has been ransacked, the table overturned, and chairs scattered. The place is a mess. The single, small window in the corner is smashed. Glass litters the floor and two pale, blood-stained legs are poking through the window into the room, kicking frantically.

"Penny, stop kicking, for goodness' sake." She doesn't stop and is making a desperate whimpering sound. She must have cut her abdomen badly trying to wriggle out of the tiny window. I can't understand her thinking, there is no way she would ever fit. I raise my voice a little, but I don't shout.

"Stop kicking your legs, Penny. You'll only make things worse." I grab her left knee firmly and she stops kicking immediately. "Good, thank you, Penny."

I can hear her panting. My head is pounding but I keep my voice calm. Penny has stopped whimpering and I know that she won't speak.

"Penny, listen to me very carefully. You have one chance to get yourself out of this mess. I'm not sure I should be giving you a chance, given that you have broken my trust, but I care about you, and I'm also rather interested in what you think you are doing. I am going to tidy up the mess in the room, and then we are going to sit down and talk."

She stops struggling but her body continues to shake with fear. "You are going to get yourself down from there. I am not going to help you. There are consequences to our actions, and we must all accept them."

My words are harsher than I had planned, but I stand by them. We have an understanding, I trusted her. She knows I need her to stay. I turn away and begin to tidy the room. Everything is unrecognisable, a complete mess.

In my periphery, I can still see Penny. She is wriggling and screaming again, trying to free herself. "If you got yourself in, then it must be physically plausible for you to get out." I realise that may not be true, but I can't help her. She starts to wail, and irritation prickles my skin. "Change of plan, my dear, you have exactly five minutes to get out." I set my watch. "If you are still hanging gracelessly out of the window at the end of those five minutes, then I will kill you and we can all get on with our lives. I have enough mess to clean up and adding you into that will make little difference to me."

She kicks and screams violently and falls onto the floor like a calf being born. She scuttles into the corner and pulls her knees up her chest. She looks pale and terrified. My throat tightens and my vision is cracked and disjointed.

"Good, well done. See what you can achieve with a little motivation." Her trembling hands are holding the bloody nightdress that is stuck to her stomach.

She speaks. "I'm bleeding, please help me, please." Her voice is thick with fear. She writhes and pushes pointlessly against the corner; there is nowhere to go. Her human instinct has kicked in. It is perfectly natural behaviour to try and escape danger.

"Go to the bathroom and get yourself cleaned up. Then we can talk."

I sit on the bed, close my eyes, and concentrate on my breathing. I hear the bathroom door close. I close myself off from the helpless cries and moans emanating from behind the door. I don't want to face what has just happened, or what might happen next. Everything was fine, what we had was working. I was coping. I felt better than I had in years. I can't let her see how shaken I am, so I speak to her through the door.

"I can't get you a doctor or take you to a hospital." She doesn't say anything. The crying has become fast, shallow breathing. She has moved past tears. "I am sorry that we have found ourselves here today, Penny. I hope you believe me when I say that." I hear her gasp, but she doesn't speak. "I am going to clean everything up in here. When I am finished, I will leave, and you can come out. Then we can continue with our arrangement as if all of this ugliness didn't happen." I hear muffled sounds but still no words. I know she is upset and scared. I am upset too. I hope she can see that she has made a terrible mistake.

"Penny, this is your home. We have an understanding. I give you everything you could ever need. I don't ask anything..." I'm struggling for the right words "...of you"

She's still sobbing. I imagine her, small and childlike. Weeping. Tears dripping down her face and through her fingers. I listen to the crying and a heaviness develops in my chest. I don't ask any questions. They would have no bearing on what happens next, and we have both been through enough already.

This isn't what was supposed to happen. I stare at the wall, feeling a sting of sadness and confusion. I do not want to hurt Penny, I have never wanted to hurt anyone. All I want is for her to stay. I don't want to be alone again.

I clean and tidy the room meticulously, removing any evidence of what has occurred. Making it calm and quiet again. I leave the window as it is, I will fix it tomorrow. I'd be very surprised if she attempted to go through it again. I don't know how much time passes. Many hours, I am sure.

When I am finally too tired to do anything further, I leave Penny's room and climb the stairs slowly. My body feels numb and hollow. My heart is twisted.

I clamber into my bed. My chest feels hollowed out and a sob rises in my throat.

Eventually, I drift into a deep sleep. Thankfully, nothing wakes me this time.

Chapter Nine

Before

Everyone thinks I hate school. I don't hate school at all. I can understand why they think that though, they don't understand that it is so much better than being at home. All the boys at school are mean to me, and most of the girls are pretty horrible too. But it doesn't bother me, school is safe, and no one is going to properly hurt me here. The kids at school don't like me because they think I am weird. I think they're right, I am weird, but I don't understand why that's necessarily such a terrible thing. I've got one friend and one friend is all I need.

I have Dotty.

Everyone thinks Dotty is weird too. I don't at all, Dotty is wonderful. She has a bright red mark on her face that covers her left cheek and goes over her eye, and her teeth are too big and poke out of her mouth even when she's not smiling. Her wild, curly hair sticks out at all angles. Something could easily live in Dotty's hair, a mouse, or a small bird perhaps, and nobody would ever know. Her hair smells like mints and bounces when she runs. I'd love to touch her hair, to gently stroke the wiry, brown curls, but even Dotty would think that was weird.

Dotty and I tend to hang out together at playtime and

lunchtime. Being together definitely attracts more attention and cruel jibes from the cool kids, but it's all much easier to handle when she's standing next to me. The insults just fall away, and they don't hurt my feelings when I'm with her.

Dotty's dad picks her up from school every day. I often wonder why it's always her dad and never her mum, but I don't ask. I don't want to invite any return questions about my own parents. Plus, lying to Dotty would make me sad. Nobody picks me up from school, I live less than a five-minute walk from school, and I always tell people that my parents trust me to walk home by myself.

Dotty's dad is big. Not just tall, but big and square all over, like a refrigerator. He looks kind and strong, and his face always lights up when he sees Dotty come out of school. He envelopes her in huge squishy hugs and holds her face in his giant hands. I always imagine what that must feel like. To have a father who loves you and is proud of you. I know men are usually good and kind, especially fathers, I know my father is not how it's supposed to be.

Dotty and I walk out of school. It's a cold, biting afternoon and our breath creates clouds that swirl together as we chatter about our day. I can see right away that Dotty's dad isn't here. Even if he was at the back of the crowd of parents, his head and wide shoulders would still be visible. Dotty doesn't seem concerned. She doesn't jump to the worst possible explanation as I do. She knows her dad is simply caught up somewhere, I'm already thinking he's probably dead.

"Can I come to yours?" Dotty asks without hesitation.

Everything inside me suddenly starts screaming.

No. Absolutely not. There is no way that Dotty can come to my house. Nobody is allowed to come to my house. My heart is racing and despite the cold, my face is burning with heat. But what can I say? I can't leave her here by herself. I have never been to Dotty's house, but I know it's much further away than mine. I could offer to wait with her, but my house is so close. I am taking too long to answer, and Dotty is looking at me sideways.

"Sure." I shrug with as much nonchalance as I can muster and hide my shaking hands deep in my coat pockets.

"Cool! I've never seen your house."

Dotty's face is wide and her eyes gleam with excitement. I twist at the fraying fabric inside my pocket, desperately trying to think of a way out of this. We keep walking towards my house, and I can't think of anything to do or say to change our inevitable journey. Going to your friend's house is a perfectly normal thing to do, so I guess we'll just have to go.

Nobody will be in, and as long as Dotty is out of here before Dad comes home, then everything might just be okay.

My chest tightens at the thought of my bedroom. How can I possibly explain why my room is like it is? My mouth is dry as I conjure up a plausible lie.

"We can't go in my room though, it's being decorated, so it's not as... nice as it usually is."

I blush and attempt to unstick my dry lips from my teeth with my tongue. Dotty doesn't seem to notice, I'm not even sure that she heard me, she's too busy twirling and skipping down the road in front of me. It's beautiful to watch.

The walk to my house truthfully is less than five minutes. I try to drag it out as long as I can, but if anything, we get there quicker than I usually do dawdling on my own. I gesture to the house and study Dotty's face as we both look up at the completely unremarkable building. It looks the same as every other semi-detached, red-brick house in the street. The garden is clean and tidy, the door is nicely painted, and there is not a hair out of place. Nothing that would make you look up and notice this house. It is entirely ordinary.

I know that the house is empty, so I don't worry as I put the key in the lock and slowly open the door. I can feel it when someone is inside the house, somehow my body just knows.

The ground floor of the house follows the same theme as the outside. Everything is immaculate and unmemorable. Beige and boring are how I would describe it. Dad spends a lot of money on the downstairs of the house to keep it looking like this. Carpets and furniture are always replaced if they're damaged or stained. Dotty is clearly impressed though.

"Wow, nice house, Monty."

I suddenly notice the tiniest edge of a balled-up duvet poking out from behind the sofa. I try to control my breathing and usher Dotty swiftly past, and thankfully, she doesn't seem to notice it.

Dotty suddenly runs up the first three stairs. My heart almost stops.

"Let's go play in your room!"

I start explaining about the decorating again, but my words are lost by the sound of Dotty's feet pounding up the stairs. She leans over the banister, her hair falling over her forehead and into her eyes, and beckons to me. Listening is not one of Dotty's strong points, and I usually love her for it. Not today.

I run up the stairs as fast as I can. As much as I don't want Dotty in my room, I simply cannot risk her opening the wrong door. This is a house of two halves. Everything appears nice and normal downstairs. Nobody is allowed upstairs except me, Mum, and Dad. Nobody. If Dad comes home or finds out, I am dead.

I point at my door and make a final attempt to explain away the appearance of my bedroom.

"All my stuff is at my Granny's while my room is being done."

I have no idea where that came from. I'm not even sure if I

still have a Granny. My father never mentioned his mum really. I know his dad was a soldier. He doesn't speak to them anymore, and I have no idea if either of them is still alive. I have a memory of Father calling his dad a 'vicious bastard' one day when he'd had some whisky. I always remember that, as I think it's a pretty accurate description of my own father. Perhaps that's just the way the men in our family are. Doomed to be vicious bastards.

Mum isn't allowed to see her parents. I think she'd like to. I don't ask her in case it makes her sad. I can vaguely picture them, but they don't have faces. I wonder if I've made them up.

Dotty flings my bedroom door open with enthusiasm. I see her nose wrinkle and she raises her hand to her mouth. The stench of stale urine seeps from the room. Heat rises quickly to my face, and I do everything I can to sound casual as another lie falls seamlessly from my mouth.

"That's from our new kitten. She loves my room."

Dotty looks around the room for the imaginary cat, her nose still turned up at the smell. It seems much more pungent today than usual.

"She's at the vet. With Mum. Yes, that's where Mum is, she'd usually be here."

Dotty looks at me quizzically but eventually smiles. I'm not sure she believes me, but she has a kind heart, and I know she won't question me further.

Dotty scans the room with her piercing blue eyes, they stop for a moment as they reach my tired-looking, unmade bed. This whole room radiates a feeling of neglect. There is no love or warmth here, and I know that she sees it. Dotty shrugs dramatically and suddenly sits down on the floor where she was standing, crossing her legs. She yanks her school bag into her lap, pulls out a crumpled packet of blackcurrant and liquorice sweets and pats the floor in front of her.

"Want to share these?"

She smiles, her sticky-out teeth shining in the dreariness of the room.

I sit down slowly and take a sweet from her.

"Can I come back and see your room when it's finished?"

The sickly-sweet smell of blackcurrant fills the air between us.

"Definitely. It's going to be amazing. I'm getting new everything. New bed, new carpets, they're painting the walls. Mum and Dad are really going to town on it."

My heart flutters with excitement. I almost believe it myself.

"I need to go at 4ish, Monty. I don't know why Dad didn't show, but Mum gets home at four and I've got swimming tonight. She works in a shoe shop. Don't you think that's gross? All those feet."

I'm flooded with relief that I don't need to invent a reason for her to leave before Father gets home, but at the same time, I am floored by a deep, painful knot in my chest that desperately wants her to stay. I'd love a sister and Dotty is the closest thing I have. I don't want her to leave me here. I don't want to be alone.

I listen to Dotty talk animatedly at a hundred miles an hour about her swimming lessons. She waves her skinny arms around and shows me the special positions she needs to put her hands in for each stroke. I don't interrupt. I've never been swimming, what would I say? I don't mind though, I love watching her, and she loves to tell stories.

Dotty jumps to her feet, reaches for the half-empty packet of sweets and places them on my bare and dusty bedside table.

"I better go now. You can have those."

She smiles and looks briefly around the room again. I push my hands deep into my pockets and walk towards the door, leaning against it. Dotty does a swimming motion with her arms towards me, opening and closing her mouth like a fish. I can't help laughing, but unwanted tears prick my eyes at the same time. I don't want Dotty to go. I want her to stay so desperately that, for a moment, I want to push her backwards.

Father coming home and finding her here terrifies me, but the thought of being left alone here again scares me more than I could have ever imagined. Dotty's eyebrows furrow.

"What you doing?"

I don't answer her. I turn away from her and rest my forehead against the cold, hard door. I press my hands against the door so fiercely that my wrists burn.

"Move, Monty. Stop being weird."

She grabs my shoulder and spins me around, so our eyes are only inches from each other. There is fear and anger swimming in her beautiful eyes, and tears in mine. Shame washes over me, my cheeks are flushed and my whole body feels itchy inside.

Dotty's face softens when she sees my expression. I want to touch her hair so desperately, I want to stroke her soft face, and kiss the red mark she hates so much.

I step to the side, no longer blocking the door. Dotty tries to lighten the mood as she leaves my room.

"Come on. See me out at least!"

I wipe my face on the sleeve of my scratchy school jumper and plod down the stairs after her. My chest hurts. She's already opened the front door by the time I get to the bottom step. I know she was worried I'd stand in front of this door too. She was right though, I do want to. She waves but doesn't say anything, her expression unreadable. I clear my throat and try to find a vaguely normal-sounding voice in my dry throat.

"Bye, Dotty. Bye."

She wrestles her backpack onto her back and crosses her arms.

"Yeah. Bye, Monty. This was... nice. Bit weird though. Nice but weird."

Dotty attempts a laugh, but it comes out more like a snort. I have never seen her look so uncomfortable.

I push my hands back into my pockets and look down as I hear the door close. Dotty is gone. I am all alone. Again. I let the tears fall freely down my face. I choke and splutter as the tears come faster, and I begin to sob uncontrollably.

Once again, I have nobody. I am alone.

Chapter Ten

"George, can you please hold all my calls for today? I have some personal things to attend to."

I pinch the bridge of my nose. My head is pounding with possibilities, always racing towards the worst possible scenario. I haven't seen May yet today, but she will need to go straight home when she arrives. Having extra people around today won't be helpful. George can tell May that something has come up last minute, and I need to close the office. I'll make sure that she gets full pay. "Would you answer any calls that come in and I'll come and see you when I'm finished?"

My voice is thick and unsteady.

"Of course, sir." George's eyes look heavy. I hope our conversation yesterday evening isn't the cause of his noticeable weariness.

Thankfully, I have no other commitments today, other than Penny. Memories of last night squirm inside my mind.

Life is not difficult for me regarding money or workload. Although May and George are certainly surplus to requirements, I like having them here and I pay them both very well. I would be sad to see May go. I would be devastated to see George go.

I collect everything I need and make my way down to the basement, glancing over my shoulder constantly. I can feel the beginnings of a headache gnawing at the back of my head. Thankfully, the basement is quiet, and I hope Penny doesn't cause any further disruption. I swallow a lump in my throat.

The powerful smell of bleach hits me as I open the door. Penny is lying on the bed, uncovered but in fresh clothes. She is completely still. Uncomfortably still.

I scan the room; it appears to be exactly as I left it, but my gut is telling me something isn't right. Self-doubt creeps over me. I look at the broken window with its sharp edges, and I hope that she hasn't done something stupid and unnecessary.

Thankfully, she stirs. But something is wrong. Dread and uncertainty climb up my spine. I walk cautiously towards her, licking my dry lips. Her eyes are squeezed tightly shut and I can see her mouth twitching as she mutters silently to herself. She smells sour. There is the briefest of flashes in my peripheral vision, and I realise that I was right about the window. Blood rushes to my head and I fight the overwhelming urge to run to safety.

"Penny, I know what you have there." I'm relieved that I don't need to say anything further, she throws the shard of glass she was holding immediately, and it hits the floor with a tiny clink. Penny springs to life and crawls away from me across the bed, frantically shaking her head and mumbling nonsensically before she finally manages to speak.

"It's not what you think, I wasn't going to hurt you, it was..." She points to her wrists which are completely untouched.

A sense of weariness sweeps over me. I had hoped that we could talk and go back to how things were. She knows that I am not a bad person; that I only want her to stay. But she has gone too far this time.

I take a deep breath and take a step towards the bed. Penny's face contorts with disgust, and I am momentarily taken aback. Her wretched face saddens me. I shake it away and clear my throat.

"Lie completely flat on your back on the bed and turn your head to look at the window. Do not move or turn your head as I move towards you." My voice is monotone and carries an air of authority that I do not feel inside. I walk purposefully towards the bed and inject the needle into her neck without hesitation. "Thank you, Penny. When you wake up, everything will be just as it should be."

I stand back and look at the room. I am trembling, my body yet to catch up with the elimination of danger.

Penny is still. Sleeping peacefully.

My eyes feel heavy, and I slump, resting my hand on Penny's bed to catch myself. Why did this have to happen? We are all trying to cope in this hideous world. Why couldn't she just stay?

I right myself and pace around the room slowly, admiring the beautiful, lavish décor. I had hoped that she would love this room. I had imagined this would be the room of her dreams.

I will come back and visit Penny later, but I will need to be prepared. When people wake from sedation, they are often very unruly, and violent even. They can behave as though in a drunken rage, completely oblivious to their actions and surroundings.

I check in with George when I am finished, he is taking the car for a service and won't be back until after lunch, so I sleep for the remainder of the morning. I know that I am sleeping too much, but I have become so tired. My whole body craves rest. Far too much has happened.

My nap achieves little. I feel sluggish and my body aches for more sleep. I splash water on my pale face and then run my fingertips over the dark circles under my eyes. My body seems able to sleep, but it feels as though my mind stays awake, and I know that my reactions are not at their best.

I enter Penny's room cautiously. My breathing is ragged and shallow, and the room feels like it is closing in on me. I have another syringe tucked behind my wrist. I am taking no chances. I know I can't keep sedating her indefinitely, but I can't think clearly enough to decide what to do next. I just need a couple of days to figure things out.

She is still completely comatose, lying in precisely the same position she was when I left. I breathe a sigh of relief. I may need to lower her dose; she is so thin. I reach out my hand to touch one of her feet. She looks lifeless. Pale and unresponsive, like a beautiful porcelain doll. I stroke the top of her elegant foot gently.

Without warning she leaps off the bed and to her feet violently; her eyes are wide and full of fire. There is fight and pure determination in her stare. Fear takes hold of me. In a split second, she emits a blood-curdling scream and lunges at me. Her teeth are bared, and saliva is dripping from her snarling mouth.

I move instinctively out of her path. She is still under the effects of the sedation, and her movements are not as quick or as accurate as her brain is ordering them to be. Her body is clumsy and ungainly, as though she is wading through water. She has thrust herself towards me with such intensity that she cannot stop, and she tumbles past me and into the open doorway. Her head hits the hard floor with a sickly thud.

All she needs to do is close the door on me and she is free.

Of course, I have a key and I could instantly leave the room after her. She scrambles to her feet and tries to close the door with every ounce of strength she has. I get to it in time, she is waiflike and easy to overcome. I push the door back and she is knocked off her feet. She is flailing frantically, scrambling and moaning. She makes it to her feet momentarily before she loses her footing and stumbles backwards. I watch the colour drain from her face when she doesn't hit the ground this time. She hits something hard and solid and is lifted to her feet. Her brow furrows and her face twists into a scowl as she tries to turn. I watch, mesmerised, and completely glued to the spot.

There is an ear-splitting scream as he wraps his strong arms around her and holds her tightly. Their bodies morph into one animal. Her screams quickly turn to whimpers as terror swells within her and tears fall down her horror-stricken face. She has lost all hope. I am torn between anger and relief at his presence. I feel tears falling down my own face. I am still unable to move but I manage a whisper.

"George?"

"Yes, sir. Yes. Are you okay?"

My body is numb. I feel overwhelmed by his sudden and unexpected arrival. My eyes mist over. I want to cry at the horror of this whole, unbearable situation. How did I get here? I didn't want any of this to happen.

I don't look at Penny, I focus on the face of my rescuer, a haunted look in his eyes. My friend. My wonderful George. I want to scream at him to leave, but the words get lost in my throat. I don't want George caught up in something that will harm him. This is my responsibility, not his. George may have gone against my wishes by coming down here, but somehow, he knew I was in danger.

"I think you should leave, George." My words are croaky,

and I feel unsteady. The blood that belongs in my head feels like it is in my legs. They are heavy and my head is light and airy.

George is insistent. "No. Stay with me, sir. Talk to me." His voice is unsteady and heavy with emotion.

He takes a deep breath and turns away from me, his eyes dull with sadness. Penny is swallowed up in his huge form. His broad back is towards me, protecting me. He is speaking to her. His words are stifled, I listen carefully but I can't make out any of what he is saying. There are black spots in front of my eyes and the room has begun to sway nauseatingly.

Unexpectedly, I hear a sharp, hideous sound. An atrocious crack that splits the atmosphere. My blood freezes. George rotates slowly to face me once more, his face contorted, and I hear a sickening thump as the body falls to the floor. I hold my breath and I don't dare to move.

Penny is no longer in George's arms. Indeed, Penny is no longer anything at all. George looks at me and his eyes are watery and hard to read. He is watching me, waiting for my reaction.

Fear has stolen my words. I am stunned. I stare at him, adrenaline crashing around my body. We stand in silence for what seems like hours, but I know is barely even seconds. The blood begins to return to my head, and I stifle a scream. I have to hold it together somehow. My throat is sealed with raw panic.

George is still watching me intently. Eventually, I find my voice.

"George, I..."

George is staring at me, his eyes swimming with fear. I need to get him away from here. Away from what he has done. Before he breaks.

I take George's hand in mine and lead him towards the stairs. His palms are clammy and radiate heat. He looks at the floor and I mirror him. His veil of calm and control is crashing down. I squeeze his hand gently.

"You are afraid," I say.

"Yes." His voice is childlike and loaded with fear. "I think maybe we should call someone?"

George's whole body is shaking. I want to throw my arms around him and hold him close.

"No," I say simply. My tone is calm but secure. The way a parent would speak to a child after a nightmare. "No, George. I don't think we need to call anyone."

His brow furrows and I hear his breath catch in the back of his throat.

We arrive at my office. I'm not sure how we managed to walk here. I want to close the door and shut us both in here forever, away from the nightmare downstairs. George doesn't look up at me. He looks like a ghost, his eyes hollow and darting across the floor, never quite focusing on anything.

Eventually, he sinks into one of the chairs at my desk and rubs his thinning hair. I stand behind him and place a hand on his shoulder. He is still in a state of shock, but I know he will be okay in time. He is stronger than he thinks.

"George, I am going to go back downstairs. Alone. I don't want you to come with me."

He looks up, alarmed, and clearly about to protest.

"There are some things I need to do by myself, and then I need you to drive me somewhere later."

George's expression is one of bewilderment.

"I need you to trust me, George. I know what to do. I can fix all of this." I take big, deep breaths and pull my shoulders back. It's easier to appear in control when someone is more consumed by fear than you are. George stares into my eyes intimately. I don't flinch and I don't look away. Finally, there is a shift in his posture, and I hear him exhale forcibly. He nods resignedly and we share a moment of silent understanding.

The reality of what has just happened is beginning to affect my body. I can't let George see the panic rising within me. I turn and walk away from George, fear and dread mounting with every footstep. I haven't felt true terror like this for so long, it gnaws at my insides and multiplies like cancer.

I keep walking. I don't look back.

Chapter Eleven

George is waiting in my office. He did exactly as I asked and did not follow me downstairs. He looks defeated. It has been almost six hours since we parted ways. I'm worried about him.

"Have you eaten?"

"No. But... that's not..." George is struggling for words. "Can I... anything you need me to... help with?"

"No, everything is okay." I recognise the absurdity of the statement, but I don't need to add anything further to George's mental load right now.

"Could you meet me outside in an hour with the car please, George? That drive I mentioned." I doubt he will remember. He nods and flops back down into the chair.

I am beyond weary. I squeeze my eyes tightly shut and then open them as wide as I can. I need to find the strength to deal with Penny's body. There is no point thinking about it or discussing it any further, neither of us can change what has happened. Regret can have its time later, there is no place for it tonight.

I am desperate for a shower, and I urgently need something

to eat. I need to focus and take each small task one by one. One step at a time. One thing at a time.

I am running late, which is not like me at all. I normally shower quickly, but I must have stayed under the water much longer than I realised. There is a lot to wash and rinse away from today.

I can hear the car idling outside my window, but I know George will wait. I look at myself in the mirror. I have dressed for the occasion and as such, I don't look like myself. Thankfully, I have never borne any physical resemblance to my father, there is nothing in my appearance that reminds me of him. He had a shock of unruly, black hair and eyes so dark they looked like holes. I can't recall the detail of my mother's appearance. I don't think about her at all; there's nothing good for me in those thoughts. They hurt.

George says nothing as I get in the car. I stay silent too, this is an unavoidable and painful journey and pleasantries are inappropriate. I didn't want this to happen, but now that it has, I have to fix it.

George drives me to the back of the house and everything I need is outside, just as I left it. George unbuckles his seat belt and I hold up a hand. He understands and fastens the seat belt again. I am not as physically strong as George, but there are consequences to what I have done, and I must take them on my shoulders.

We drive in silence for over an hour, and I work hard to stay focused on the task at hand. Eventually, we arrive. I shiver and my face prickles with goosebumps. Without the sound of the car engine, the silence is oppressive. It is pitch black outside, but the night is calm, and I know this place. Even after all these years, the memories are crystal clear. I had hoped that I would never return, but some things are unavoidable, no matter how hard you try.

I speak for the first time.

"Stay in the car, George. I'll come back when everything is done." George doesn't respond and he doesn't turn around. The air is heavy with anticipation. The hairs on the back of my neck stand up. I close my eyes and prepare myself and, for a moment, time stands still. I feel myself getting out of the car.

It will take me several trips to complete everything. I will leave the body until last. Carry everything else first, dig the hole second, and transport the body third. It's safer that way.

I can hear the gravel crunching under my boots, I can almost feel it inside my head. The darkness is all-consuming and a big part of me wants to run away. I mustn't and I won't. I will myself to keep walking.

I dig my nails into my hands to try and feel something. Anything. But there is nothing.

I bury Penny's body. That's all I want to say about it.

If only she would have stayed, she would still be alive. If only she had given me a chance.

I can't think about it anymore, it sickens me, and I am surer than ever that I am hurtling towards hell. If I could, I would claw my skin off to wash away the evil that lives inside me.

The return journey seems to pass in an instant. I think I must have fallen asleep at some point. My mouth is bone-dry, and my temples are thumping and painful to the touch. George opens the door for me, and I struggle out of the car. I can see he wants to take care of me but is lost as to the right thing to do. I cut him off before he says anything.

"George, I need a few quiet days. I shan't be around much, but I would like you to be here."

He nods. "Certainly, sir. I will be here every day. As always."

There is so much that I want to say to George, but everything will have to wait. I am spent.

"George, will you find some work for May to do? Tell her that I have back-to-back meetings or something."

George smiles at me with watery, dazed eyes.

"I have my appointment with Dr Pathirana on Tuesday, so, if I don't see you before..." George manages a weary nod as my voice trails off. I hate what this is doing to him. I feel a wave of sadness and turn away before the inevitable tears begin to fall. "I am so sorry about all of this, George." I force myself to walk away with a purpose that I don't feel. It takes every ounce of my strength. I don't want to see George's reaction. My head is swimming and I need time to process everything and pack it all away. Create an order somehow. I also need to work out what happens next.

Penny is gone.

There was no other choice, but I think her absence will leave a hole in my life. A hole I'm worried I can't live with.

I get ready for bed in the same methodical way I always do. Hunger is eating away at my stomach, but the urge to sleep is winning and food will have to wait until the morning. I climb under my covers, curl into a ball, and I am asleep within seconds.

The days pass in a blur. The exhaustion is crushing. I sleep, but not always at night and I eat, but not always at mealtimes. I embrace it and go with what my body and mind are telling me is right. A dark, inescapable cloud of shame is my constant companion. It presses down on me, and I feel myself changing. I allow myself to think about my father. Relieved to find that the thought of him still disgusts me. I take out the memories carefully and pack them away again when I am done each day.

It has been many years since my father died, but time doesn't matter. The effects on my humanity are permanent. Not simply injuries, but deep, jagged scars that can't heal. I have tried to live a good life. I have tried so very hard.

As the days pass, I feel a sense of stability return. My days line up again, and I am ready to face the world.

I have done a bad thing. A terrible, unforgivable thing. I'm not yet sure if I am a bad person.

All the while, I know George is waiting patiently. I picture his face many times. The image of him brings me warmth. I know he will be worrying about me, just as I am about him. I didn't tell him how long I would need.

Tonight will be my last night alone. Tomorrow is Tuesday and I am ready to speak to Dr Pathirana. I am done with the incessant fighting and self-flagellation.

These days have brought me clarity, and I am ready. I either face the world and live, or I don't. I'm not ready to give up. Tomorrow is a new chapter in my life, and I hope that George will be with me. I pray that I haven't lost him.

Chapter Twelve

George's face softens when I enter my office the next morning. There is such tenderness in his expression, and I can see that these days have brought uncertainty and fear for him.

"Good morning, George. I'm sorry it took me so long." I raise my eyebrows and George gives me a tentative smile.

"Shall we leave at 9.30am for your appointment like last week?"

I nod. "Yes, thank you."

This all feels so normal.

"Anything else you need before then?"

"No, that's it for now. But could we chat this evening if that is okay with you?" George nods and I smile at him and sit at my desk.

Completely normal.

"Can you ask May to come in? Has she been... okay?"

George smiles and walks towards the door. "She's been happily working away. No problems at all, sir. I'm sure she'll be happy to see you."

"Perfect. I'll see you out front at 9.30am." I hear George and

May's muffled conversation, followed by May's polite knocking on the door.

"Good morning, May, how lovely to see you!" I am not usually this friendly or upbeat and she is thrown. I want her to see me as approachable, but perhaps I am overdoing it. Overcompensating. She appears embarrassed and looks around the room for a reason for my unusual behaviour.

"Good morning, sir, it's good to see you."

"Thank you, May, it's good to see you, too. George tells me you've been working very hard."

"Uh... George said... Uh... thank you, sir."

"Excellent. George and I will be gone for most of the morning and all I would like you to do is take calls. You can take the afternoon off if you'd like. Do something nice."

May tilts her head. She is watching me with a mixture of suspicion and confusion. I like May but I know she is somewhat wary of me. I genuinely would like her to feel more comfortable and relaxed at work, and happy to be here. I don't want to make her any more uncomfortable than I have already.

"Can I have some tea please, May?"

"Yes, sir, right away, sir." She lets out a shaky laugh before pressing her hand to her mouth with embarrassment and rushing out of the room. She can't get away from me quick enough. I was trying to be nice, perhaps I need to tone it down a bit at first.

I am still in a positive mood when George pulls the car around to pick me up. He is surprised to see me standing outside and I see him frantically checking his watch. I don't wait for him to get out of the car and open my door, I simply get in.

"You're not late, George. I just fancied some fresh air." He tries to hide his surprise and I detect a hint of nervousness in there, too. I put my hand out and touch his forearm. George raises his eyebrows and nods

He drives with care, and I study his strong profile. He is swallowing needlessly and is focusing hard, despite driving down a straight, empty road. It's obvious we need to clear the air. I want him to know that no question is off-limits. I know I can trust this man. We have less than thirty minutes before my appointment with Dr Pathirana.

"Is there anything you want to ask me, George?"

He continues to look at the road, but his cheeks flush slightly. I can see he is nervous. He shakes his head.

"Come on, George. I'm sure you have questions, and I will answer anything. I trust you."

He doesn't answer.

If I were George, there would be one burning question. I know he must be thinking about it.

"Do you want to know what I did when I got out of the car?"

He shakes his head again, but I notice prominent goosebumps appear on his tanned forearms. He answers me clearly, despite avoiding the question entirely. "I think maybe you should talk to the doctor about it all."

That's not the response I was expecting, but I know what he means. The effects of Penny's death have caused us both huge mental strain. I need to find a way to talk it through with Dr Pathirana without revealing any details.

I'm surprised he doesn't want to know. The curiosity would eat me up. Plus, if there was even a small chance I could be implicated in a crime, I'd want to know that everything had been taken care of.

Something is brooding within him though, it's palpable. I try one last time.

"I can see there is something you want to say or ask. Please do. It doesn't matter what it is." I will give him this final chance. If he doesn't want to talk about it, I have to respect that. I know what it's like to decide something needs to be locked away inside your mind.

"It's..." His eyes glaze over, and his voice is quiet and shaky. I wonder if the guilt is becoming too much for him.

"Go on," I say.

"It's just..." He takes a deep breath in and starts tapping the steering wheel. I give him the space and time that he needs. Eventually, he puffs out his cheeks and audibly exhales. "It's nothing. I'm just concerned about you, that's all."

As I promised myself, I don't push him. But his face gives everything away. I can see the painful thoughts and fears etched into the lines of his face. I want to comfort him, to tell him that what he did was brave and, in many ways, kind.

Instead, I change the subject. "Let's chat this evening, George?"

"No problem, sir."

In my solitary days, after Penny left, I had the chance to think about the future. I'd like to share my thoughts with George. I am devastated by the loss of Penny, but I can't change that now; I have to look forwards. Everything is beginning to take shape in my mind.

George parks the car outside Dr Pathirana's office. I am five minutes early. I check in with Elizabeth, who seems a little downtrodden today. I relax into the buttery soft chair. There is a luxurious citrus scent in the room, like a refreshing breath of fresh air. I'm looking forward to seeing Dr Pathirana again. I haven't been able to deduce a lot about her, despite knowing her for such a long time. She is very good at keeping me away from herself, which of course she is right to do.

She invites me in at exactly 10am, we shake hands and greet each other warmly and I sit.

"How has this week been for you, Monty?" She has her expensive pen poised. For me to get the benefit of being here, I need to be as truthful as possible. I know I can't tell her everything that has occurred this week as she has certain legal responsibilities. However, if I tell blatant lies, there is no point in me speaking with her. I think it would be detrimental and frustrating for me.

"It's safe to say I have had an eventful week. I have done a lot of soul-searching and I feel ready to begin a new chapter in my life. I feel very positive about it, excited even."

She looks pleased.

"That does indeed sound positive, Monty. Let's look into things in a little more detail." I relax and lean forward. "I've been thinking about you a lot this week, Monty. What I'd like to do in this session is spend some time discussing your new friendship, but make sure we leave time to discuss your romantic relationship in more detail. I think we came to that too late in our last session and didn't give it the attention it deserved. How does that sound to you?"

"Thank you, Doctor. I'd definitely like to discuss my new friend. It's going really well, and I have lots to tell you." She is writing and thankfully not making eye contact. "But I won't be seeing Penny again."

She looks up suddenly. "Oh... what happened? You seemed to speak so positively of your relationship when we last spoke."

"Yes, but I realised we wanted different things, and, after some difficult discussions, she made it clear that she didn't want a long-term relationship with me."

She seems unusually disappointed. "I am so sorry to hear that, that must have been very hard to hear."

"Yes. Yes, I suppose it was. Although I didn't handle it as

well as I would have liked. But I've done a lot of thinking and I have realised it is for the best. There was a lot of good that came from my relationship with Penny, things I have learned."

This piques her interest. "Can you tell me what they are?"

"Certainly." Some of them at least. "I know now that I want a partner in my life. I want someone to share my time with, but I need someone who gives me the things I need out of the relationship. I want commitment and loyalty; I need someone who wants to stay."

"So, you'd like to find another partner?"

"Yes, I would, and I don't want to be too presumptuous, but I can imagine something happening very soon. I have made space in my life for someone and I'm very hopeful. I have realised that not all relationships have to look or feel the same."

She smiles, but I can tell she has follow-up questions.

"That's all great to hear. Truly it is. But you seem quite certain of a new partner, is there anyone on the horizon? Somebody you'd like to get closer to?" From my words, that's not an unreasonable deduction.

"No, sorry, Doctor. I'm not speaking of anyone specific, just that I'm feeling more open and confident. I have had one relationship now, and although it ended... differently than I had first hoped, I know that means I can have another, and I think future relationships will turn out much better for me."

She continues her line of questioning. We discuss my hopes and my concerns about romantic relationships. I answer honestly and vaguely where necessary.

"Thank you for sharing all of that with me, Monty. We will pick up your progress at every session, but I will be led by you. Please know that you only need to share what you feel is relevant at these sessions. You are entitled to private relationships, as the rest of us are. There may be things that you wish to keep private and special between you and your future partners. Please know that is entirely normal."

I smile as she speaks. Entirely normal. This is exactly what I was hoping to hear from her.

"That's good to know. Therapy has only worked for me because of my complete honesty. Sometimes I want to hold things back because I worry about what people will think. Does that make sense?"

She nods in complete agreement. "I fully understand how you feel. Your experiences have been unique, and in your previous circumstances, I agree that a complete disclosure approach has worked in your favour. However, this is different. You are most certainly allowed to have private moments with a partner."

I struggle to hide the wave of relief that courses through me. She is giving me permission, in fact telling me it is entirely normal and appropriate, to keep the details of my future relationships from her.

"Thank you, Doctor. That is immensely reassuring."

"So, let's move on to your friendship, shall we? You mentioned you had lots to tell me. What's your friend's name?"

"His name is George."

She sits back in her chair and opens a new page in her notebook, simultaneously crossing her slim legs. I consider her for a moment. She is a very beautiful and well-put-together woman, but I have no attraction to her whatsoever. I don't think it's because she is older, I suspect it's because she knows too much. She holds too much power.

"Tell me about George."

"George and I have become closer this week. I have a feeling we'll be spending a lot more time together. He makes me feel good about myself and he seems to admire me."

She interrupts me and I sense I've triggered something. "Do you like that?"

"Do I like that he admires me?" I am taken aback by the question. Who wouldn't like that? "Yes, of course, it makes me feel like a good person, someone worthy. Is that not okay?" I feel a flicker of irritation, but I am also concerned that I have said something inappropriate.

"Please don't worry, it's just not a word I've heard you use before. I simply wanted to find out how that made you feel."

I'm not sure I believe her. I think I may have missed something. I gloss over the rest, treading carefully and avoiding detail.

I talk about taking some thinking time after Penny left. I describe going for a drive with George and making plans to talk with him. She doesn't interrupt me to clarify anything again. I'm not surprised, as everything I am saying is remarkably mundane. I glance at the clock, and I am thankful to see that there is less than ten minutes of our session remaining.

"You had some worries about making a friend who was like you in some way. Does that still concern you?"

"No, not anymore. He is calm and measured, perhaps a little more closed off than I would like. But everything is fine." I'm surprised to find that I'm not enjoying speaking with her anymore. I feel as though I'm asking her for permission. I've never found Dr Pathirana to be anything but helpful, but it's not working this time. I needed her help in the past, but I'm not sure what she can offer me now.

"You talked about sharing with him. How do you feel about that?"

I'm tired now and I want to get out of here. I am giving terrible responses, just to be done with it. I press my palms into the arms of the chair.

"I feel comfortable around him, but I've realised I don't need to share my past to have a close friendship."

She presses me. "Really? I thought that was the whole point?"

I stop myself from sighing. I do wish she would just leave it alone. I know what I am doing. I wasn't expecting to have to explain myself like this.

"No. It's not. I've been looking for the wrong thing. Being myself doesn't necessarily mean talking about myself. I think George and I can be friends. That is enough."

She is writing down everything I say.

We both look up at the clock. Finally, the session is over. I am itching to get back to George. I don't feel any better, if anything I feel worse. Feeling exasperated can't possibly be the point of therapy. I know now that it was a mistake coming back here. I panicked and gravitated towards something that once brought me strength and gave me hope. I can see now that coming back here is simply going backwards. I'm not the same person I was then. I can make my own decisions now.

I don't want to set off any alarm bells, so I agree to another session and shake her hand before I leave. I take a moment to look at her striking face. This woman has helped me enormously. I wouldn't be here without her, but it's time for a new chapter.

It's time for me to start living.

Chapter Thirteen

I don't jump into the car as I did this morning. I climb in slowly and roll my neck from side to side. I had hoped George and I could chat and listen to music on the way home, but I have little to give. I check my phone and see a missed call and a text message from Susannah. I've been keeping her at arm's length. Miles was my only connection to her; I can't understand why we'd need to stay in touch now he's dead. All we would do is talk about Miles. How can that be good for either of us?

I read her message. It's an invite to a special dinner to honour Miles on his birthday this weekend. It is a lovely gesture. I message her back to say that I would love to, but I will be away on an important business trip that can't be cancelled. She texts back immediately:

> I understand. We will miss you. I hope you are okay. The grief is just unbearable x.

Susannah loved Miles deeply and I know that she misses him dreadfully. But grief is much more complicated than most people realise. What she is feeling is not just the loss of Miles's

77

life, his lost potential, and all the things he will miss out on. She is also grieving for herself. The unwelcome changes to her life, the loneliness, and the inconvenience of it all. That part of it is much harder to process.

I message her back to say I hope she is okay too and put my phone away. I've had quite enough of everything for today. My head is throbbing, and I rub my temples to no great effect. George turns to look at me but says nothing.

"I'm sorry, George, my session was not great, and to top it off I've just had a text from Susannah wanting to see me." I close my eyes, lean my head back against the car seat and exhale loudly. "I'm so tired, and sick of the constant pressure."

"That sounds hard. What was wrong with your appointment though?" George asks. He surprises me with his question. It's not like him to be so forward.

"Dr Pathirana has been a huge help. I think she is brilliant. I owe her my life in some ways." I wince a little at how dramatic that sounds, but it's certainly a fair comment. "But I'm not going to see her again. It's not good for me anymore." My eyes are still closed, and my headache is increasing exponentially.

"And why is that?" Another question.

"Because I will have to lie to her, and it defeats the purpose. I have spent my entire life censoring and lying by omission. It's exhausting. I'm certainly not going to pay hundreds of pounds to do the same with her."

I take deep breaths in and out. Slow and steady.

"What did you talk about?" I suspect George is concerned about me discussing recent events.

"I told her what I needed to. Got it off my chest." I open one eye slightly to watch George's reaction. He nods knowingly and we sit in silence.

"Anyway, let's not talk about that anymore. I'm going to

cancel my next appointment. I'll come up with something convincing and that will be the end of it."

"And Susannah?"

"I'll just keep making excuses until she gets the message." George opens his mouth to speak but then closes it quickly and stops himself. I open my eyes and catch his in the rear-view mirror. "It's okay, George, what is it?"

"Sorry, sir, something just occurred to me, but I think it's overstepping the line."

Even if that is the case, I still want to hear what he has to say.

"No, go on, please."

"It's just... You seem to be your most content, at your best, when you are being honest and not hiding away. I wonder whether that applies to Susannah, too?"

He's got an extremely good point. Why am I behaving like this with her? He is right, and I feel stupid and weak for not acting on it myself. I'm not sure what makes me do it, but I lean towards him and place my hand gently on his forearm. He doesn't flinch when I touch him.

"You're right, George. I'm not being fair. I'll call her tomorrow."

He looks over his shoulder briefly and smiles. "I'm glad, sir. You need to start doing things that make you feel good." I meet George's eye in the mirror again and we smile together. Is it that simple? I wonder. Perhaps if we are willing to accept the consequences of our actions, we can all be whoever we want to be.

I remember that I'd asked George to talk with me tonight, but I'm not at my best and the conversation I want to have with him is extremely important.

"Could we cancel tonight please, George? I think dinner tomorrow evening would be better. I am so sorry to let you down, but I need to get my head straight first. Would that be okay?"

"Of course, sir. You know I am always here any time you need me."

We complete our journey in silence. Tiredness is pressing down on me. My head is swimming with imaginary discussions with Susannah. I'm anxious about the conversation but looking forward to the result. I know she will be upset, but we will both just have to deal with it. Despite it still being the morning, I doze off for the remainder of the short journey.

I'm woken gently by George's calming voice and his outstretched hand. "We are home now, sir, let's get you inside, it's freezing." I take his big, warm hand and let him lead me indoors.

Chapter Fourteen

I wake suddenly and in a cold sweat. The light shining through the gap in my curtains tells me it's morning, but I don't feel rested. My mouth is dry, and my throat feels scratchy. I can see my dreams before my eyes, but they start to pull away from me before I can commit anything real to memory. I can't remember anything of value, but I know I am scared. I'm not a stranger to nightmares.

I shower and dress and try to shake the after-effects of my nightmare. I make my bed, ensuring the sheet has neat folds at all the mattress corners, before draping the duvet evenly over the bed. I straighten the few, functional possessions on my dresser and walk slowly to my office. I know I have some meetings this morning, my accountant being the first one.

May is busy typing and George is waiting in my office. My tea tray is there as always, and everything looks just as it should.

To distract my mind, I send Susannah a text.

Could we talk later, please? Around 5pm?

She messages back immediately.

Sure. Everything okay? Xx.

I ignore it.

George will be running errands while I am busy with meetings.

I hand him a list. "Could you add these items to your 'to-do list' today, please? They are things for our dinner tonight. I will be cooking; I'd like it to be special."

He takes the list and studies it carefully but gives me very little reaction.

"Sorry, I realise it was supposed to be last night. Do you have plans?"

"No, it's not that, sir. I was just reading." He folds the list in half and tucks it into his pocket. "Is there anything else I can help with?"

"No, thank you, George." He leaves and I pour myself some tea. My stomach rumbles. I sip my tea and reach into my brain to remember my dreams once more. Nothing but blackness.

I look up and see that George has left his wallet on the desk. He'll have a completely wasted journey without it, and an embarrassing moment at the checkout, too. My car is still in the driveway, so I grab the wallet and hope I can catch him. I run quickly but carefully over the polished wooden floors. I shout his name as he closes the front door, but I am too late.

I slip George's wallet into the top drawer of my desk and spend the next hour speaking to my accountant. It's all good news with regard to my finances, it always is. I pay excellent people a lot of money to invest my money and make even more money.

I decide to call George and tell him that he has left his wallet behind, although I'm surprised he hasn't noticed and come back by now. I lift the well-worn, brown leather wallet out of the drawer and bring it to my face. I recognise George's scent immediately. Warm, and almost peppery. I turn the wallet over in my hands. Receipts bulge from the straining sides and there is a faint metallic rattle as I pass it between my hands. I open it with care and smile as I see George's stern face staring back at me from his driving licence. He looks so different now.

I pick up the phone to call George, but something stops me and makes me take a closer look. I study George's eyes, empty and staring in the mini-portrait photo, and then I see it.

My blood runs icy cold, and I can feel a wave of sickness rising inside me. I trace my finger over the photo, willing it not to be true. I trusted George completely, but evidently, everything I thought I knew about George is a lie.

It can't be. It doesn't make any sense at all.

There is no denying it. The photograph is small and at least ten years old, but still, the resemblance to my father is unquestionable. George has managed to alter his appearance just enough that I didn't see it right away, and time has aided the deception and softened his face. I focus again on the photo. I can hear blood pulsing in my ears and anger is thrumming in my veins.

I take a deep breath and summon my fight for survival. I've had to survive much worse things than this in my life, but the fact George has been lying to me feels like a knife through my heart. I thought George was my friend, more than a friend even. The betrayal is sickening.

I pace around my office, trying to dispel some of the energy surging through me. George will be back any minute to collect his wallet; he can't complete his errands without it. Although George is now striking me as a man who may have thought of every eventuality. I can't let my feelings for George hamper my need to protect myself. The George I care for isn't real. My stomach clenches at the thought that our entire relationship has been a lie. What does he have planned for me? He has been working for me for over a year, why has he waited all this time? What does he want?

And then I understand. The world begins to fall away beneath me. My brain stutters and I stand impossibly still, adjusting to this new and devastating reality. George has been watching and waiting. Biding his time. Waiting for the perfect opportunity. I know exactly what he wants.

He wants revenge.

He is going to frame me for murder, and he knows that nobody will believe me.

Despite everything crashing down around me, there is no choice but to act immediately. Even if I act now, it may already be too late. My chest constricts sharply as I realise that I have played into his hands completely. I think of where Penny lies. The police will never believe that I didn't kill her.

I call George.

"Hello, sir." His voice is unusually quiet. I don't say a word. He knows, I can hear it in the silence. Mentioning the wallet seems pointless now, and I'm not playing along with this charade a moment longer.

"Hello, George." I am quivering and failing to control the volume of my voice. I slam down the phone as the fear and anger spreading through me erupts. I regret it instantly and try to call back, but his phone is engaged or switched off.

I have to assume he is coming for me. I must be ready.

May is at her desk, happily typing.

"Good morning, May." She raises her eyes and a look of uncertainty flickers across her face.

"Good morning, sir." She is swallowing and blinking too much. She looks down at my hands and I realise that I am still trembling. "Are you okay, sir?"

I manage an unconvincing smile and walk past May's desk to the large arched window at the far end of the room. I have a clear view of the drive from where I am standing, and there is no sign of George or my car. I need the doors locked and to get back to my office as quickly as possible. I can see both the driveway and all the cameras from there and I will be best placed to get the measure of what he is planning for me. I consider sending May home, but perhaps her presence will be a deterrent for George.

"Sorry, sir, it's just..."

My heart is galloping. Time is not on my side, and I feel like George currently holds all the power. "What is it, May?"

"Are you going to fire me?" she blurts out. I blink with astonishment. I don't know why she would think that. Unless this is part of George's plan. "It's just I really need this job; I need the money. I have bills to pay. Please."

I can't work out where any of this is coming from. I don't want May to be worried, but I certainly don't have time to deal with any of this now. I look at her properly for the first time. She looks so desperate and little in her chair. In my haste, I hadn't noticed her obvious upset. Her eyes are puffy and red-rimmed. A make-up-stained tissue rests in her hands.

"No, May. I am not going to let you go. Please don't worry."

She looks relieved and a wide smile fills her whole face. "Oh, thank you, sir. It's just that things have been... Anyway, it doesn't matter. Thank you, sir."

I am curious to know what she means, but it will have to wait. There are more pressing matters.

"If George comes back, will you pass on a message for me?"

"Yes, no problem, sir. And thank you, sir, thank you so much." Her palpable relief prompts a stab of guilt inside me. I had no idea that this job was so important to her.

"No need to thank me, May. If you think about it, nothing has actually happened. Just a misunderstanding. No thanks required."

She smiles and wipes an escaped tear from her cheek with the now partially shredded tissue.

"Would you tell George that he left his wallet in my office? He can get it from my desk. I am going out for an urgent meeting." She is writing. "Did you get all of that?"

"Yes, sir." She reads it back word for word. "Do you need anything else, sir? Should I arrange a car for you?"

"That's okay, May, but thank you. I will be heading out on my own today. You can pass that on to George, too." She nods and writes, thankfully smiling once again. "Goodbye, May." I walk quickly out of the room taking one last glance through the window before I go. Still no sign of George.

I walk around every room on the first floor. The car has not returned, and I wouldn't imagine he has had the time to walk. I make my way back to my office and close the door. I check my phone incessantly, but he hasn't called. I sit at my desk and watch the cameras. My thoughts are clouded by a mix of trepidation and resentment.

May works diligently and then leaves at 5pm. I don't eat. I stay alert. I am all alone, but at least for the moment, I am safe. I am shocked that George managed to fool me, and I know that makes him dangerous.

Chapter Fifteen

Despite every effort, I know I have dozed off in the chair a few times and I finally give up my watch and go to bed shortly before midnight. George is not coming back today. He's in no rush, he's proven that already. His absence is hugely unnerving, I almost wish he'd get it over with. Whatever "it" is.

I wake to a sound that I can't quite place. It is pitch black but I know that I fell asleep with the light on. I reach for my phone on the bedside table, and my scalp prickles when I discover that it is gone. My breathing is too fast, and there are no options here that don't leave me vulnerable. I blindly reach onto the floor and under the bed in the vain hope that I knocked my phone onto the floor. Instead, I touch skin. Warm, alive, moving skin.

I scream and try to sit up. I scramble furiously, my legs and arms get caught in the covers of my bed, and I am flailing like a helpless animal in the dark. I see the figure emerge and it looms, blacker than the darkness that surrounds us both. Fear paralyses me. There is nowhere to go, there is no escape this time.

I stop and sit quietly. Just as Penny was, I am out of options. The consequences will be whatever they will be. The figure leans over me and reaches out. I close my eyes and try to think of a happy memory, my one final thought on this earth. Nothing comes and I am not surprised.

My bedside light comes on suddenly, blinding me. My eyes are slow to adjust but I know without looking that the figure leaning over me is George. Fear pulses through me but I force myself to remain still. I wait for the knife or the strong hands around my throat, but they do not come. You don't wait patiently to kill someone quickly and painlessly.

I reluctantly meet his gaze, shocked to see that his eyes are sad and concerned with no trace of anger. He moves towards me gently and sits beside me on the bed, like a mother who's just finished a bedtime story and is about to tuck in their beloved child for the night. I am not surprised that he is torn. It shocks me that I'm willing to go down without a fight.

"Hello, Uncle George."

He closes his eyes, bows his head and exhales deeply. He shakes his head but still doesn't speak.

I don't know how I could have missed it. Now that I know, it's so obvious. He looks so much like him. Although I avoid remembering Father as much as possible, his evil face is etched onto my mind with hideous accuracy. I knew that he had a brother, but I'd never met my uncle and I didn't know his name. My father said he was a useless, insignificant piece of shit and they hadn't been in touch since he left home. I didn't give it a second thought my entire life.

The big difference is deep inside their eyes. Father's eyes were dark and deep yet always so full of emotion. Father was never dead behind the eyes, no matter what was happening. That's one of the things that scared me about him the most. The fact that nothing ever dulled him in any way.

George continues to sit calmly and quietly. His head remains bowed, and his eyes are squeezed tightly shut. This man has shown me something that I want, something I've been missing my whole adult life, he's taunted me with friendship. Losing him will hurt me deeply.

"So, Uncle George, what will you do with me? Should I be expecting the police? Are you here to serve justice to the little boy who betrayed his father?"

The colour rises on his face, and he flexes the fingers on his strong hands. I don't care anymore; he can do as he wishes.

"Perhaps framing me for murder is not sufficient revenge." I hold up my hands in mock surrender. "If you want to kill me, George, just fucking do it. I am past caring."

George flinches as I let my hands crash down onto the bed.

"I know your father was a terrible man..." he starts.

I hold out a hand to stop him. I'm not interested in anything he has to say about my father's childhood. I know this story. It is pathetic and I don't wish to hear it again. My father's parents knew he was wicked. Apparently, they "didn't know what to do with him" and "it was different times then". Essentially, they turned their backs and disowned him.

I force myself to look at George.

"I'm not here to hurt you. I am here to help you." He looks so genuine, but he has betrayed me. He has proven that I can't trust him. I mustn't be fooled again. "I can help you find a way through this." I look deep into his eyes, and I see the pain and the toll that the years have taken on him. "I am not here to frame you for murder, or to harm you in any way. I know I haven't handled things in the best possible way, but I am here for you. That's it. That's all I want to do."

I don't want to let my guard down too quickly. George's dishonesty can't be ignored, but I wonder if I have been looking at his deception in completely the wrong way. Jumping to all the wrong conclusions. I can see that George has suffered, too. We both have the same blood running in our veins, we can't escape that.

I start to soften; I can see that perhaps he has lied to protect me. Misguided, certainly, but I am beginning to doubt that the deceit was for his own personal gain.

We sit in silence. My head is a jumble of thoughts and feelings, but I am no longer scared. The longer we sit here, the more I trust that George wishes me no harm. He may not be the kindred spirit I thought he was. In fact, he is something more. He is my family, my blood. My twisted, broken, damaged blood.

I can certainly understand why George stayed away after Father died. I had a wonderful adoptive family; I was happy and well cared for.

"I am so sorry if I scared you. I wasn't sure what to do, but I am now. Trust me." He smiles at me, and I return the smile. I have so much to say, but I say nothing. We sit in comfortable silence for a long time. Our breathing, slowly returning to normal is the only sound in the room. My eyelids begin to feel heavy, and I feel my legs jerk suddenly as sleep threatens to take over. George stands up slowly and straightens the covers on my bed before walking towards the door. He hovers there a little too long and I can tell he's waiting for me to say something.

"Let's talk tomorrow, can we, George? I'm tired." Tired is an understatement. My body and mind feel as though they have just survived a battle. The torrent of emotions has left me completely spent.

"Of course." George closes the door behind him, and I pass out into the welcome blackness.

Chapter Sixteen

Night has become morning. I dress and stand by my bedroom window, watching the tree branches swaying gently in the soft breeze. Calmness has descended. My heart is a soft, steady drumbeat, and my breathing is quiet and free. Aside from the morning birdsong in the gardens, all is quiet and serene.

I walk to my office to meet George. No feelings of fear or anger flow through me. It's a wonderful feeling. There is so much that needs to be said between us, but I am ready.

I am fascinated by George and where our new relationship could take us. Nobody can change the past events etched upon their soul, and more damage can be done by pretending.

My office is bathed in sunlight and the aroma of fresh coffee is invigorating. George and I sit across from each other. He is very smartly dressed today. I've never considered George to be handsome, but today that's how he looks. George squints and rubs his eyes, and I pat my hand gently on the soft velvet of the seat closest to me, away from the direct sunlight. He moves to sit closer to me.

"George, can I say something?" George gestures for me to

continue. "Since Miles died, I've been thinking about my life more and more. Too much of my life has been filled with fear and self-loathing."

George looks deep into my eyes. The intensity is disarming. "Tell me more, sir, I want to help you."

Our relationship has changed. It is stronger now. I don't care that he lied to me about his relationship with my father, and now I understand why he kept it from me. He didn't know how I would react, and I believe him completely when he says he wants to help me. And I want his help. I want him in my life. And so, I am honest with him.

"What happened with Penny was horrible. I hate myself for it." I chase away the lump that rises in my throat. "But I think I want to try again with someone else."

George's mouth forms a lipless line, and he forcibly exhales through his nose. I lean forwards and clasp my hands together.

"Hear me out, George, please." I let the emotion in the room settle before continuing. "I don't want to hurt anyone. I need you to know that. I just want someone to stay with me, to want to be here and share their life with me. I've had a lot of time to think, and I think I know what I need to do to make that happen." George nods and clears his throat. "I need to find the right person, and I'm going to need your help."

I don't take my eyes off George. There is much more to say, but I can't risk overwhelming him at this point. George tilts his head back slightly and rests his hand on his chin.

"Okay, sir. Tell me what you need. Tell me everything."

Chapter Seventeen

Before

Today was number four. Number four was definitely the worst one yet. There is so much blood. I can't fathom how there could possibly be so much. Father has a nasty, weeping cut on his face and his eye is swollen. I know this is a big problem for him as he'll have to explain to the people he works with why his face looks like that. Father is usually happy afterwards, at least he was after the last three. Today he is crashing around the room, kicking things and shouting all the worst swear words.

I stand with my back to him. My current task is to mop the floor. I blur out the rest of the room and the thunderous noises he is making and look down at the wet mop and the floor. I stifle a cough. I know if I cough it will anger him, but the combination of metallic blood and bleach burns my throat. The floor isn't getting any cleaner. It has changed from bright red to a foamy, pink mess. I push the frothy bubble-gum-coloured liquid around the laminate floor. It seeps through the cracks and rolled-up edges of the damaged flooring. It must be soaking through to whatever lies beneath. I shudder as I realise it will probably live there forever, like a ghost.

I can see Father in my peripheral vision. He doesn't know I am looking. At least, I pray he doesn't. Without warning, he marches across the room towards me. I don't choose my reaction, and I have no idea what made me say it. I cradle the back of my head and bow down and away from him. The word escapes my mouth before I have a chance to stop it.

"Mummy!"

He stops suddenly, skidding a little on the sopping floor before finding his feet. I feel the blood freeze in my veins, and I am too petrified to lift my head. His voice is eerily quiet.

"What did you just say?"

I need to answer but I am mute with terror. My legs suddenly lose all their strength, as though turned to water. I crouch and wait for the inevitable kicking or beating that is sure to come my way.

"Look at me!" His voice is no longer quiet. I flinch and almost topple over. I have to put my right hand into the blood and bleach concoction on the floor to save myself. I twist my neck to look at him but stay hunched over and keep my dry hand over my head. His jaw is clenched tightly and combined with the gash on his cheek and misshapen eye, he looks utterly terrifying. His remaining eye looks different though, it is not burning with anger. It is big and sad. He's hurt. What I have said has hurt him.

He crouches down, the bottoms of his trousers soaking up the liquid from the floor. He turns his face towards me and stops with his lips almost touching my ear. His voice is a menacing whisper and pellets of spit hit my ear as he speaks.

"She didn't love you. She wanted me to leave you here and go with her. She hated you. But *I* stayed!"

His terrible words squeeze the air from my lungs and my chest aches with actual, physical pain. His knees crack loudly as he stands and turns away from me, placing his hands on his hips.

"Don't ever speak her name to me again."

I don't.

I start mopping.

Chapter Eighteen

Moving away from obligation towards honesty will not be an easy shift, but nothing in this world that's worth having comes easy. I decide to start with Susannah. I call and tell her that it is best we don't see each other again. She cries and tries to tell me that I don't mean it and that I am just grieving. That she will be here for me when I am ready. I absolutely believe her. Susannah is a kind person, and the last thing I want to do is hurt her any further. I know it is best for both of us if we lead separate lives from here on.

George and I spend almost every waking moment together. We talk, and we laugh, but most of all we make plans for the future. I can't go out and meet someone, I need them to come to me. I know that if I can choose the right person, then they will want everything that I want.

There are five applications for my new "personal assistant". I have them in my hand, ready to look over.

George has continued to call me "sir". I thought it would feel odd, but it doesn't. We are exactly as we should be.

I have placed the adverts for our new arrival very carefully. There is no way to trace them to me, and there are no details of the company or the location. These desperate times in the job market are certainly playing to my advantage. I tell George that I will choose a successful candidate today.

"Please could you book a table for you and the lady in question at the Grace Garden hotel for tomorrow afternoon? Then you can bring her back here to meet with me."

I spend the day looking over the applications in my room. Penny's arrival was unplanned, and I think that's one of the main reasons it wasn't successful. Things always work out better for me when I plan meticulously. Hope rises inside me as I read. I don't let any of the negative thoughts take over. I know this is an unusual way to meet a partner, but I also know that this is the best way for me. I have to believe in myself and my plans. Self-doubt and a desire to confirm can no longer rule my decisions.

There is one application that stands out above the others. I feel an instant connection. Her name is Miriam, and I have a new life to offer her. I commit Miriam's number to memory, and I shred the remaining applications.

I wonder what Dr Pathirana would have to say about my plans. I replay my last phone call to her office in my mind. I'm still concerned about how hasty my sudden cancellation will have appeared.

"Hello, Elizabeth, it's Montague Barclay. Could you please apologise to Dr Pathirana for me, I won't be able to make my appointment tomorrow?" I frown and curse internally. I'm disappointed at how I've worded that. Of course, I can make it. The fact is I don't want to.

I rectify this before she can respond. "Actually, can you cancel all my future appointments, please, and do thank Dr

Pathirana for me." I am about to wish Elizabeth a good day when she interrupts.

"Please hold for one moment, Mr Barclay." My ear is filled with loud but pleasant hold music. Before I can contemplate hanging up, I hear Dr Pathirana's voice replace Elizabeth's.

"Hello, Montague, how are you?" I'm sure she knows what I have just said to Elizabeth.

"I'm fine, Dr Pathirana. As I'm sure you heard me saying to your receptionist, I am cancelling my appointment tomorrow and any future appointments. I'm very happy to pay for tomorrow's session because of the short notice. I'm sorry, cancelling simply slipped my mind." I can hear her breathing quicken and I know she is going to try and convince me to stay.

"I think..."

"Please don't worry, Doctor, I know what I am doing, and I no longer require my appointments with you." I know she won't be easily put off and, once again, I regret restarting my sessions with her. It was an error of judgement.

"If you could..."

I remain calm and polite, but I don't let her finish.

"Thank you for your concern, Dr Pathirana. I appreciate everything you have done for me. Please believe that. Goodbye, Doctor." I hang up the phone. There's nothing she can do. I'm not required to see her anymore. I mean it when I say that I appreciate all she has done, but I need to move on now.

Chapter Nineteen

I have Miriam's number memorised, and I decide to call it so I can hear her voice.

"Hello." She answers straight away, but she sounds unsure and says the word like it is a question, her intonation rising at the end of the word. I consider speaking, but I decide against it. She does what I expect her to do. She repeats "Hello" a couple more times, followed by "Is somebody there?" and then sighs and hangs up.

George and I continue to be close. We chat at the beginning and the end of every day, at least. We have agreed that we don't discuss anything personal while May is here, and nothing is ever discussed over the phone, in text messages or in emails. Only face to face, and only when we are sure we are alone.

George is clearly on edge about tomorrow. He doesn't sit still in his chair as he usually does and he's bouncing his knees up and down, creating an irritating squeak.

In hindsight, I should have chosen a different location. The Grace Garden is an old, prestigious hotel. Its defining feature is opulence and exclusivity. George will feel out of place there and, as such, he may look out of place. His insecurity is bubbling over as we talk this morning. He is a person who likes instructions and certainties. For this to work, he needs to feel at ease, to feel in control. I stare blatantly at his bouncing knees. He stops immediately and smiles apologetically.

"George, please listen. I can see you are nervous about tomorrow. It is completely normal; I hope you realise that. Neither of us knows what will happen. You need to try and be okay with that."

He nods his head and smiles softly. "And you, sir? Are you okay with that? You seem... relaxed."

"Why, of course." The knee bouncing has been replaced by hand wringing, which is still annoying but noiseless at least. He looks at his squirming hands and shakes his head as I speak. I wish he believed in himself more. "You will arrive first, and the staff will bring her to your table."

He continues to look down, avoiding me. Almost as though he is trying to block out what I am saying.

"George." He doesn't look at me. "George!" I startle him and he looks at me with sad, bemused eyes. "What is wrong with you?"

"Nothing, sir. Sorry. I'm just thinking, but I don't think any of it will help. We just need to wait. See what happens. I just... I don't want to let you down. I don't want to do the wrong thing."

I understand his concerns, and I know that he will feel overwhelmed. I want to put my hand on his, but instead, I simply watch him and let him self-soothe his anxiety. I think it will look odd if we change the location now, so I don't offer. Suddenly he straightens himself up and gives himself a shake.

"Anything else this morning, sir? Otherwise, I'll be getting on with things."

"Nothing just now, thank you."

I know that George will be absolutely fine. He gets too deep inside his head sometimes.

I have imagined my encounter with Miriam from start to finish and I can already see her sitting across from George at the Grace Garden Hotel. Her delicate hands rested on the spotless, white tablecloth. Even though I haven't met Miriam, I know that George will be more nervous than she is. I don't think he has conducted an interview before.

George doesn't have any business experience that I know of. His employment history consists of jobs similar to the role he has with me. At fifty-eight, I don't suspect he will make any major changes in that respect. We need to work with what we have.

I think about our changing relationship. In such a short space of time, we have both chosen to forget who we really are. Now, we are a team. It works for us both, we are happy, and we fit.

I have made an extra special effort for this evening. I have changed into my favourite navy wool suit and a crisp white shirt. I have also applied a little of the cologne that Susannah bought me for Christmas. The box describes it as a mixture of bergamot and bitter orange, which is nonsense, but it still has an agreeable smell. My nightly meetings with George have become a welcome end to my day. May has arranged coffee and tea for us and I am surprised to feel a hint of nerves developing in my stomach. I hope tomorrow goes well for George; I need it to. I've busied myself with administrative tasks today, so George and I haven't seen much of each other. I reach for the teapot.

"Let's have a drink before we start, George, calm our nerves, shall we?"

He sits in his chair. I've come to think of it as his. It has come to bear the shape and scent of him. I pour carefully for us, but my hand is a little unsteady. I try my best to hide it and push away the flush of embarrassment that threatens to redden the tips of my cheeks.

George holds a piece of paper in his hands, most likely an aide-mémoire. It is overworked and ragged in his hands, a visible representation of his inner nervousness. He folds and twists it absent-mindedly. He has obviously spent a lot of time with it today. I nod to the paper.

"How has today been, George?"

He tears the page as he tries to open it the wrong way and I hear him curse under his breath.

"George, it's okay. Please. It's only me, I am here to help you."

He shrugs and attempts a light-hearted response. "That's not the way this is supposed to work is it, sir?" I can see some writing in ink on the page, but I'm not able to make out the detail. I don't ask. I don't want him to feel he doesn't have any autonomy or privacy here. That won't help improve his confidence. I can see the worry lines across his forehead, the questions running through his busy mind. I wish I could empathise more with his worries.

I do, however, know what he is worried about.

"My suggestion is this. Ask Miriam the questions that we have prepared. Tell her that if she passes this first part of the interview then she can ask me any further questions when she arrives here. That way you don't have to worry."

George looks at me with unease. He shakes his head, and I can see he is trying to find the words to express himself.

"Ask anything you like, George," I say, and open my arms widely as an invitation.

He focuses again and looks at me as if trying to see directly into my brain.

"It's just... I can't work out how you switch so quickly from one thing to another?"

I'm not completely sure what he means, and I ask him to elaborate.

"Sorry, I'm not explaining myself very well. It's not my place anyway..." He trails off and looks down at his hands self-consciously.

"I guess that's just how my mind works, George." I'm conscious of not offending him, and I want him to know that he has many other just as important and valuable qualities. "Why don't we enjoy our evening and see how tomorrow goes. How does that sound?"

He relaxes a little, but not completely. George's manner is changeable, too, but in a different way to mine. He ranges from unsure and overly apologetic, to almost military, occasionally bordering on aggressive. I accept him exactly as he is.

We sit and talk together for what feels like hours. I encourage him when I can sense his confidence wavering and, by the end of the evening, I feel assured that he feels much more positive about the interview tomorrow. I haven't mentioned the interview specifically for most of our conversation. But there are a few things I want to clarify before he leaves.

"George, this has been a really lovely evening, thank you. I don't want to put you on edge, but there are just a few things I want to say before we go our separate ways." He nods and bites his bottom lip nervously. "Remember to stay distant and detached. Stick to the questions, and don't ask her any personal questions. At the end of the interview, tell her that you will take her for a tour of the office. Make her think that she has got the job and that it is a simple formality. She will come with you; I am sure of it."

George says nothing, but there is a quiet understanding, and we take a moment to reflect.

The silence is broken by a sound at the front door. George doesn't move. The knocking is polite but insistent. A visitor is unexpected, to say the least. I never have unannounced visitors and especially not outside of working hours. I turn on my computer screen to view the security camera. The blue glow from the screen illuminates the room. George is watching me, waiting.

"What's wrong, sir?" The feed from the security camera is unclear at first, and I can't quite see the face of the person standing at my door. Soon the image becomes clearer, the features emerge, and I know exactly who it is.

"Sir?"

"It's fine, George. Don't answer. Don't do anything. She'll go away."

I hear the knocking again. Louder this time. I realise I have underestimated the lengths people will go to when you remove them from your life. She looks down and all I can see is the top of her head. George is standing next to me now. Looking at the screen and then back to me. I won't stop watching, I barely blink. She leans in close to the camera and her face suddenly fills the entire screen as she mouths words at me. I can see instantly what she is saying. "Let me in please, Monty." I shake my head insistently, even though she has no way of seeing me.

"Is there anything I can do, sir?" There is a quivering edge to George's voice. I continue to shake my head. I take long, slow breaths.

"We don't need this tonight, George, tomorrow is too important. I don't know what she wants at this hour. I will sort it out tomorrow. Don't worry about anything."

Dr Pathirana stands at the front door for over fifteen minutes. I am sure she means well and simply wants to check how I am after I cancelled my sessions with her. But this is not the time nor the place. This is my home.

George has started to pace around the room, running his hands through his thinning hair. Eventually, Dr Pathirana leaves. George looks a little shaken.

"Are you okay, George?"

"Yes. Yes, I'm fine. I just think that I should stay here tonight. I... I need to make a phone call first though. Is that okay? I'll be right outside the door."

He is worried for my safety. There is no reason to be. I am sure Dr Pathirana's visit was borne out of professional obligation. She is a good woman, and I'm sure she will understand when I explain that an unannounced visit is something that simply doesn't work for me.

I like the idea of George staying here though. I don't invite people to stay with me readily, but George is different. I want him to feel at home here with me. What I'd actually like is for him to be here permanently. There is a beautiful guest room with an en suite bathroom at the top of the house. I will show it to him once he has made his arrangements.

I don't know who he is speaking to but it's nice to know that he has someone who cares for him outside of here. Despite planning to, I haven't made any effort to ask him about his circumstances outside of his time here. This is even more important now I know that we are family. He must think me terribly self-involved, and I vow to ask him next time we meet.

George enters the room, and I am pleased to see that his anxiety level has dialled down a notch or two.

"Will you be staying, George?" I ask, even though I already know the answer.

"Yes, no question, sir." He smiles gently.

"Great, I think we both need to get some rest." He opens his mouth to speak but I beat him to it.

"There's everything you need for an overnight stay in the

guest room. Please treat it as your own. Tomorrow is a big day for us, and I'm glad you're staying here tonight."

George thanks me as I show him to his room. If George ends up living here in the future, then this would be his room. I hope he likes it. I'll make any changes that he needs.

"Goodnight, George, get some rest and don't worry about any more uninvited guests. I will sort it all out tomorrow. It is simply a misunderstanding, I promise you."

George looks at me with hooded, weary eyes. "Goodnight, sir." He closes the door quietly. I make my way to my bedroom. Tomorrow certainly is an important day and I need to heed my own advice and get some rest.

I try to sleep, but I am filled with nervous excitement. It's times like this that I wish I had a penchant for alcohol or some other form of self-medication. I've tried many things over the years, particularly in those early days, but nothing ever worked. I only ever felt worse or out of control.

I breathe deeply and close my eyes. I play through the arrival of Miriam in my head. It soothes me, slows me down, and eventually I switch off.

Chapter Twenty

George seems like a different man at breakfast; he looks ready and calm. It's just the two of us this morning. I have informed May that I have a stomach virus and she shouldn't come in for a few days to avoid catching it. Full pay, of course. She seemed happy and not at all suspicious. I go back and forwards with May. Sometimes I think having her around is an unnecessary risk, but I like May, and now I know how much working here means to her. I've learned to go with my gut instincts, which is why, for now, she stays.

George will be leaving shortly. He knows that I don't want him to take any unnecessary risks. There will always be another opportunity if things don't go according to plan. I have a strong urge to hug him. I think he would like it, and I think I would like it, too, but I keep my hands down by my sides.

"Remember everything I told you. Introduce yourself and ask her the questions. Congratulate her and invite her to visit the office."

He nods. He is breathing a little faster than usual, but nerves are to be expected. "I believe in you, George." His eyes glaze over a little. George is more important to me than anyone else in the world. I need him here. "No heroics today, George, I mean it. There will always be another time, another day. There will never be another you." He says nothing and the lack of physical contact feels awkward and unusual now. I take out my phone. "I will have this with me constantly. Call me with anything. Do you understand?"

"Yes, sir. I will see you shortly. Call me if you need anything."

My body is tingling with excitement and anticipation at what today will bring and the next couple of hours will pass slowly if I don't busy myself. I go to the basement to look over our new guest's bedroom once more. I've spent a lot of time and effort creating something special. The room is beautiful. I've given it a complete overhaul and there's no trace of the unpleasantness with Penny anymore. Although there is perhaps still a hint of bleach in the air. I have had a brand-new carpet fitted. It is thick and bouncy beneath my feet. The décor is stylish and sleek, and the furniture is expensive but tasteful. The walls are painted a beautiful sky blue.

The wardrobe and chest of drawers are empty, but as soon as Miriam arrives and settles in, I will fill them for her. I need to meet her to understand what is right for her, I don't want her to be uncomfortable in any way. The same applies to the empty bookcase next to the bed. I don't want to be presumptuous about her tastes. There isn't a speck of dust or an inch of the room that isn't sparkling and clean. I am pleased with my efforts. Nothing is damaged or dirty, and that's the way it will stay. I'll buy her some fresh flowers tomorrow. I can't wait to meet Miriam. I know she will be everything I imagine.

I hear the crunch of stones as the car pulls up the driveway and, shortly afterwards, their two voices outside. I can't make out the words, but everything sounds very amicable. They sound like two friends having a lovely discussion. I stand behind my desk and wait. My skin tingles and I have the urge to fidget. Their footsteps become louder as they ascend the stairs, the clack of her heels versus the gentle thud of George's footsteps. The anticipation is excruciating. All my senses feel heightened, and I rest my palms on the desk to steady myself.

They knock and enter my office. Miriam enters first. I am surprised to see how impeccably put together she is. She wears a grey, collarless jacket over a simple white blouse, and matching slim trousers. She greets me with a beautiful but businesslike smile. Her teeth are incredible, and her make-up is subtle and perfectly applied. She has struck the perfect balance between elegance and professionalism. Subtle gold jewellery adorns her ears and neck. Before me is an assured, capable woman who looks like she knows what she wants. George is openly relieved and happy that Miriam is here, and I can tell he has enjoyed his time with her. I maintain eye contact and keep my body as still as my nerves allow. I extend my arm and invite her to sit. She chooses George's chair, but I don't comment.

I breathe her in. She smells like summer.

"Thank you, Mr Barclay."

"It's Montague Barclay, but please call me Monty." There is no need for secrecy anymore.

"Okay, Monty. It's good to meet you."

I'd prefer George to stay but I'm aware that may look a little odd.

"Miriam, can you please excuse George and me for one minute? There is some urgent business I need him to attend to. Please help yourself to a drink while I am gone, and I will be with you as soon as possible." She nods and confidently reaches to get herself a drink. I gesture to George to follow me, and we congregate at the far end of the corridor. Miriam can't hear us here, but we will see if she tries to leave my office.

George is still glowing. His eyes are sparkling with happiness. I can see that he thinks she is amazing. I don't want to burst his bubble, but I do have concerns. Miriam seems incredibly self-assured and it's setting me on edge. He senses my trepidation and I see his lips grow thin. There is a flash of something in his eyes that I can't quite place.

"What's wrong, sir?" He pinches the bridge of his nose.

I don't want to spoil the moment or bring George down after everything he has done today. That would be selfish of me.

"Nothing. Nothing at all. I just wanted to see you for a moment. You've done an amazing job, George. Let me have half an hour alone with Miriam and then knock and bring in a second tea tray once you have everything ready. Miriam and I can get to know each other until then."

George nods and unexpectedly puts his hand on my shoulder.

I can see that this is the beginning of something special.

Chapter Twenty-One

When I enter, Miriam is sitting back, legs crossed and sipping tea. She looks comfortable in George's chair and stands when I enter.

"Sorry for the delay, Miriam, and please, do sit." She sits again and recrosses her legs. She looks athletic and strong. "Please do relax, I'm not going to ask you any difficult questions. I'd like us to get to know each other a bit better. I'm sure you have questions too and I'd be happy to answer anything."

She nods and smiles. Her face lifts. I could get used to looking at her face every day. She is absolutely charming. Our conversation is open and easy. The discussion flows effortlessly.

I keep it general; I want her to interpret the questions as she sees fit and get a genuine sense of who she is and what she wants from life. It would be easy to focus on the negatives around her opportunity here, but I want her to find the positives. She will never have to worry about money again. She can live in a safe, secure environment, with magnificent surroundings, beautiful food, and access to anything else her heart desires.

Miriam is clearly well prepared but still manages to come

across as natural. It is a perfect start. She takes lots of notes as we speak and effortlessly comes across as hardworking and dedicated. Her interview technique is impressive, but it feels a little rehearsed at times, and some of what she says feels unrelated to why she is here. Although perhaps not from her perspective. I'd rather know more about her, so I interrupt.

"Tell me about your family. Where are you from?" During our discussion, I think I detected a hint of an American accent somewhere. She raises her eyebrows and fine lines appear on her previously unblemished forehead. I've hit a nerve. She tries to hide it but doesn't cover it up quickly enough. She picks up her pen and starts writing, avoiding eye contact.

"Actually, I don't think it's appropriate to talk about my family."

That was not the response I was anticipating. Of course, it's acceptable to ask about her background. I wonder if I've uncovered something. Perhaps she is estranged from her family or not on good terms. I don't want to push her into uncomfortable territory during our first meeting.

I consider asking her what she does in her spare time, but this is an interview, and I will get a prepared and appropriate answer. I want to know who she really is. The intimate questions will need to wait until she is a permanent addition to the house.

I watch her intently and take in everything about her. I consider every word carefully and every expression on her face. There are lots of things that impress me about Miriam. For a start, she is undoubtedly very comfortable in her own skin. As she should be. But something is living in the background, something that reveals itself even though she tries so hard to keep it hidden. I wonder what her story is. I look forward to finding out more.

I have seen enough of Miriam today to know that I have

made the right decision. What she says is not important, it's who she is behind the words that interests me.

There is a light tapping at the door. I glance at my watch; time has flown by.

"Come in, George."

George enters, peering first before standing in the doorway stiffly. He looks to Miriam before me. He relaxes his posture and puts the tray down on the table confidently. There is a new, subtle addition to the tray.

George addresses Miriam first. "Would you like another drink?"

She smiles gratefully. "Yes, please." She leans forward. "Shall I pour?"

George shakes his head and Miriam nods appreciatively at the chivalry.

"George, why don't you join us?" I say.

He pours for us all and sits down, shifting his position several times before flushing slightly and placing his hands in his lap. The air is heavy with expectation, and I enjoy it a second longer than necessary before speaking. Miriam and George watch me closely.

"Miriam, I think you would be an excellent fit here. We run things a little differently than most and you'll find your role here unlike anything else you will have experienced in the past. I'm less interested in your skills and credentials and much more interested in who you are as a person."

She nods and exchanges an enthusiastic look with George. I can sense they like each other, and I feel a sudden surge of happiness.

"I am glad you'd like to work with me, Monty. I hope this is the start of something positive."

I smile at her and continue to speak. "There is one thing. Something I maybe should have mentioned from the outset."

All my senses feel sharper as I choose my words carefully. "I do hope it won't be an issue. It is a deal-breaker, I'm afraid."

She is silent, raising her eyebrows subtly.

"The commitment I require is rather more than you may be used to in typical personal assistant roles. You may find you can't do some of the things you are used to."

She butts in. "Monty, I wonder if—"

I don't let her finish. I can feel my heart rate and breathing quicken. What I have to say is important and I don't want to leave anything out or be distracted by any further questions.

I watch her closely as I say the words.

"I would like you to live here."

She barely reacts. I wonder if it's shock or whether that simply doesn't seem like a sacrifice for her. I can't read her this time.

"You will have your room and everything you could need. All expenses will be taken care of."

I can see her mind ticking over, her eyes flitting back and forwards. She opens her mouth to ask a question but then stops, and reconsiders for a moment before finally speaking.

"What are your... expectations of me, Monty?" She watches me closely as I consider her question. She doesn't hide the fact that she is observing my body language, studying my face.

"Well, Miriam, I hope that we can finalise that together. I'd rather you didn't see this as a job with strict and specific hours, more that you become a part of the family here. Does that make sense?"

She taps her index finger gently against her bottom lip. It is very distracting. She clears her throat before addressing me confidently.

"What if I were to say no?" The question is phrased more as a test than a genuine question and there is a degree of challenge in her tone that I do not like.

"I think that would be... disappointing. For everyone." She nods and tilts her head upwards as she thinks. I notice she has a rather long and slender neck. "Plus, I will need a commitment from you now. I hope you understand."

She crosses her legs and leans forward, resting her steady hands on her knee.

"I understand that you are a very busy man, Monty. I know we can work very well together." It hasn't gone unnoticed that she hasn't directly answered my question. I lean forward and look deep into her dark eyes.

"That's excellent news. We are delighted." I look to George who has barely moved a muscle. He smiles on cue but is still half-lost in thought. "George will get all the paperwork ready for the morning and I will show you to your room."

Miriam's confident façade dissipates instantly, and her cheeks turn pink. "Uh, okay. Do you want me to come with you? Both?" She looks over to George. Perhaps the thought of being shown to a bedroom by two men has frightened her. I can understand that. Women have many more things to be afraid of than men, and there is already plenty for men to be afraid of.

George defers to me, shrugging his shoulders, before returning to sitting statue-like.

I imagine that Miriam thinks we will show her the room and then she will leave. I have discovered over the years that people like information drip-fed to them. If you tell them everything all at once, they become overwhelmed. The most sensible course of action is to show her the room now. Drip. Allow this discussion to sink in a little deeper while she looks around. Drip. And finally, tell her that she won't be leaving. Drip.

How she reacts will determine everything else.

I stand and point to the tray so George can see, and Miriam cannot. The new addition to the tea tray is a simple napkin. Under it is a syringe loaded with sedatives. Thankfully, it has not been needed yet and I truly hope that it won't be. But I am not a man who likes to take chances. George sees and understands my signal.

"George, I am going to show Miriam to her room. Will you come with us, please?"

Miriam has been deep in thought, packing away her notebook and pen, and gathering her belongings. She has missed our entire exchange.

I gesture to the door, and Miriam and I walk together. I sense a reluctance as I walk towards the basement stairs. She is taking in every inch of her surroundings as she walks and clutches her coat and bag to her chest as she takes careful steps.

"Are you okay, Miriam, you seem a little distracted?"

She straightens herself up, back in job interview mode. "My apologies if it seems that way, Monty." She is trying hard to make her voice fill the space, but it still sounds small, and she can't disguise her nerves entirely. "I wasn't expecting anything other than a sit-down discussion, but I am glad to be able to see the rest of your home." She smiles, but it doesn't reach her eyes. Her eyes are vigilant. Waiting.

I watch her take in the surroundings as we continue our walk. The walk from my office to the basement is pure, baronial splendour. Sometimes I think that the décor is pretentious, but it simply matches the architecture, and it's what the decorator suggested. I am used to this place, but many people have confused it for a country house hotel or even a grammar school. When the ostentatiousness gets to me, I spend time in my room. My room is the palate cleanser of the house.

"Your home is very grand. Clearly, you are a very successful..." She stops herself for a moment and I know what she is thinking. She has no idea how to finish that sentence accurately and she is torn between looking unprepared and genuine worry at the lack of information that has been made available to her.

I interrupt. "Thank you, Miriam. Yes, I am lucky to have this wonderful home. I have a catalogue of investments that the staff here help me manage." We continue to walk. Miriam gives me a quick, nervous glance. Her pace has slowed, and I mirror her. Her rate and rhythm of breathing have changed. I would imagine she would like to turn and run back. To her credit, she continues. I can't decide whether she is comforted or concerned by George's presence. Either way, she is keeping a close eye on him too.

"Almost there, Miriam. I do apologise that the room is rather far away from the office, although I do think that in time you will come to appreciate the tranquillity. It's so quiet here."

She mumbles something. I don't hear it, and I don't ask her to repeat herself.

"You see, my living space is on the first floor and George has a room available to him on the second floor."

I think I see her relax at the mention of George living here. If I were her, George wouldn't concern me in any way. There is nothing predatory about his appearance or behaviour at all.

I open the door to her room. My stomach flutters as I stand aside so as not to block her view. Miriam takes in the scene before her. Her eyes widen and the corners of her mouth curve upwards as she scans the room. The beautiful sky-blue walls create a peaceful yet bright atmosphere. Botanical and flower-themed artwork completes the serene décor. Miriam is now focusing her attention on the bed. Crisp, white Egyptian cotton bedding.

This is a room that dreams are made of, but this time it's not imaginary.

"This is your room, Miriam. This is where you live now." My heart speeds up as I wait in anticipation of her response. I hear George's footsteps behind me, and I walk behind Miriam as she wanders slowly into the room. I see her head whip around as she realises that we are all inside the room now, and she is the furthest from the door. "Do you like it?"

She inhales quickly and holds her breath for a moment. The professionalism drops for a fraction, and I get a glimpse of something more genuine from her. "This is a very fine room, Monty." She continues to look around, her eyes stopping every once in a while to take in more detail. I was unsure about the pomegranate and wildflower-scented candles on the bedside tables, but their wonderful aroma finishes off the room perfectly.

"I think I must have left my phone upstairs," she says apologetically while searching her empty pockets and bag for the phone. Her voice is a little higher than previously.

I can't avoid the inevitable any longer. I've thought long and hard about how to say this all to her. George is right, I need to be honest about who I am and what I want. I want an honest life without lies. I deserve someone like Miriam. I want that perfect person who will understand me. Someone who wants me. Just me. Exactly as I am. I gesture to the two chairs and sofa to our right. I sought out the same luxurious furniture that Dr Pathirana has in her waiting room.

"Could we all sit a minute, please?" I ask. George quietly closes the door and Miriam throws me a nervous glance. I take two deep, slow breaths, and I watch her carefully as I begin to speak. "Miriam, your phone is upstairs, please don't worry about that now." Her eyes check the closed door. She looks to George, her face a mask of alarm. I try to engage her again. "Wouldn't you love a beautiful home like this, Miriam? Somewhere safe." She ignores my question and makes a show of gathering her coat and bag, even though they are already in her arms.

"Thank you so much for today, Monty. I'm absolutely

looking forward to us working together, but I have several other engagements so I will have to leave now." She stands and holds out her hand for me to shake, her face flat. She's trembling slightly and trying to hide it. She looks to the door again. "I've enjoyed speaking with you, Monty." She is not being honest with me. I feel my jaw tense, and pull it back, doing my best to keep my expression as welcoming as possible.

I reach out and shake her unsteady hand, but she pulls away from me a little too quickly and turns to walk away. I fight against a rising panic. George moves to be close to her without me needing to prompt him. So far, this has been very civilised, but I can sense that the next part will not go as smoothly. She will not stay voluntarily, and I don't want things to escalate too quickly. I would rather tackle this with words.

"Maybe it's best if we start being honest with one another. You can't leave now, Miriam." She stares at me and then at George, a sense of hysteria in her wide eyes. The natural reaction would be for her to run for the door, and I'm sure she will at any minute. I nod my head towards the door.

"Before you try and leave, just take a minute and listen to what I have to say. I can see that you think you are in trouble, that you are about to be hurt or harmed in some way. That couldn't be further from my intention. Switch off everything you know, everything you've been told, and just listen with an open mind for a minute. Can you do that for me?"

She turns back to look at me, confused, with dread intensifying within her. I can understand why she is confused. I'm calm, professional, and outwardly middle-class. What she's afraid of doesn't match what she is seeing.

"Miriam, please, this was going so well. All I am asking you to do now is sit and listen. I think you'll understand after you have heard what I have to say." She sits slowly. "Thank you. Now, just listen, okay?"

She nods, sniffs, and forces a small smile. I sense that I am losing her. George looks at her and taps his suit jacket pocket discreetly. I shake my head. We won't be needing that quite yet. "Miriam, I'd like you to stay here with me. I'd like you to live here and I don't want you to leave. And I won't let you leave." She takes a deep breath, and her expression hardens. "It's not what you think. I will give you everything you need, and exactly as you want it. You will never have to pay another bill and you will never have to work another day. You'll never have to do anything that upsets you or makes you uncomfortable. It's a different kind of freedom. You can have this beautiful room, and you will be safe. The world out there is a horrible place. You just need to let go of everything you know and see this as an opportunity for a better life."

To her credit, she gives the impression of listening to everything I have just told her. She doesn't interrupt and she shows respect.

"Thank you for telling me all that, Monty. But as I said, I have run out of time for today, I'm afraid. We will have many opportunities to discuss this in more detail. But I really must be going." She gives a businesslike nod and stands up as if that is the end of that. She may have heard me, but she hasn't listened.

"Have you actually heard a single word of anything I have just said? I am taking the time to explain this opportunity to you." I'm speaking louder than I want to. I don't want this to end badly, I just want her to stay. Why can't she see that?

The atmosphere in the room changes at my irritated tone. I am dangerously close to losing control of the situation. Both George and Miriam are on high alert. For different reasons, of course, but suddenly the room is supercharged with energy.

"Nothing I have said is anything other than kind. I want to offer you the kind of life that others can only dream of." I'm trying to rescue the situation, but I'm coming across as desperate. The familiar feelings of a panic attack begin to creep up on me. My heart is racing and I'm starting to feel short of breath. I just want her to stay. I need her to stay. "I can completely understand that this is a lot of information to take in and I know that you must have concerns and questions."

I'm doing my best to control the panic; my fingers are tingling, and my scalp is buzzing. I can't let her leave here. I don't want to be alone again.

I focus on my breathing. I have had panic attacks for many years, an unwanted gift from surviving my father, but I desperately don't want Miriam to see me like this.

"I'm sorry, Monty, I think we need to..."

My breathing is now uncontrollable, and the pain in my chest is severe.

"You think we need to what?" My words are barely a whisper and punctuated with haggard breaths and choking sounds. Miriam walks with purpose now towards the door. George leaves her side and comes to stand behind me. He knows that she can't open the door and will want to make sure I am safe. He has comforted me through previous attacks.

I try to find words, but I can't speak. My legs are shaky now, but I refuse to sit down. Whatever happens, will happen. Even though my body feels like it is dying, I know deep down that it is not. This will pass.

I hear Miriam appeal to George. He stays behind me and I feel his hands on my shoulders. Steadying me. His warm hands comfort me, but the excruciating attack continues. I'm sure that I am going to pass out any minute.

Chapter Twenty-Two

There are always choices, even when it seems that there are none. But choices are limited by your ability to make them, and I have lost control of my body. Every effort I make to dial back the panic is failing. Colours are blurring into each other and the noise of the blood pumping through my head is louder than anything else. I feel as though I am on a carousel. Spinning out of control, never quite able to see clearly, and constantly nauseated.

Disappointed doesn't even come close. Why did this have to happen now? Miriam is watching me. She is doing a fine job of controlling her fear. Her eyes continue to flit from mine to George's. She is afraid, but I can see her contemplating her next movements, weighing up her options.

I have lots to say, but the ability to form a coherent sentence is long gone.

I take a risk. I summon any remaining strength within me, reach out and grab her hands. She flinches, but she lets me.

I stare deep into her eyes. I am pleading now, and I hate myself for it. I look up at George who is still standing behind me with his gentle hands on my shoulders. His eyes are kind, and his face is caring.

I hold on to Miriam's hands. I can feel a pulse and I don't know if it's mine or hers. I manage one last word. "Please." We watch each other for several seconds. Neither of us looks away.

Finally, she speaks. "I am sorry, Monty. I am going to leave now." She pulls her hands away from mine. I let her go with no fight at all. Even if I had wanted to, I have nothing left. She turns her back on me to walk away and the panic attack peaks. The pressure inside my head is so strong that I don't think I could close my eyes if I tried. I can feel them bulging under the strain. The heat radiates throughout my body and my skin prickles. It feels like I am being stung by a thousand bees and I bite my tongue to suppress the pain. Crushing, heavy pains rip through my chest and my lungs are empty. Dread and despair consume me. I begin to fall to the floor. Like a building that has been demolished. Just crumbling where I stand.

I feel myself being scooped up by George before I hit the ground. He grabs me awkwardly. I don't have control of my head and my neck jolts as he lifts me. I look at Miriam through the haze that has become my vision. She is petrified.

I hear George yell at her to stay in the room as he whisks me out of there and takes me to the safety of my room. I tuck myself into his body. He will keep me safe. He won't let me down. He takes me to my bedroom and lays me down softly on my bed.

"George..." I mouth his name but don't follow it up with anything. There isn't anything to say.

George sits beside me and speaks slowly, stroking my head. He is out of breath from the effort of getting me here, but his voice still manages to sound soothing.

"Don't try and speak, sir. Just rest. Everything will be fine. I promise. Just rest." I don't feel like I have a choice. My body is going to rest anyway. I can feel it falling away.

Charlotte Stevenson

I go with it and slip into nothingness.
"I don't want to hurt you, Miriam. Please stay with me."

Part Two

Chapter Twenty-Three

I don't know how long I have been asleep. My body is stiff, and I feel as though I have aged twenty years. My memory of what happened is good. I can still feel all of it. I wish that I couldn't. I must have been sleeping in an awkward position, my muscles ache as I lift my arm. I put my hand to my forehead and the temperature difference is extreme. My fingers are icy cold, and my head is wet, clammy, and very hot. My back is soaked with sweat. I sit with effort and peel myself away from my sheets. My head is fuzzy and there is a metallic taste in my mouth. I remember the panicked choking; my throat is now raw and painful. I swallow with difficulty and push the memory away. I scan the room. Something inside me tells me to be wary, but I can see easily that I am alone.

I swing my legs out of bed and plant my feet on the cold, hard floor. I'm not sure if I can stand up. I don't trust my body yet. It betrayed me terribly yesterday. I test putting my weight onto my feet. My reactions are slow, but my strength is fine. I stand with ease and stretch out my aching muscles. The room is bright, but I'm not sure what day it is. I feel as though I have been asleep for a long time. I take some time to freshen up and try not to look at myself in the mirror. I am not pleased with my reaction yesterday. I pride myself on my composure. Although most of what happened was beyond my control, I still feel that I behaved terribly.

I take a deep breath and decide to face the world. If I consider things carefully, there is little to be ashamed of. George is always on my side. No matter what. I try to open the door, but it is locked. I turn the handle again, both ways. Nothing.

I have always had a bedroom door that I could lock. I'm not afraid, just sensible. It's safer. But the door is locked from the outside this time and I can't get out. I bang my fist on the door. First gently and then more forcibly until I hear footsteps outside the door. The door opens and I am relieved to see George standing there. I gesture to the door and raise my eyebrows.

"For safety, sir. Can't take any chances. Best to make sure you are safe."

I understand. We don't know what Miriam is capable of, and I certainly wasn't in any state to be asked when George left me. I look at George's face. There are more lines on it, and I suspect he hasn't slept much. His cheeks look hollow and his face ashen.

George and I walk quietly together to my office. I feel my body loosening up. There are lots of little things that don't feel right, but I can't quite place any of them. I sit and George leaves to make refreshments.

I monitor the video feed to Miriam's room. I feel warmth at no longer describing it as Penny's old room. The picture quality is poor, and it is difficult to see everything unless I concentrate completely. I block everything else out and watch her. She is sitting quite still; I wonder what she is thinking. There is a microphone installed, but I leave it muted. If she is crying, I don't want to hear it. I feel a sudden pang of guilt as I realise that I have no idea if Miriam has eaten anything since her arrival. She has her own bathroom, but no access to food. I shudder at how inhospitable I have been. This is not the impression I want her to have of living here.

George returns with drinks in his hands and looks at me, inviting me to talk.

"George, have you been looking after Miriam? Has she eaten?"

He nods. "Don't worry, sir. I have taken care of everything."

I smile gratefully. I am still exhausted, and I don't quite know what else to say. Yesterday was unpleasant and I am still feeling the effects of it all very strongly. George is waiting for me to continue speaking. Not impatiently. Just waiting.

"What is it, George?"

He takes a deep breath. I know how much he cares for me, and he does truly understand why this is so important to me. "Nothing, sir. Just wanting to see how you are."

"George, we don't need to tiptoe around each other, we are family, in every sense of the word."

He looks me in the eye and gives me a half-smile.

"What are your thoughts for today, sir?"

"I will need to speak to Miriam." George looks like he is going to interrupt but changes his mind. It would be easy to catastrophise about yesterday, but things could be much worse. I could be sitting here watching an unconscious Miriam on the monitor. Or a dead Miriam.

"I know things didn't go as planned, George. But I don't want to dwell on the past. This can still be everything that we had planned. It's not over yet."

George is listening quietly. Tenting his fingers and gently tapping his thumbs together.

"Trust me, George. I know that some of my behaviour was shocking yesterday. Upsetting even. But perhaps this is how it was meant to be."

George is nodding as I speak. He understands me. We have a deep unbreakable bond, and we are in this together.

"Very well, sir."

"I will need her to sign some paperwork. I will sort it out today then go and see her later."

I look toward the screen. I don't see Miriam at first, but then I see that she has adjusted her position slightly, so she is almost hidden by the chair. She is looking around the room, as though searching for something. She doesn't look scared or trapped, just inquisitive and a little unsure. A slow smile comes across my face. This is going to work; I can feel it. She will soon forget anything she thinks she is missing out on.

"Paperwork?" George says the word as a question, arching an eyebrow.

"Only a formality." I think it will make her feel more comfortable. People always feel safer whenever they sign something. I have something drawn up already, but it will need some minor alterations to get her on board. I want her to know that she has a level of control here. I hope that will make her feel happy.

But first, I need to lie down and rest for an hour. Dr Pathirana reassured me that fatigue after a panic attack is completely normal. I'm often shaky with little appetite, it's like a hangover. I will be much better after some sleep. Miriam will have a lot of questions and I want to remain calm and collected and put her at ease.

I go to George before I leave to rest. "Please keep an eye on the monitor for me and come and get me if you are worried about anything."

George stands and holds out his hand to help me up. It's a lovely and very appreciated gesture. He understands what a drain all this is for me both physically and mentally. I am touched and I feel a little choked up as I speak.

"Thank you, George. And I mean it, come and get me anytime. These first twenty-four hours will be tricky and there is lots that could go wrong. We don't know her yet; we don't know what she might do."

I put my hand on George's large shoulder and squeeze.

"Your loyalty and friendship mean everything to me, George." I leave George to watch the monitor and go to my room to lie down.

I'd like to say I feel refreshed after my nap, but I feel somewhat disorientated, and my muscles are aching. An hour was not nearly long enough. My body needed more time, and it is protesting by refusing to wake up effectively. I struggle out of bed and get ready. It takes twice as long as it should, but I get there in the end. I can't find everything I want but can't work out why. I don't usually forget where I put things. Everything has its place. I find George in my office as expected. I know he won't have looked away from the screen for a second. I join him.

"How has it been while I've been asleep?"

George looks up and his expression dulls. I must look as exhausted as I feel because he fixes my drink without request.

"Fine. More importantly, how are you feeling? Did you get some sleep?"

I ignore the questions and check for myself. There are no obvious signs of upset. Certainly, no signs of attempted escape. I still can't make her out clearly. I must get a better system installed.

I sit and sip my coffee, waiting for it to bring me back to life. I need to be sharp and alert before I speak to Miriam. Currently, I feel foggy and irritable.

"Why don't you have a break, George? You've been stuck

here while I've been resting, and we don't know how long this next visit to Miriam will take. We need to be prepared for every eventuality."

He shrugs. "I'm okay. Thanks."

I consider insisting, but instead, I hold up the papers in my hand.

"I have been putting the finishing touches to this," I tell him, and he takes Miriam's contract and starts to read. He takes his time, occasionally raising his eyebrows or pursing his lips. George finishes reading and turns the contract over in his hands before reaching out and returning it to me.

"Sir, this is..." He shakes his head and puffs out a breath of air. I can tell that he is impressed. I take it back from him and place it into a fine leather binder. Little touches make all the difference.

"Thank you, George. I'm glad you approve. I'm extremely harsh when it comes to my own work."

Time is ticking away. George and I begin the walk to visit Miriam. I will probably have to repeat a lot of what I said yesterday, as she was in panic mode. I will talk everything through with her again, and I must remember to be patient. I think a gentle approach will be appreciated. As will kindness.

My plan is not to push things too far today. I don't want to discuss our last meeting. I hope that she won't want to ask me any questions about it, and I'll find a way around it if she does.

Today is a new start.

I'll leave her with the contract overnight, and I hope that she will sign it tomorrow. I want to make sure she enjoys her evening and night here first. I don't want any unexpected complications.

Miriam stands as we enter. The room looks just as it did yesterday. My spirits lift at the sight of it. She smiles nervously. Her face is perhaps not as pristine as it was when we last met, but she doesn't look like she has been crying. She seems ready and calm.

"Shall we all sit down?" I suggest. We take our seats, and I rest my hands out in front of me. Open and easy, non-threatening. Body language is everything and mine tells her that I am approachable and friendly.

I speak with a gentle but firm tone. "I know you have had a very challenging day and I'm sure you are very tired. I just wanted to talk things through with you again, and then we will leave you with these to read at your leisure." I push the leather folder across the table to her.

She looks at the folder but doesn't take it.

"As I said before, Miriam, there is no rush, and no questions are off-limits. We can change certain things and I will do everything I can to make sure that you are happy. You should think of this as a partnership." I see her face soften at the mention of the word partnership. For once, she looks interested to hear more. I continue. "I don't know you well enough to be completely open yet. My home and my business are private and precious to me. I hope you understand." She nods but doesn't interrupt. "This may seem like an unusual approach, but in time you will see things as I do. Then you will understand. I know you will."

She is still nodding, and the corners of her mouth are almost a smile. Her eyes are moving between me and George, and she seems more relaxed than yesterday. I point to the untouched folder on the table. "You can take tonight to read over everything in there, but it needs to be signed by tomorrow morning." She opens her mouth to speak but I cut her off. "Wouldn't you love a beautiful home like this? Somewhere safe." She closes her mouth and her eyes flit around the room. "We are all guilty of focusing on the negatives when something feels out of the ordinary. Everyone wants a better life. Don't they?"

She waits a moment and then answers. "In a way... Is that what you want, Monty?" She looks at me expectantly, a glint in her eye.

"Then trust me, Miriam. Ignore the feelings telling you that this is peculiar or wrong. It isn't. It's just not usual."

She is trying to hide her exasperation at my not answering her question. "You will have to take a chance, Miriam. I hope you can find it within yourself to do that."

She sighs and rests her index finger across her lips. I have so much to tell her and what she is hearing is the tiniest fraction of it. But I can see that what I am saying is still too much.

I stand up and George moves to stand next to me. "I am going to leave now, Miriam. You should try and get some rest. George will be down again soon to see what you'd like to eat."

Miriam has given up asking any further questions and looks almost amused when I mention food.

We say our farewells and George and I leave the room. He follows me closely.

I turn to him. "Would you excuse me for a moment please, George? I need to use the bathroom. I'll meet you in the office."

George nods but seems reluctant to leave me. He is still in sight as I enter the bathroom.

I look at myself in the bathroom mirror. I look alive again. That was an enormous improvement from the disaster that was yesterday. Outwardly I've always tried to appear confident and self-assured, but internally I've always been hiding, apologetic, and fearful of what lies within. Perhaps I'm not as unusual as I thought I was. We are all on a spectrum of humanity.

George is waiting for me in the doorway of my office and the expression on his face is tense and concerned. He doesn't speak and my head swims with possibilities.

"What is it? Has she hurt herself? Tried to escape?"

He is shaking his head as I am speaking.

"George, what on earth is it?"

I stride past him into the office and sit down at my desk.

I see that my answerphone is showing one new message. She's called again. I lift the receiver, press the button and the familiar voice fills my ear. Crackly but unmistakable. George sits down on the chair next to me. He looks awkward and unsure of where to put himself.

"It's okay." I mouth to him as I continue to listen to the recording. I instantly realise that I hadn't followed up on the extremely rude appearance on my security camera. It was an inconvenience I had packed away at the back of my mind, overshadowed by more pressing events. I don't often forget things, I simply move them somewhere, to be picked up later. This was not on my list of things I wanted to deal with today.

"Hello, Monty." Dr Pathirana's voice is professional, but there is an accusatory tone. "I was disappointed that you ignored my last visit." I hear her sigh before continuing. "Our last discussion ended rather briefly and there are things I'd like to discuss. I'll come and see you again at 5pm this evening."

She cuts off the call without saying goodbye. My head is fizzing, she has no right to make any demands of me and she certainly does not have the power to hold me to ransom in my own house.

"Are you okay, sir? You look a bit light-headed."

I manage a "Yes", but he's right. I'm not breathing properly, and my head is pounding. The panic attack hangover is still plaguing me, and Dr Pathirana's insistence on speaking to me is not helping in the slightest.

George speaks tentatively. "Are you sure? It's just that you look..."

I try my hardest to hold everything in, but I am struggling.

135

Flagging. It must be obvious as I feel George's strong body press closer to me. I concentrate on his calm voice. I focus on only him and block everything else out.

And then I remember something that she said.

She said 5pm.

I take a deep breath. Rest and recovery will have to wait.

She said 5pm.

That's in five minutes.

Chapter Twenty-Four

Before

A ll of the blood has gone from my skin and hair. At the start, my skin hurt from all the scrubbing, but it's okay now. I don't think the smell will ever leave my nose. A hot, metallic rotting inside my head.

I'm in a bed now, supposedly clean, and safe. I'm almost certain that this is a hospital. The bed is hospital-like and one of the walls is basically one big window. I watch the thin, white clouds move slowly across the blue-grey sky. Life is still moving out there. Tyres rolling across the roads, the occasional shout or beep of a horn. It's only my life that has stopped.

I've been to lots of rooms and spoken to lots of people since I was rescued. Horrified, pale faces have become sing-song voices and sympathetic head tilts since I got cleaned up. I wonder if anyone will ever look at me normally again. Even the nurses here have heartbreak in their eyes.

I don't remember most of the people I've met in the last few days, but one lady sticks in my head. She was taller than Father with bright red, bushy hair, and soft hands. Her skin was even paler than mine, but it looked right on her. I look dead. She told me I am going to get a new family. I almost laughed when she told me. If I knew that was even possible, I wouldn't be here now. I'd have changed families a long time ago. At ten years old, I don't know much, but I do know that any family would have been better than mine. I'd have taken a chance on anyone who would have me.

I've been poked and prodded a lot. Nobody has hurt me, but the weird stick they put in my mouth made me gag a bit. Everyone has been really nice, but everything is still horrible. I've cried a lot. My eyes are red and dry, and my head is pounding from being so empty of tears. The sleeves of my new pyjamas are damp and stick to my wrists. I don't know who bought me these pyjamas, but they aren't hospital ones. They have animals on them. Zoo animals. Even though Father isn't here to see the crying, I still feel wrong for doing it. I worry someone will come and slap me.

The police know about Father now. I've told them everything I can remember. I've had to say it all a lot of times. Once is more than enough, but they keep asking. I look at my feet when they ask questions, I don't want to see what my story does to their faces. The darkness filling their eyes.

I've mostly answered questions, even though I have lots of questions of my own. The only person that I asked a question to was the flame-haired lady. She seems to stay warm when I talk, she doesn't flinch or look nauseated. She smells of fruit and flowers, and my spirits brighten just a little when she comes in. I asked her if I would have my own room, in my new house, with my new family. She said that I probably would, but it would depend on how many rooms were in my new home, and how many children were there. She supposed that I might have to stay in a few different homes before they found me somewhere to stay forever. I'm a bit confused. I don't ask any more questions because I think I'll only get more confused.

I pull the scratchy covers over me and look up at the big,

square tiles on the ceiling. Maybe they'll let me stay here. There is a lock on the door, and I don't care about being kept in here on my own. It's probably better that way. All I want at this moment is to be safe and for nobody to hurt me.

I am free here.

Chapter Twenty-Five

I turn my head and walk slowly to the window. It's already beginning to get dark, and I can feel a chill through the single-paned glass. Black trees silhouette against the grey sky, like a haunted forest. I focus on a small figure at the end of the drive, walking purposefully towards the house. She must be able to see me, my shape backlit in the long, arched window. I breathe deeply, clenching and unclenching my fists so hard that they cramp intermittently. I don't feel the pain. I don't look at George. I need to stay centred, and his reactions will not help me remain calm. I address George without turning around.

"Will you let her in, George? Show her into the small reception room." I know I don't have to let her in. I could ignore her again. The pounding in my head is easing and my thoughts are becoming clearer. Dr Pathirana wants to talk to me. Clearly, it's important or she wouldn't be so persistent. I remain at the window as George walks to the front door.

I hear their voices coming from the small room that I asked George to direct Dr Pathirana to. It's seldom used. My mind has slowed down, but options and scenarios continue to race through my head. The unknown is uncomfortable. In hindsight,

I should have spoken to Dr Pathirana the first time she visited. This unpleasantness is entirely my doing.

I don't know what is going to happen here tonight. It will depend very much on what Dr Pathirana has to say. On the purpose of her visit. Perhaps she wants to see me one last time. I could understand that. I don't like it, but I do understand. I hope that she is not planning to continue to interfere in my life. It won't happen and any insistence will not be taken kindly.

George appears and I nod to let him know I would like him to wait outside. His eyes brim with concern and he is chewing his bottom lip. I have nothing to say to her that I would be unhappy with him listening to, but I want to be left alone with her. Dr Pathirana and I always speak alone.

My mind is taken back to how George intervened with Penny, and I consider giving him more specific instructions. But it is not possible to prepare for every eventuality while the doctor is waiting.

I open the door and she stands up to greet me. Meeting her here feels unusual.

"Hello, Monty, thank you so much for seeing me." Her tone is civil and apologetic.

"Hello, Doctor. You are welcome. However, you didn't give me much choice in the matter."

"I am sorry about that. A means to an end, I guess." She shrugs and presses her lips together.

"Forgive me, Doctor, but I can't quite work out what you are doing here. I don't owe you any money, our sessions are not compulsory in any way. What is this?" There is silence. "Turning up at my home without prior agreement is not something I would have expected of you. I would hope that after all these years, after everything we have been through together, and how far I have come, you would respect my ability to make decisions about my own life." She does not interrupt me. "I am not a little broken boy anymore. You know that."

Finally, she speaks.

"Yes, I know, and I am sorry, but I needed to see you one last time and you weren't being agreeable."

"Agreeable? Why should I have to be agreeable?" My tone is clipped but I keep my frustration inside. I want this meeting over as soon as possible, becoming aggravated will not achieve that.

I am surprised at the lack of retort. "This is rather controlling behaviour from you, Doctor." I'm trying to provoke her to talk, and it works.

"Monty, I have no desire for control. This isn't exactly a profession of certainties. Almost every aspect of my job requires me to relinquish control. You have been through enough and clearly, we have reached the point that your sessions with me are not the right thing for you."

I am taken aback. This was not at all what I was expecting.

"Thank you, Doctor. I appreciate that. I will of course get back in touch should my circumstances change."

Dr Pathirana leans towards me, an unusual sadness in her eyes. "I am sorry about this, Monty. I know coming here is unorthodox, and I would never do this with any of my other patients, but please believe me when I say that my intentions are good. I care about you."

I scrutinise her as she speaks. I don't detect any signs of deception.

"I don't want this to end negatively, Monty. Please understand that I will always be here to help you. I think cancelling your appointments with me was a mistake, and now I know that we won't be seeing each other for some time, I wanted to make sure we ended things properly."

I nod. I understand completely. She wants to keep herself safe.

"What you mean is that you want to protect yourself. Make sure that you're not to blame. Although from what, I can't understand. We've had breaks in our sessions before and I would think our most recent sessions have been uneventful and mundane in comparison."

She takes a moment to consider my challenge, and the muscles in her jaw twitch.

"If this is to be our last meeting, Monty, then I suppose I should be completely honest. You have been through a lot in your life. Nobody ever gets over something like that. You just get through it. Because of that, I can't always believe you. I wish I could, but I can't."

I let her words circulate in my head.

"I think there are many successes in your life. I am amazed that you have not turned to drugs or alcohol. I am astonished that you have not broken the law or been in prison." I want her to stop. I don't want to hear any of this. "And in some ways... I don't know."

"You don't know?"

"I'm sorry, Monty. I'm not explaining this as coherently as I would like. There will forever be an 'if' with you. And when you wouldn't accept my professional help, I couldn't be held accountable should that 'if' become a reality."

I stand and walk towards the door. There is nothing more to say.

"Thank you for your honesty, Doctor."

I have often wondered what has drawn Dr Pathirana towards the path of speaking to the broken, the damaged, the evil even. But she has shown me tonight that self-preservation is at her heart. It drives her and she will fiercely protect herself if needed. I have been a burden to her. I hadn't seen myself that way.

I will miss her in many ways, and I expect there are parts of me she will miss, too.

We leave the room and join George in the corridor. "George will see you get home safely. Let's take the back door. I'll walk you both to the stairs and bid you farewell. The lighting is much better at the back of the house. It was lovely to see you again, Doctor, and I wish you the very best with everything." We talk as we walk, like two old friends. George is silent and listens.

"The same to you, Monty, take very good care of yourself. I hope everything goes well for you here." We reach the stairs and I'm glad that we have reached a better understanding of one another. There is always a common thread between people, even if it isn't always obvious.

"I think I'll leave you here, Doctor. Goodbye." She turns to walk down the stairs.

Out of my life. Forever.

Chapter Twenty-Six

I collapse into the chair and focus on the camera feed to Miriam's room. My heart feels heavy, and my eyes are hot and dry. I have to keep reminding myself to blink. Miriam is sitting on the sofa; she lifts her legs from the floor and tucks them underneath her. In the dark, she is ethereal with her movements.

My mind keeps pulling back to Dr Pathirana, and I feel a huge wrench of sadness. I wish my last memory of her wasn't so negative. I shake my head wearily. I know that I need to put our final meeting behind me. Nothing can be changed now, regret is pointless. Our entire relationship cannot be defined by this one meeting. I sigh deeply. The only healthy thing to do is to erase the events of this evening from my mind. Miriam must be the focus of my thoughts now.

I still have hope for my relationship with Miriam. Although I have been so desperate to have her here, I have not fully formed in my mind the nature of our relationship. I keep struggling with my intentions. The one thing I know for certain is that I need her to stay.

I wonder what we will be. Will we be friends? Will we be

family? Will I eventually want a romantic relationship with her? I don't know the answers to any of these questions and the only option is to take each day as it comes. Our relationship needs time and space to develop organically.

I decide to go and talk to her. A part of me knows that this is a bad idea, but I desperately want to see her. I want to make sure that Miriam is happy and cared for.

I brush my teeth and change my clothes. I can feel my mood improving, the sadness lifting and lightening my body. Already I am feeling more like myself.

I knock on Miriam's door. "May I come in, Miriam?"

She draws a sharp breath and looks behind me as I open the door. I sense a hint of nerves from her at us being alone. I look over my own shoulder to let her know I have seen her reaction. Even though this is my house, I feel as though I have intruded. Perhaps I have.

"Sorry, Miriam. I shouldn't have turned up unannounced. I could come back another time if you prefer?" I wait in the doorway. Showing her that I do in fact respect her space and boundaries. She glances and nods at the chair opposite her, and I sit, grateful that she appears calm.

"How have you been, Miriam?"

"Okay, thank you, Monty. How are you?" She is polite but cold. Her expression closed.

I can't tell what she is thinking. I consider telling her that I am proud of her. I don't know where that thought comes from and it feels inappropriate. Instead, I say, "I'm sorry if there has been some noise, I had a visitor, I hope we haven't disturbed you too much?"

She shakes her head and draws her lower lip beneath her teeth. She looks exasperated and drained suddenly. Like she can't find the energy to continue the conversation. Exhaustion can be like that. It can hit you suddenly. I need to make sure that I'm looking after her properly.

"I'll make sure you get some food as soon as I leave. We can have breakfast together tomorrow. Does 10am sound okay? You can have a long lie-in. Of course, you can call up to the house anytime should you need anything."

She runs her hands through her hair and gives me a pinched smile and a nod.

"Okay, Monty, 10am."

There is an awkwardness in the room now. I can see she wants me to leave. I close the door quietly without saying goodbye. I know that developing our relationship will take time and I am prepared to be patient.

George is waiting for me outside. His eyes and cheeks are red and blotchy. I don't draw attention to it. He looks exhausted, too.

"Are you okay?" I ask him.

"Yes. Yes, I'm okay." He looks like he's struggling to breathe. His nose sounds blocked, and he is breathing mostly through his open mouth. I have never seen him do that. He looks unwell.

"Good. Miriam is hungry. Can you get her..."

George's breathing has quickened. He covers his face with his hands briefly before speaking. "Please. Stop. Let's just..."

I cut him off and stare deep into his eyes. My expression is grave, and I leave him with no doubt. I know how his sentence ends. Miriam cannot leave. We've come too far to change our minds now. I continue my sentence as though I hadn't been interrupted. He is listening, but he is shaking his head and moving his lips soundlessly, although he doesn't butt in again.

I walk away and leave George alone with his thoughts.

Chapter Twenty-Seven

Miriam and I sit down together in the basement the next morning as planned. She has chosen her clothes impeccably and she looks beautiful. George has clearly added the new clothes I purchased to her wardrobe.

"Miriam, I hope you don't mind, but I took the liberty of buying a few items for you. My intention is that you choose what you would like, but I didn't want to leave you without fresh clothes to wear."

She responds with a brief smile. I am tired and not at all at my best. I look across the table at her. If I am honest, her cool disposition annoys me. I want our relationship to be special. I want to feel that wonderful bond that has been missing for so long.

She makes small talk, and the atmosphere is comfortable, just as I had always hoped it would be. I hate it. It is so ordinary. I recognise the absurdness of my feelings, but nevertheless, it is how I feel. I play my part in the conversation, willing it to be over as soon as possible.

"Did you sleep well, Miriam?"

"Yes, thank you." She answers politely and smiles affably.

I force my face into an appropriate expression. "That's wonderful to hear. Beautiful choice." I gesture to her outfit. She blanches at the compliment and looks down at the gorgeous cashmere jumper she is wearing.

"As I said, everything in your room is here for you to enjoy. Everything is yours." She doesn't answer, instead, she smooths the front of her jumper and leans back in the chair. I am exasperated at how comfortable she is. I can't understand why she is so relaxed. I wonder what she thinks of me.

"May I ask you something, Miriam?"

She senses the change in my mood, and she does her best to answer confidently. "Yes, of course you can."

"Good. Do you have any intention of giving this arrangement a chance?" My face screws up. I try to rearrange my features, but they stay put. She's getting anxious now, and I'm sickened to find that it makes me feel better. "Because you can't blame me for thinking that you aren't. Can you?" She looks confused and I know that I am expressing myself poorly. But I can't find another way. "You don't seem very grateful, Miriam." She stares at me, poker-faced. She may be troubled by the way I am speaking to her, but she is not backing down.

"Monty, please. Can we just talk?"

I relax my face and slowly exhale through my nose. Her reactions do bother me, but I need to do better. After all, I can't control her completely. I take another deep breath in and count slowly. I hold out my hands, as a sign of apology.

"I am sorry if I upset you, Miriam. I just want to make sure we are on the same page. That we have a mutual understanding." She nods slowly and the corners of her eyes crinkle. I must remember that we are only at the very beginning of our relationship. "We are still getting to know each other. No relationship, whether professional or otherwise, is perfect. It takes work. Do you agree?"

She is listening carefully now. "Yes. That makes perfect sense."

"I'd like you to do something for me this week, Miriam. I'd like you to make a list. Have a think about what you'd like to get out of being here, short-term, and long-term. I'll do the same and then we can see where we are."

She nods, and I'm surprised to see her face light up a fraction. "Actually, Monty, I think that is a really good idea."

I'm surprised by her willingness but glad we are in agreement. "There's going to have to be a bit of give and take if we want this to be a success." She is looking down and I can see she is thinking rather than listening.

"Monty, if you don't mind, I think that's enough for today."

The silence between us is uncomfortable. I leave us in it for a moment.

"I'll leave you to your thoughts now, Miriam. I'm sure you have a lot to think about. George can help you with anything for the rest of the day. We can meet again tomorrow morning and then we can discuss you coming up to the rest of the house."

She raises her brows, and I can see that I have piqued her interest. Her behaviour this morning may have irritated me, but I'm willing to see it as a hiccup and as part of the teething process. I can't expect this to be smooth sailing, we will make mistakes, we are only human. And I do still hope that this goes well, despite the increasing and gnawing doubt in my stomach.

"This room is yours, but I want you to feel welcome in my home too." I smile and I leave her.

I had planned to talk to George about his behaviour last night, and get him to share his feelings, but I don't have the energy today. Thankfully, he seems back to his old self. Not a hint of the teary and emotional man I saw last night. We arrive at my office. He smiles and pulls out my seat for me; there is warmth in his eyes, not sadness.

"How was your meeting, sir?"

My sigh says it all.

"To be honest, it was absolutely average." I tell him how I became irritated with her, but that we left on better terms, and agreed to consider what we both want.

George strokes his chin and thinks things over for a minute. "I don't know what to say, sir."

I take my mind back to my meeting with Miriam, and I picture her still face. None of it makes any sense. Perhaps she's just playing along, waiting to catch me off-guard. I would imagine that any escape attempt by Miriam would be more sophisticated and have a much better chance of success than Penny's. I have not been keeping as close an eye on the camera as I would have liked to.

I'm definitely missing something important about Miriam. I rub my eyes. My head is buzzing and feels heavy. I am quite simply exhausted.

George is watching me intently. He has such a wonderful way of making me feel relaxed and free to share without uttering a single word.

"Everything is different, George. It's all wrong. We sat together; we had a polite conversation for the most part. But it all felt so completely pointless. So ordinary. A complete waste of my time." George nods sympathetically. "Does any of this make any sense, George? I know Miriam hasn't been here long. Am I being ridiculous?" I feed off the kindness on George's face. "Maybe I'm expecting too much. But I'm not getting anything that I hoped I would from Miriam. I don't feel the way I thought I would."

"No, you're not being ridiculous, sir. Not at all." George

exhales loudly. "Do you mind if I say something?" His neck flushes and his eyes take on a haunted look. "You might not like it."

He's probably right, I don't like much of anything this morning. Fatigue is making me grumpy and unreasonable. But at least I know with George that everything he says comes from a good place. I gesture with my hand for him to continue and sit quietly as he speaks.

"You probably know this already, but I think how you are feeling has nothing to do with Miriam or her behaviour. I think it's just how you feel. Inside." He holds his hand over his own heart as he tells me this.

"Yes, yes exactly. That's what I thought." I stand and pace the room to quell the rising emotion. "I made a mistake. I thought I wanted somebody here, someone to want me. But that's not the case." I think as I walk. What would happen if I just let her go?

"I'm sorry, sir, I'm not making myself clear at all. I think it's about how you see your relationship with her, how it makes you feel, and that what you need has... changed." He stops himself and chooses his next words cautiously before continuing. "Don't you see? Everything for you is different now."

He stops and waits for my response, inspecting his nails rather than looking at me. I sit back down and consider what George has said.

I have changed. There is no disputing that.

Miriam doesn't want to be here. Keeping her here against her will feels completely dissatisfying. She doesn't want to stay with me, and if I gave her the chance to, she would leave without a second thought. But if I let her go, my life and George's will be over. I can't let that happen.

George's voice brings me back into the room. I run my hands through my hair as the room comes back into focus.

"I think you should get some rest, sir."

I nod and rub my temples in slow circles with my index fingers as I slowly stand up. George and I leave the office, and as we walk towards my room I think about Penny. Penny didn't want to be here either, but at least she didn't leave me. In a way, a part of her still lives here with me. I grimace and feel nausea swell as I realise that the thought actually gives me a degree of comfort.

Penny can't leave me now.

There is nothing wrong with terrible thoughts. Everyone has them. It's what you do with them that counts.

Miriam doesn't want a life here. I can't choose to let her go and I can't face the idea of her leaving me. Perhaps the only solution left is that a part of her stays.

I look at my hands then I look up at George. Walking here with him, I have no desire to hurt anyone. I don't consider myself to be a terrible person. I am not driven by anger or hate. If all that is true, then what am I?

We walk in silence and a sense of sadness creeps over me.

With my recovery, I have always felt in control. Since Miles died, everything has broken. He was the last link to the family that made me who I am, where I vowed to be a better person, even if only on the outside. They saved me and I owed it to them to show that their acts of kindness had worked.

There's no one left now. No meaning left.

We arrive at my door, and I smile weakly at George.

"Thank you for everything, George. I don't know what I'd do without you."

George smiles. "Always here, sir." I can feel tears on my cheeks. "Don't worry about a thing, sir. You need some rest. Call me if you need anything." As he leaves, I breathe in his scent, familiar and comforting. I collapse on top of the bed covers and I'm not sure whether I fall asleep or lose consciousness.

Chapter Twenty-Eight

Nightmares plague me as they often do in times of inner turmoil. I often dream about Father, and tonight is no exception.

"Well done, son..." I hear his repulsive voice. It penetrates the corners of my mind and my soul, digging deeper with every word.

"Well done, son. You're really getting the hang of it now."

"Thank you, sir."

His darkness must be relentlessly pushed away. It is strong and persuasive, but it can only go as far as you let it. If you allow it to grow, it will take over everything.

"Now go and clean up like a good boy."

"Yes, sir."

"Don't worry, son. They deserve it."

"Do they?"

"Don't question me, boy."

"Sorry, sir."

"They owe us."

"Yes, sir."

Chapter Twenty-Nine

I hear the hammer striking. The bones cracking. I hear the shovel collide with the ground. Slow at first and then faster, relentless.

When I wake, I am sitting bolt upright in bed. My mouth is wide in a silent scream. My skin is slick with sweat, and my heart is trying to escape from my chest.

The persistent thumping from my nightmare is replaced by a familiar, unthreatening noise. It is George. He is banging on my door. My reactions are slow, and I stumble out of bed and rub my face. George continues to knock; he knows I am in here.

"One minute, George," I shout, and he stops knocking immediately. I look at my reflection in the mirror. Even in the gloominess of the room, I can see I look terrible. My skin is pale and blotchy, and my eyes are dark and ringed with shadows. My hair is messy and sticking out at unusual angles. I look nothing like Montague Barclay. I turn my head from left to right, taking in all the details of my face. I stick my tongue out and waggle it from side to side, watching my reflection change.

"Sir?"

"Yes. I'm coming."

I go to the door and George is surprised by my appearance. I laugh.

"Sorry, George, I know I look like shit." He's taken aback by my casual swearing; I hardly ever swear. The Barclay family never swore, so therefore I never swore. I might take it up now though.

"Sir, I'm sorry to wake you. It's just that the police are here. They want to speak to you."

"Fuck." That really raises his eyebrows. I laugh and beckon George into the room. "Come in. Have a seat on the bed." He is looking at me like I have two heads.

"What do they want?" I ask.

"They want to talk to you. They said it is about Dr Pathirana."

I keep my face as still as I can. In a strange way, I was expecting this, but I can't quite understand why. George studies my face. "Sir, I can see you're a little... different this morning. Just please be careful."

He's right. I'm probably making him very nervous and that's not fair.

"I'm sorry. Yes, absolutely."

I wonder what it is specifically about Dr Pathirana. I can only surmise that it is something to do with her coming to see me here, in my home. I run over our last meeting carefully in my head. Our discussions were a little tense, but nothing that would require reporting to the police. Plus, I know that she at least got to her car safely. George made sure of that.

I lean into George's ear. "Don't worry, George." I follow it quickly with, "Would you please tell the police I'll be with them as soon as possible? I will get dressed and make myself presentable. Please offer them tea and send my apologies for their wait."

George nods. "Of course, sir, I'll let them know you'll be with them shortly."

This is important. George is exactly right; I need to be careful. I know I have nothing to hide regarding Dr Pathirana, but I need to give the right impression to the police. I don't want them pursuing me for anything, their presence is an unwelcome risk.

I dress smartly and practise my expressions in the mirror. There's a part of me that wants to go out there exactly as I am and tell them to fuck off and leave me alone, but I need to tackle this properly.

There are two police officers, one male, and one female. It strikes me how comical they look. He is at least a foot taller than she is and probably twice as heavy. He could certainly use a size larger in his police uniform. They introduce themselves as PC Colin Bowman and PC Jamila Afzal. I shake their hands firmly and greet them with warmth and concern.

"Good morning, officers, I hope George has been looking after you. I am terribly sorry it took me so long."

PC Afzal answers, pushing her thick, black, oversized glasses up her nose as she does so. Her manner is formal but friendly. "No problem, and yes, thank you, we've been well looked after." They nod to George almost in unison.

We all sit, and I lean forward as I speak.

"How can I help you?"

They inform me that they have received a report that Doctor Pathirana is missing and that her last recorded appointment was with me. I nod along, making all the right noises and shaking my head at the right moments, nothing too emphatic and no interruptions.

It's clear Afzal is the more experienced of the two and she leads the questioning. Bowman has a notebook and an angry stare. I sense his annoyance at being second fiddle to a woman, possibly even a hint of racism. He is clean-shaven, but his skin looks irritated and itchy.

"Can you tell us what you know, Mr Barclay?" Afzal asks.

"Yes. Happy to help." I give them my most gracious smile. I know what happened that evening, and I won't embellish or deviate. Liars add too much detail and it's the details that catch you out. I know exactly how the evening went. If you ask me questions about it, I will simply recall the facts. I have altered a few details in my mind, to direct the police away from me as a suspect. To create the perfect lie, you have to first recreate the alternative story. The alternative story must be as close to the truth as possible. Every detail must be considered. Never come up with anything on the spot. I have created this perfect version of my evening with Dr Pathirana. I can replay every detail in my mind.

"I don't usually see Dr Pathirana at home. In fact, I know that for her, home visits are highly unusual." I pause but they say nothing. "I had cancelled all of my upcoming appointments with Dr Pathirana." They look at each other as I say this. Not subtly either. "I didn't think I needed to see her anymore. She felt differently and turned up unannounced." Bowman sniffs noisily and writes something down with his hairy paw. "She called the day before, too. I think she was worried about me." Afzal and Bowman both shift in their seats and exchange a look, a look that says they think they are onto something. George mirrors their movements unconsciously; I can see he would rather I had answered that differently.

Afzal speaks. "Please continue, Mr Barclay."

"I asked George to show her to one of my meeting rooms. This is my home but also my place of work." They look around in disbelief as I say this. "I was a little annoyed that she had turned up without an invitation. I thought it was rude, so I just needed a few moments before I spoke to her." They exchange another look and I continue. They should really work on being more subtle. "She had upset me. I thought she would respect my decision not to attend, but she hadn't. We talked for a while and... it's probably worth mentioning at this point that I had taken up sessions with the doctor after the sudden and unexpected death of my brother." Both officers perform the traditional sympathetic head nod and Bowman continues to write. "We only had a couple of sessions before I cancelled. I think she thought that was too soon." They are both looking at me compassionately. I can tell that I am not in any trouble. If anything, I think I am boring them with this extra information.

"Anyway, I have a lot of good support here and I didn't think I needed any more sessions and I'd paid for everything."

Afzal leans forward before asking me, "Anything else you'd like to say to us? Now, while we are here?" They are obviously keen to wrap this up and get on with their day.

"Not particularly. Just that she felt it was important to see me one last time before ending our sessions. End it properly. Make sure everything was okay. She didn't say it, but I think she wanted to see that I was looking after myself." They nod along. "Once we started talking, everything was fine. She stayed for maybe an hour and then left."

"Do you and Dr Pathirana have a relationship outside of your professional one?"

That was a question I wasn't expecting but I do my best to hide my surprise.

"No, not at all. Purely professional." I remind myself of the rules. Stick to the facts, don't answer any questions that you aren't asked, and don't offer up any voluntary information unless it is of benefit to me. "After we had finished talking, we said our goodbyes. I told her that I would get in touch if I needed to book in again, and George walked her to her car."

They look over at George, and Afzal addresses him. "We'll ask you some questions shortly if that's okay?"

"Yes, no problem." He looks so kind and accommodating. I'm proud of him.

"Is there anything else, officers?" They both exchange another look and I know their thoughts have turned away from me. But I add one last thing just to be sure. "There is one more thing you may find useful. She parked her car on the street rather than driving up to the house. I thought that was unusual. Visitors usually drive up here, it's a long walk. She said that she thought it was unprofessional to drive onto my property when we didn't have an appointment. That made sense and that's why I asked George to accompany her to her car. It was dark and her expensive car had been sitting on the road unattended for over an hour." They nod along, hopefully considering the possible source of threat I have just planted in their mind. They turn to George to ask him some follow-up questions. I tune out and run through my checklist, making sure I have covered everything. George's natural manner lends itself to brevity and his tone is kind and concerned.

When they are finished, George sees the officers out. I wish them well with their endeavours and offer my assistance should they need it. But they won't. As far as I can deduce, we have been crossed off the list and they won't be back.

In any case, I'm sure that Dr Pathirana is not missing in any way. Clearly, this is just a misunderstanding. She's a grown woman, I'm sure there is a very good reason for her absence. I know that she visits her family in Sri Lanka regularly.

The thought that something may have happened to her is too awful to consider. There is rarely a good end if a woman has been abducted. I shudder as an image of Dr Pathirana's face springs into my mind without warning. Her hair is no longer smooth and glossy but is instead tangled and matted with blood.

Her own blood. Her beautiful dark eyes are creamy and bulging with death. Anyone who knows her will spend their days waiting for news, hoping for closure. Thinking that they'll feel better if they only knew what had happened to her and justice could be served. That's not true, of course. They are much better living with uncertainty and hope rather than the cold, hard facts of murder. I squeeze my eyes tightly and force the nightmarish thoughts away. Dr Pathirana is alive and well. Nobody would have any reason to hurt her.

"Let's get some breakfast, George. That wasn't a very nice way to start the day. I'm sure there is nothing to worry about. She'll turn up in no time."

"You did well, sir. I'm sure that wasn't easy."

"They didn't ask me anything too difficult. I just kept it simple. And you seemed very relaxed too, George."

He doesn't answer, but I hope he is pleased with my compliment.

I'm due to meet Miriam this morning, but I'd rather stay with George. We walk back into the office, and I take my usual seat in front of the monitor.

Immediately, I can see that there is something very wrong. The room has changed dramatically since I last saw it. I lean in closer. There is a large pile by the door. The display resolution isn't high enough for me to identify the individual items. Miriam is running around the room, grabbing things, and adding them to the growing mountain. Piling up objects from the room like a bonfire. She scurries, like a little mouse. Sometimes I lose her. But she always returns to the pile at the door.

I can see she has tried to move furniture, too, but unsuccessfully. The furniture is heavy and solid wood, she'd have no chance. I watch her for a while, back and forward she goes. Adding bits and pieces, like an animal building a nest.

George joins me.

"What's wrong, sir?"

"She's trying to barricade herself in. Look, she's tried to move the furniture and now she's just throwing anything she can find on a pile in front of the door."

George doesn't speak, he rests both his hands on my shoulders to comfort me. I point at the screen.

"Look, George. Watch her. It doesn't make any sense; the door will open right up and push all that to the side."

George watches the screen with me. I suspect she knows it's futile, but perhaps she feels like she needs to do something. She's clearly had a change of heart, to say the least.

"Let's watch and see what she does, shall we? Then if you don't mind, George, I think I'll send you in to see her first before I meet with her."

"When are you due to see Miriam today?"

"This morning. Now, in fact. But I'd like you to see how she is first." I reach out and grasp his arm. "Please don't put yourself in danger. If she starts throwing things or being erratic, then just come away. She's not worth getting hurt for."

She continues to wander around the room, fruitlessly adding things to her barricade and occasionally trying to move the same pieces of furniture. She starts pulling the beautiful clothes out of the wardrobe, treating them like rags. She's looking through them and tossing some aside. One by one, the cameras go black as she covers them with the clothes. Clever move, Miriam.

"Go. Now, George." George looks hesitant but leaves anyway. I shout after him, "Tell her to tidy up and take those clothes down before you leave." He doesn't answer.

This has been quite a morning.

I have to admit I'm a little impressed. Even though her actions are pointless, it shows determination and guts.

I turn the sound up on the cameras. I should have thought of that earlier. There's nothing, just a crackling in my ears. I turn the volume all the way up, and I hold my breath to quieten my shallow breathing. Nothing. Only static.

George must be down there by now, but there are no voices and no movement. Unease prickles at my skin. I think I hear a rustling noise, but little else. There's no way she could overpower George, and I can't imagine why he would hurt her, but I can't think of any other explanations for the silence. I know what I have to do.

Chapter Thirty

As I approach Miriam's room, I can see that the door isn't fully closed. George must be inside. There is no noise coming from the room, and anyone inside will have been able to hear my footsteps on the stairs.

My whole body is trembling. I should grab a weapon, but curiosity wins, and I push the door wider. There is some resistance and the grating noise of all the broken and smashed things behind the door as I struggle against them. I push the door again, hard. It opens a further foot and sticks. I still can't see or hear anyone, but there is more than enough room for me to get in. Panic surges through me but I need to get to George. I hold back and wait, listening intently for any movement inside. They must know that I am here.

My heart is pounding, and anxiety gnaws painfully at my insides. Something could have happened to George already, and I know I need to act fast; Miriam clearly isn't thinking straight. I step sideways and quickly into the room, avoiding the monstrous pile of beautiful, damaged things at my feet.

It takes a moment for my eyes to adjust to the scene in front of me. Fear pulses through me relentlessly. I see them, and my eyes dart between them. At first, it seems as though they are talking, embracing even. They are close together, wrapped around each other. But then I see what is really happening.

George is sitting on the edge of the bed, and she is behind him, her arm around his neck. I shrink backwards on wobbly legs before righting myself again. George's eyes flare. He is more than strong enough to fight her off, but I notice something in her hand. It looks like a small knife at first. I can't see it completely, but after a second look, I think it is only a nail file. She must have brought it with her. We should have checked. There have been so many little mistakes and this one may cost us dearly.

George is sitting very still, and I can see that he is petrified. His face is pale, and sweat is dripping down his forehead. Miriam, in complete contrast, is consumed with anger. Her eyes bore deep into me, her mouth twisted. I hold my hands out and start to walk slowly towards the bed.

"Miriam, what's going on here?" I try to sound strong, but my voice is shaky and shrill. She tightens her grip and pushes her weapon into George's neck. I expect to hear a cry from George, but he is silent, and his jaw is set. She has not pushed deep enough to draw blood.

"Nothing, Monty. How are you?" Her voice is acerbic, and her once beautiful face is now an evil grimace. She looks demonic. I stay where I am, but keep my arms held out like I'm offering a hug. Panic is the only thing fuelling me.

"Okay, Miriam, I won't come any closer. Can you tell me what's happening here?"

"Nothing is *happening*." She is spitting as she's talking, all her airs and graces are gone. She pokes George again. He closes his eyes but remains resolute.

"Let's just talk. You don't want to hurt George." My voice is thick, and I feel like I might vomit at any moment.

"Of course, I don't want to hurt George." Her tone is mocking.

I look at George's head. He is a big man and I wonder if she hit him on the head with something before holding him hostage. He looks fine, there is no blood. The room is weirdly silent. The smashed scented candles are nauseatingly strong.

"I don't know what you think you are doing, Miriam. Clearly, you are upset and frightened. But I am standing here unarmed and you are the one holding a nail file to my friend's throat."

George is as still as a statue. I take another tentative step towards the bed. She either doesn't notice or chooses not to react. I look George in the eye, and silently make him a promise. I know I have to end this for him. He's terrified and confused, and I don't want him to be. I am not letting her hold us to ransom like this. I summon every ounce of strength and poise that I have. I know I can do this. Miriam is nothing compared to Father, and I am a man now, not a mere child.

"You see, this is how I view this situation, *Miriam*," I pronounce her name with distaste. "You're holding a nail file to his neck. You could probably kill him with that nail file, probably although not definitely, which is why he is sitting so still and why I'm being a little more cautious than I would like."

I take another step, more assured this time. As I get closer, I see that the nail file isn't very sharp at all. It looks flimsy and it is more likely to bend against his neck than anything else. Her eyes are swimming with tears, and I take another step towards her, continuing to speak. "Plus, even if it were strong or sharp enough to penetrate through his skin, you'd have to make quite an effort to kill him. It would be messy, he'd probably start thrashing around, lashing out at you."

She looks disturbed by the thought of it. Tears begin to cascade down her cheeks and she chews roughly on her bottom lip. "Monty, please." She tries to convey authority with her words, but I am not buying it. She is consumed with fear, and I can hear it. Confidence swells inside me.

"You haven't really thought any of this through, have you? You don't hold the power here, Miriam. You've made a real mess of things." The tears come faster and are accompanied by anguished sobs. "So, what I say is this. Go ahead. Try and kill him. Give it your best shot. But I am going to keep walking towards you." I feel an overwhelming sense of control and a surge of adrenaline. With a primal moan, she flings herself backwards and lets him go. George is on his feet and standing next to me almost immediately. There's no need to control my voice now and I don't try. "How dare you try and hurt my George! You fucking bitch!"

I turn and touch George on the shoulder gently. He isn't shaking and I am flooded with relief.

"Go and prepare, please, George. Miriam needs to sleep this off." He understands my request but is understandably reluctant.

"Sorry, sir. I can't leave you here."

"Please don't worry about that, George, you'll only be gone minutes. Miriam and I still have a few things to sort out. You'll be good, won't you, Miriam?"

She is still watching me, vibrating with anxiety. Waiting for what happens next. I look around the destroyed room. There is no sense to any of it. Meaningless damage to all of these beautiful things.

George is quick; he is beside me again before I know it.

"This is more than you deserve. It's just sleep, Miriam. Not death." I leave the room; I don't want to watch.

George follows me shortly afterwards. He didn't delay and I don't blame him.

"I hope you gave her a big dose, George? I don't want to risk anything else like that. We can't trust her." I look at his neck but there is no sign of damage. "Do we need to take a look at you, George?"

He shrugs it off in his strong manner, but a suggestion of panic remains on his face.

"Don't worry about me, sir. Let's get you sorted first, shall we?"

My body is still on high alert, with no signs of calming. I consider asking George why he just sat there. We both know that she couldn't and wouldn't have killed him with that ridiculous nail file. He could have easily overpowered her. But I think I already know the answer.

It was the door.

"The door was open," I say out loud. He smiles at me. He knows she could have gotten away and out of the door if something had gone wrong, and he wouldn't have risked my safety. I look at his sincere face and I am again so grateful to have him in my life. He has shown me the true meaning of kindness and has cared for me in a way I could never have expected.

"Thank you, George. From the bottom of my heart."

"No need, sir. No need at all." He says it so casually. He has an amazing way of making everything feel good again.

Miriam will be sleeping for some considerable time. Even when she wakes, she won't be able to move efficiently. I sit in my office and watch her on the monitor for a while. Her chest is rising and falling, her eyelids fluttering occasionally. We all have that thing that lurks in our nightmares. I wonder if tonight I will be hers.

Thankfully, George is fine, but I know he is lucky. I must not forget that. She planned to hurt him. Maybe even kill him. I will remember that before I start feeling merciful. She is dangerous.

We are right back to where we started with Penny. It is infuriating and ever so disappointing. I had considered not letting Miriam wake up at all. In some ways, I think it would be kinder. But I'm not ready yet. Too much has happened, and I know I'm being pushed towards something that I'm not prepared for. I need time and space.

George comes in to check on me.

"George, I want to have a few normal days."

I can see that's not what he expected me to say.

"What do you mean, sir?"

"I need to take some time for myself. I'm not... feeling so good. I'm tired and running on empty." George's face is filled with empathy and understanding. "I want you to keep her lightly sedated for a day or two, but make sure her needs are taken care of. We are not animals. I'm not thinking clearly, and I need to get this all straight in my head. Does that make sense?"

"Okay, sir. Normal days."

Chapter Thirty-One

The normal days are just that. I attempt to make small talk. I sit at my computer. I still have lots of money. Everything is fine. On the surface. But in reality, everything is far from fine.

The police don't come back. Not even a follow-up phone call. I'm relieved, but in some ways disappointed. I would like to know if Dr Pathirana is okay.

I don't ask George about Miriam. He will tell me if there is anything to report. I quite like not knowing. I only ever ask George about himself; I want him to know he is still important to me.

The days drag, and George and I sit together every evening. It's my favourite part of the day, it's what keeps me going. The events of this week have taken a lot from him, both physically and mentally. He looks exhausted.

"Please make sure you take some rest, George, you look so tired. I'm worried about you."

He always laughs it off. Some days it is more convincing than others.

"Don't worry about me, sir, I'm fine."

"Are you sure?" I ask.

"Yes, honestly." He assures me.

But I still worry. I worry a lot.

"Actually, sir. Just one thing." I am delighted and gesture with my arms for him to continue. "Miriam," he says. "She is asking..." He trails off, trying to find the right words, but he doesn't have to say anything further.

I realise the uncertainty around Miriam's future is taking its toll on him more than I had anticipated. I don't say anything. It seems easier than lying. And I suppose the honest answer would be that I don't know.

He looks at me, his expression pleading. I think that we all, Miriam included, know how this is going to end and I have been selfish in dragging it out. I know that keeping Miriam here is wrong, and I know that what happened to Penny was wrong. Nobody in their right mind would think these were good things to do. I don't tell him any of these background thoughts. He has been through enough.

"I will come with you tomorrow morning, George. To see her." His face brightens, and one corner of his mouth turns up a touch. "Please don't warn her. I feel it will only cause her unnecessary alarm."

I can't help thinking that things could have been very different. How was I to know that what I wanted wouldn't be enough? George's face is solemn. I wish him a good night's sleep and I withdraw to my room.

I try not to think too much when I am alone. I need to come to terms with what I have done, but it is exhausting and confusing. My thoughts are attacking me.

I crawl into bed and pull the covers up high. This room is no longer a sanctuary. Nightmares crawl out of the walls and bury themselves into my head as I sleep. In a short space of time, I have stepped out of the life that I spent decades so carefully crafting. It was my masterpiece, and I am abandoning it.

But I think I always knew that the life I built could only ever be temporary.

You reap what you sow.

Chapter Thirty-Two

Morning comes and as promised, I accompany George to Miriam's room. Heavy rain is bouncing off the windows, and everything is grey and sorrowful. I don't ask George about Miriam's behaviour, and he doesn't volunteer an update. If there had been any trouble, I would know about it. George wouldn't take the risk of her harming us and I would be surprised if she had tried to hurt herself.

I can't keep wallowing in shame and regret. Nothing can ever change the past; I need to move forward. I have to trust my instincts and live each day as it comes. Self-pity will get me nowhere.

"I've thought carefully about this, George. There is no sense in dragging this out. I am happy to see Miriam alone. I know you are worried, but there will be no risk to me, I assure you. You have been through quite enough." He nods as I start to speak, but then immediately shakes his head and crosses his arms when I mention visiting Miriam by myself.

"No, sorry, sir. I'll be coming in with you. I won't interfere though. Not unless I have to."

I don't try and convince him otherwise. He is not being difficult. He is simply doing what he thinks is right for me.

I walk into Miriam's room, and she is completely calm. She is staring straight ahead, but as I enter, she turns her head to look at me and seems both relieved and surprised to see me. She gives me a quick once-over and smiles.

"Good morning, Miriam," I say, without emotion.

"Good morning, Monty." Her tone is easy and friendly, completely at odds with her current predicament. "I was hoping you'd come."

I look at the pillow on the bed to my right. It seems like the most humane way out of this. It will be over quickly, and I know that everything will be better afterwards. She has proven herself to be a danger to us. I don't doubt she'll attack either me or George again

She sees me looking and recognition dawns on her face. She looks at me urgently, eyes wide and blood draining from her face. "Monty?"

"I'm sorry, Miriam, I just don't see another way." My heart is thrashing against my ribs and bile rises in my throat. I walk towards the bed and George moves behind me.

"Wait," she says loudly, standing with alarm and raising her arms as though to push me away.

I reach for the pillow, shaking my head. An icy calm replaces the fear coursing inside me. I have to do this. This is the only way.

"Wait, Monty. Hear me out. Please."

I ignore her and lift the pillow to my chest.

"Goodbye, Miriam."

"I can help you, Monty. I can help you if you just listen!"

I was expecting "Please" or "No", but certainly not that. She takes full advantage of her reprieve.

"Give me five minutes, Monty. Listen to me. Really listen. Can you do that?"

Her voice is frantic and punctuated with ragged breaths.

I promised myself I wouldn't delay, that I wouldn't listen to her. I know that dragging this out is useless and unpleasant for everyone. George appears at my shoulder.

"It's okay, George," I say. He stays next to me and crosses his arms across his wide chest. I look at Miriam's face. She is clearly stalling, but I'm intrigued. "Okay, Miriam. This won't change things, I'm sad to say, but I will give you your five minutes." I take a step forward. I need to see her face as she talks. "Go ahead."

She thinks carefully before speaking. A touch of colour returns to her cheeks.

"I want this to stop, Monty." Her eyes do not falter. Her jaw clenches. She is completely serious. "I can help you, Monty. I can help you get what you need. I want to know what drives you. What you need to feel fulfilled." Her words are fast and frenzied, but it is difficult not to listen. "I know I can help you. I know I can be of value. But you have to let me in. Let go of this idea of me being your prisoner. Think of me as an ally. I can be an ally, Monty. But you have to trust me."

I take a step back. I am still holding the pillow and suddenly I feel childlike with it in my hands. She has blindsided me. I mustn't listen. Her words are simply a desperate, final attempt to save herself.

"But I don't trust you, Miriam. I don't trust you at all."

She is not deterred. "Of course, you don't. I know that you feel I haven't proven myself to be trustworthy yet. But I know we can change that."

I stop and let what she has just said wash over me. Her eyes gleam and she becomes animated when she sees I am considering it and, in honesty, I am. I don't know what it is. I am certain that I was prepared to kill her. Or am I simply looking for a way out of doing the unthinkable? If she hadn't spoken up, would she really be dead now?

"I am running out of options here, Monty. I know I can be of value to you, but I don't know how to make you see that."

I put the pillow down and her whole face floods with relief.

"You're not out of the woods yet, Miriam, I'm just getting fed up with holding it."

George stiffens beside me.

Miriam continues to speak. "Take a chance, Monty. If this doesn't work, then you have lost nothing. You may look back and think it's the best decision you ever made."

"Or the worst," I add, somewhat petulantly. She has got me thinking, but I can't help feeling that I am being manipulated.

"Tell me what you want out of life, Monty. I will help you. I will help you find it." I nod slowly. Perhaps there is another way. "Let's start afresh, Monty. Let's try and move forward. We can't change what has been before." She is speaking more quickly and persuasively as she senses me yielding. And I am.

Could this actually work? She wants to help me. She repeats my thought back to me. "I will help you get what you need." I allow her to continue.

She sits down hesitantly, never taking her eyes off mine, and adjusts her position in the chair. She looks at the pillow on the floor. "You don't want things to be like this. Do you?" I shake my head. She's right. This isn't what I want, I just couldn't see any other option. "Monty, I think our job in life is to make the best out of the situations we find ourselves in. We all have a role to play. Some roles are harder than others. I'm prepared to make a commitment. I am here and so are you. Working against each other won't benefit either of us."

I don't want to agree to anything now, here in front of her. I need some time to think things through. I turn away from her, giving no assurances.

"I need some time," I say to George.

"You do." He agrees and flashes a look at Miriam.

I don't process anything else until I sleep. I think I have hit an internal limit. I try, but I don't have the capacity. This whole situation has become too much for me and I hate how inconsistent I've become. I crawl into bed; the cool sheets are calming and comfortable. I breathe in and out slowly, trying to empty my head and slow my thoughts. I yield and let sleep wash over me.

I sleep like the dead. Nothing disturbs me.

Chapter Thirty-Three

I have an awful feeling that George is angry with me the next day. He doesn't say that he is, but I can't help feeling that way. He brings me breakfast and we talk. He looks different today. There is a deep black line between his eyebrows and irritation flickers in his eyes.

"What is it, George?"

"Nothing, sir, how are you feeling?"

"Are you angry about how I handled things yesterday?"

"No." He doesn't elaborate. He closes his eyes briefly and softens his face. "Tell me what you're thinking. Talk to me."

Things still feel strained, but I do my best to ignore it. "I've been thinking about my next meeting with Miriam. I need to spend some time contemplating what I want to say. I feel a lot clearer in my head, I want to make sure I can articulate it properly."

George seems to agree with me. "Okay, sir. If that's what you need. I'm sure there is a lot to get clear in your head." His responses feel rehearsed, as though he is reading from a script. Something isn't right.

"Thank you, George. I hope you know how much I appreciate you."

"It's my job, sir. I will always be here if you need anything." He smiles and his eyes crinkle at the sides in a way I hadn't noticed before.

"Have you been looking after Miriam for me?"

"Miriam is fine, sir. I hope your next meeting with her goes well."

He doesn't say anything further but the look on his face tells me that he has concerns. I suspect he thinks I've made a huge mistake in trusting Miriam.

George goes back to his duties. There are some minor things that need fixing around the house and today is his weekly trip to the pharmacy. I sit and plan out how everything will work if Miriam is going to stay. I write it all down and make my asks of Miriam very clear. I have come to the conclusion that my methods were not flawed, but my choice of person was. I am also much clearer about what I want now. I see now that Miriam has a place here, just not the place I had expected.

I take care of my appearance. I enjoy a hot shower and make sure my hair is neat. I have decided to wear a full suit today. I feel a strange urge to impress Miriam with my plans for the future. George knocks on the door and I gather my papers.

"Hello, sir, is there anything you need before your meeting?"

"No, George, but thank you for checking on me. I have thought everything through very carefully. I've been conflicted, but things couldn't be clearer now."

Miriam is waiting in my office, and she looks extremely professional. She has a folder of her own and I am impressed to see that she has taken some time to prepare. She is taking this new arrangement seriously and, unlike before, I now believe her intentions to be good.

"Good morning, Monty."

"Good morning, Miriam, how did you sleep? I hope George has been looking after you?"

She smiles graciously. "I'm good, thank you, Monty. How are you? Did you sleep well?"

She seems genuinely interested in how I am. I am taken aback, given what I have put her through. Our recent struggles seem so far away now, almost like two different people. I sit and place my papers on the table.

"I have prepared carefully for this meeting, Miriam. I hope you don't mind listening for a while. I have lots of things I want to say to you, and I don't want to lose my train of thought." She nods to show her interest and picks up her pen. "It's been a stressful few days. I hope you will bear with me."

"Yes, that's no problem. I hope you don't mind if I take notes while you speak. I don't want to forget anything important."

"Yes, most definitely." I'm delighted to see how ready and committed she is.

"And one other thing, Monty, please be honest. It doesn't matter what you say as long as it is the truth. If we are going to do this together then we need to have trust. Don't sugar-coat anything and don't hold anything back. There is no judgement here. Is that okay?"

She is back to the Miriam I met on the first day. I am impressed that her experiences here haven't changed her. She's not a victim, she's a fighter.

"What I'd like to tell you, Miriam, is how you came to be here and what I think needs to be different next time." She nods but doesn't say anything. "I'm sorry if some of what I say upsets you. I'm glad things are different between us now, but I think it's necessary."

I take a deep breath and, without leaving anything out,

describe how George and I came up with the plan for Miriam's arrival.

"Can I ask a question?" she interjects towards the end of my story.

"Please do." I'm grateful for the interruption. I feel like I've been talking for far too long.

"You say you sent George to meet with me? Why did you not come yourself?"

I'm surprised at the practical nature of her question.

"For my safety. You will know by now how much George cares and looks after me. It may appear to be an unusual relationship from the outside looking in."

"Not at all, Monty. We all need to feel that people care for us. It's a basic human necessity."

"As you rightly pointed out though, Miriam, I think that asking George may have been a mistake. I agree, I think you will be a much better choice.

"I'd like to move quickly on this, please, Miriam. I'd like the advert to go out today. The same process as before." I tap the pages in front of her.

"I'm going to need some time to read these, Monty. Can I please keep them?"

She gathers up the papers and flicks through them. Her eyebrows furrow.

"Yes, of course," I say.

She nods while continuing to scan the papers. I can see she understands.

"Can I ask one final question, please, Monty?" She holds up one of the pages I have given her. "You describe here how you plan to choose someone."

"Yes." I know what she's going to ask, and I don't want her to upset herself by having to say the words. "Yes, this is how I chose you. I'm sorry if you find any of this insulting or upsetting.

It really isn't meant to be taken that way. I need someone who is going to see this as an opportunity. As it turns out, I was wrong about you. I hope you see the fact that we are now working together as a testament to you as a person."

She places the piece of paper back with the others and piles them up in front of her, showing no outward signs of upset.

There is a knock on the door. I know it will be George. He still doesn't trust Miriam and I can hardly blame him.

"Come in," Miriam and I both say at the same time. It's a little bold of her to answer, but I let it go.

George enters. "Sorry to interrupt, but I just wanted to see if there is anything you need?" He is looking pointedly at Miriam, making sure she knows that he has his eyes on her. He can't forgive and forget as quickly as I can.

I answer. "We are fine, George, but excellent timing. I was just about to leave Miriam with my plans. Would you like to walk with me to my room? I can catch you up on our developments."

"Yes, sir, I'll bring you some lunch. You haven't been eating much lately."

He's right. I need to concentrate on my health more. I need to be at my best, and nutrition is so important.

"Very well," I say as I turn to Miriam. "I'll leave you to your reading. If you have any questions, just call George and he'll let me know."

She collects my papers along with her own notes.

"Thank you for today, Monty. I think we should meet daily, given the seriousness and importance of all of this. Do you agree?" I'm glad to see her taking the initiative, but I want her to focus on what I have asked of her.

"Yes, I completely agree. But I want the advert out today, please."

Miriam and I say our goodbyes and I walk with George to my room.

"How did that go, sir?" George is being respectful, but I sense the undercurrent of concern.

"I know how you feel about Miriam, and I completely understand why, I do. But I think we need to give her a chance. I've really warmed to her. I think she can be a real asset to us." He doesn't respond. "I'm surprised she is so calm and understanding after everything that has happened, but she seems genuine so I'm going to trust my instincts."

He nods but purposefully keeps looking forward as we walk side by side.

"How are you feeling?" I point at his neck as I ask so he knows what I mean.

"Don't worry about me, sir, just focus on yourself and what you need to do." I have the urge to envelop him in a hug. "I'll bring you some lunch shortly, sir."

"Thank you, George. And despite what I have just said, do keep an eye on Miriam for me, won't you? She has surprised us before."

He places his hand on my shoulder. "Take some rest, sir. It will be good for you."

I eat lunch and lie on my bed. An inner peace flows through me. I'm pleased with how this morning went. I take George's advice and spend the remainder of the day resting. I am overtired and I haven't been looking after myself properly. I fall asleep easily and deeply.

Dreams twist into my brain. I try to pull my eyes open with every ounce of strength I have, but the dreams continue. I am frozen and cannot shake myself awake. Penny stands over my bed. She opens and closes her mouth, but my father's voice comes out. I scream and I hear it inside my head. Piercing and real. But nothing comes out of my mouth. The walls are closing in on me and his voice is getting louder and louder. It is rhythmical, like a drum, pounding in my head.

"My son. My son. My son."

I picture his face. He is laughing. Taunting me.

His voice washes over me and soaks into me.

Deep into my soul.

Chapter Thirty-Four

When I wake, my bedsheets are soaked with sweat. The nightmares arrive most nights now. My bedroom used to feel like my sanctuary. Now it feels infected.

I clean myself up, but I'm still not happy with how I look. The exhaustion is etched on my face. I can't seem to get past it at the moment. My once-sharp jawline looks baggy and pitiful.

I find George in the corridor. He takes in the sight of me and frowns.

"Hello, George. How has your day been?"

"Good, thank you, sir. Did you manage some rest?"

I consider telling him the truth, but I don't have the energy to explain.

"Of sorts. Thank you, George. How is Miriam? I hope she has been following my instructions and hasn't been difficult for you?"

George gives me a pinched smile. His eyes look unusual; watery and small. I wonder if he has been crying. I don't push it. If there had been any issues with my instructions, then Miriam would have let George know.

"Can I do anything at all for you, sir? I was about to finish for the day."

I forget George in all of this sometimes. He has a life outside of here. He gives so much of himself to me.

"Yes, of course, George. I know we usually meet every evening but I think you should take this evening to yourself and rest."

He gives an embarrassed smile and turns to leave. His shoulders are hunched forwards, the weight of the world resting upon them. I say goodnight to him and walk along the corridor. I look out of the window at the sweeping drive and the vast beautifully landscaped and maintained gardens. I often forget to stop and really look. When I remember to, it's like seeing it all for the first time.

I could never have imagined I would end up living somewhere like this. Sometimes, I have to stop and remind myself of what I have and how far I have come in life. Things could have been very different, after all. Mostly I feel safe here in this picture-perfect world that I have created. I've never had to endure the drudgery of a soul-crushing job. I have lots to be grateful for.

I don't think I am a bad person and, if I am becoming one, it is not for want of decades of trying. I have to believe that my plans are the way forward.

Otherwise, I have nothing.

Chapter Thirty-Five

I am impressed. Miriam has produced a written brief that George delivered to my room this morning. I found it pushed under my door and it is of excellent quality. I feel a surge of happiness. I like her taking the initiative and using this as an opportunity to prove herself to me. All my instructions have been followed to the letter and, I am assured, we can expect a new visitor within days. I have arranged a post-breakfast meeting in my office with Miriam and George.

George asks how I slept, as he always does. I lie. Lying wasn't part of the plan, but I'm hoping my experiences at night are not permanent. I am only human, after all. These are the physical effects of what has happened. I am not in control of them, but that is okay. My body is adjusting and will catch up with my waking mind soon enough. George would only worry. I put the envelope of professionally prepared documents onto the table.

"Thank you for these, Miriam. I have to say, they impressed me hugely and it is good to see that everything is in order. You have clearly worked very hard, and please be assured, it has not gone unnoticed." I look at Miriam pointedly. "Do you have any questions, Miriam?"

She hooks a finger through the fine gold chain of her necklace and begins rubbing the small open-heart pendant that hangs from it.

"Yes, Monty, I do have some questions."

"Go ahead. Ask me anything."

What Miriam asks me knocks me off my feet. My brain stutters briefly but catches up quickly. This is a very important moment.

"Are you planning to kill this woman?" She asks the question in a monotone, matter-of-fact way, her face an emotionless mask. I mirror her behaviour and answer her truthfully and without hesitation.

"I don't want to kill anyone, Miriam. But I will need her to stay one way or another."

Her expression doesn't alter, and she keeps looking me in the eye. Her hand unconsciously drifts to stroke the back of her neck.

"If this one doesn't... work out, do you expect there to be more?"

She continues her questions in a businesslike fashion. It is unexpected, but I don't dislike the approach. I decide to continue with honesty. I owe her the truth.

"Miriam, this isn't what I want. Please believe me. I have suffered horribly with shame and disgust over the past few weeks. This is everything I despise, everything I wanted to avoid at all costs. I have tried unsuccessfully to live a different life. I have discussed this many times with George." I look over at George. His face is grey, and he is holding himself so stiffly it looks painful. "George, it's okay. I know what I'm doing. There is simply no point in keeping things from her."

George remains rigid, his eyes lined with concern.

I continue, unperturbed. "I am who I am. I have tried to be somebody else my entire adult life. The Monty you see now has been developing all these years right alongside the person I presented to the world. In parallel." Miriam is listening carefully and taking notes. She is engrossed in my every word. "The airs, the graces, they are all a façade. One I have been so proud of. One I would prefer to continue with if it were possible. But it is all a lie. I am a creature born out of necessity."

If Miriam is appalled, she doesn't show it. If anything, she seems enthusiastic and enthralled. She continues with her questions.

"So, there could be a situation where there are multiple women. Dead women. Surely you know that's... a problem?"

She pauses for effect after "dead women", but I don't react. I can't explain it to her in a way she will comprehend. Only someone who has my experiences can truly understand.

"You said you wanted to help me, so you are going to have to trust me. It's something that I simply know will work if I get it right, and, as time passes, I will prove it to you. This is the path I have to take. I am not a monster, but all other roads have closed for me."

We finish our meeting. What is there to say after that?

I know that Miriam will deliver what she has promised. Despite my exhaustion and the nightmares, I have become more in tune with my natural instincts recently and I can tell that she is on my side.

George and I leave my office together. He accompanies me to my room.

"You looked shocked in there. You weren't expecting me to say that to her, were you?" George shakes his head and puffs out his pink cheeks. "I know you don't trust her yet, George, but there is no point in lying. I've been living a lie for too long. But now, I am ready to accept what I am."

George shrugs and smiles warmly.

We stop for a moment outside my room. George and I are standing so close that I can feel his warm breath on my skin. "George, you've begun to make this a bit of a habit. You must stop worrying about my safety. Nothing is going to happen to me."

George nods, leans across my body, and opens my door for me with his usual chivalry. He doesn't argue, but I know he will feel more comfortable looking after me until Miriam has been here a little longer. "You can talk to me you know, George. I will always be here for you. I'm sorry if I don't always make that as clear as I should."

George forces a smile and lowers his eyes. "Just focus on yourself, sir."

George and I have arranged to meet later and I decide I am going to spend the afternoon in my office. Catch up on some correspondence and clear my head a bit. On my way there, I discover that May is not at her desk, and neither are any of her things. I glance around the room, confusion furrowing my brow. I know I told May to take some time off but I thought she would be back by now. I hope she's not unwell. George is quick to assure me that she's taken some extra planned leave. He's a little on edge and stumbles somewhat over his reply, eyes darting everywhere but towards me. He seems particularly anxious today and he isn't walking as tall and strong as he usually does.

I work for hours. My concentration seems to have improved today and my energy levels are up. I've let the business side of things slide a little recently. I've cancelled far too many meetings and there is much to catch up on. Everything is starting to feel much more ordered again.

George and I meet for our usual catch-up in the evening. I'm hoping George will open up a little more. He has been particularly quiet today, so my expectations are not too high.

"What was your childhood like, George?"

There is a lingering sadness in George's eyes as I realise too late that he won't want to talk about my father. I wish I'd been more specific with my question. "You don't have to talk about him. I'm wondering more about you." The haunted look does not lift and it is obvious that, despite my clarification, he still doesn't want to answer the question.

"I'm sorry, sir. I don't think that's something I can answer."

"Why?" I ask the question gently. Letting him know there is no pressure.

"I'm sorry, sir." His words are thick and heavy. He looks down at his hands and begins picking at the already ragged skin around his thumbnail. His reluctance bothers me, but I know I must learn to let him be who he is.

We sit quietly and drink tea.

"Did you hear that, George?" I look around, searching for the source of the voices I clearly heard.

"What, sir?"

It was as clear as day. I stand and walk to each wall in turn, searching for the sound. "The talking? I heard a man and a woman talking, quite loudly. Only briefly, but I definitely heard it."

"I'm not sure, sir. I wasn't paying attention." He's looking at me, jaw slack, as if waiting for me to say something else. "Can you still hear it?"

"No," I say honestly. I can't even remember what direction the sound came from.

"Did you hear what they said?"

"No." The voices were loud but conversational. It didn't sound like an argument.

George stands and joins me, and I check the corridor outside. There's nobody here but us.

"Do you think you imagined it?"

"I don't know." But I do know. The voices were far too clear to be imagined. Those voices were real. I reach deep into my memory, but I can't put any faces to them.

I watch George closely. He is trying to disappear into the soft chair, and his remaining fingernails are getting the same treatment as his now painful-looking thumb. George is not being honest with me.

"It was only brief, George, and I couldn't hear what they were saying, but I know they were there."

George is definitely breathing faster. He gets out of the chair clumsily. I don't take my eyes off him. He doesn't even glance at me.

"Would you like me to get–"

I cut him off quickly. "No, I don't need anything. I'm sure I'm only tired. I think I'll get an early night."

"Are you sure, sir?"

"Yes, I'm sure." I draw my lips in tightly before forcing a smile.

And I am sure of one thing. I heard two people talking in my house, and I don't believe that George didn't hear them too. Why would he lie to me?

I consider pushing it with George. Clearly, he is withholding information. But I know that pushing him at this moment is not the answer.

George has been dishonest with me once. Have I been stupid to trust him again? My gut instinct tells me that my faith in George is not misplaced, but I will find out what he is hiding.

Chapter Thirty-Six

Before

I hear a whisper. I feel warm breath against my ear and the faint smell of lavender hovering over me.

"Shh. Don't wake Miles."

I instantly remember where I am, and I feel the weight of Lois as she lowers herself onto my bed. She ruffles my hair playfully and I force my dry, sleepy eyes open. Her face slowly comes into focus. She is beaming and there are streaks of what looks like flour on her forehead and in her hair. She puts her finger to her mouth and whispers again.

"Come downstairs."

She performs an exaggerated tiptoe out of the room and beckons for me to follow her. I stifle a giggle and mime zipping my mouth closed before following her downstairs.

Today is Miles' 11th birthday. There hasn't been a birthday since I arrived here. That seems impossible, I feel like I've been here for ages. My 11th birthday will be next month.

I walk silently into the kitchen and Henry closes the door behind me. The kitchen is even more chaotic than usual. There are balloons everywhere. All different colours, shapes, and sizes.

Birthday banners and streamers adorn the walls and hang from the ceiling.

"Do you think we need more balloons?" Henry says as he laughs and rolls his eyes. Lois hits him playfully with a tea towel and a spray of flour coats the front of his navy shirt and the bottom of his beard.

"Oops!" Lois giggles, as she whips the towel back and covers them both in even more flour. We are all laughing now. Hands over our mouths, trying and failing to stay quiet for Miles.

Lois gestures with a flourish to the cake in the centre of the kitchen table. It is the most perfect cake I have ever seen. It is wonderfully wonky and splattered with icing and covered with strawberries. Eleven candles haphazardly cover the top. A sugary, buttery aroma fills the kitchen. I give her a wide smile and marvel at her creation.

"It's wonderful," I say as my eyes fill with tears. It really is just wonderful.

Henry and I wait in the kitchen as Lois runs upstairs to wake Miles. His warm, heavy hand rests on my shoulder. I look up at him and his eyes are warm and filled with excitement. Miles enters the room and Henry booms.

"Happy birthday!"

The volume of his voice makes me jump. I try to settle myself and join in with Lois' and Henry's clapping. My face is flushed and I'm hoping I don't look as anxious as I feel. This is Miles' birthday, and the last thing I want is to ruin it by acting weird.

Lois squeezes Miles and plants a noisy kiss on his cheek, before leaving the kitchen suddenly. She returns with a small pile of presents and places them on the table next to the cake and then stands next to Henry. The cake seems to have shifted slightly and now resembles the leaning tower of Pisa. I like it even more.

I know that Lois and Henry are very wealthy. Henry began his working life as a lorry driver, before deciding to open his own haulage firm shortly after Miles was born. All Lois ever wanted was a big family and Henry wanted nothing more than for her to be able to stay at home and enjoy being a mother while he earned a good living for his family. They are not showy with their wealth at all. In fact, they are the most humble and down-to-earth people I have ever met.

Miles looks at both of his parents with what is obviously pure love and gratitude. He embraces them both, burying his head into their bodies and squeezing tightly.

I feel awkward and out of place. An intruder in a perfect family.

Miles turns and I don't manage to change the uneasy look on my face quickly enough. The tips of my cheeks flush and I have to stop myself from running for the kitchen door. My heart is beating too fast, and the once delicious cake smell now feels sickly and overpowering. I know I'm going to spoil everything. Most of the last few months have been about me. Today is Miles' birthday and I should be able to act normally for him. I clear my dry throat.

"Happy birthday, Miles," I manage, but it sounds weak and pathetic. I follow it with, "I'm sorry," and I cast my eyes down to the floor and poke my toe at a stray red balloon on the floor. It floats for a second and returns to the floor, bobbing away from me.

Suddenly Miles throws his arms around me and laughs.

"What are you sorry for, silly?"

He pulls away and moves his head comically to try and look into my eyes. I lift my gaze reluctantly and Miles and I lock eyes. We stare at each other for what feels like an eternity. At first, I want to look away. It is as though nobody else is in the room. I watch Miles' mouth closely as he speaks again.

"Thank you, Monty. Just having you here makes this the best birthday ever."

He pulls me towards him again, and then Henry and Lois surround us, hugging us both tightly. I can hardly breathe but in the nicest possible way. My body floods with a wonderfully warm, satisfying feeling. I would smile but my face is squished against Miles' cheek.

"Aargh! Get off!" Miles shrieks playfully.

Henry and Lois loosen their grip but don't let go of us and I feel Lois plant a soft kiss on my forehead. I don't think I have ever felt this happy.

My life before was a living nightmare. A constant tirade of fear, pain, and dread. In the arms of these wonderful people, I know that everything is going to be fine. I will never heal from the things that happened to me, but with their warmth and love, I don't need to. I will always be okay.

Just as long as they never leave me.

Chapter Thirty-Seven

There are many applications for the personal assistant position. I'm not sure how Miriam has achieved this so quickly, but I am delighted to find a well-presented list for my consideration first thing in the morning. She must have been working all night.

I read and contemplate each one as I get ready for the day. She has exceeded my expectations yet again. There is one that stands out clearly above all the rest. Miriam has clearly noticed this too; I don't think it is an accident that it is at the top of the pile. I throw the remainder of them in the wastepaper bin.

Miriam and George are waiting for me, in my office. Punctual and well prepared. We all greet each other professionally and I put the application I have chosen down on the table.

"Have you seen this, George?" George has cut his hair and taken extra special care with his grooming today. His skin is smoother and there is colour in his cheeks. It is very pleasing to see him making time for himself.

"No, sir."

Miriam pulls the application towards her.

"I don't think my choice will surprise you, Miriam. Thank you for all your hard work, but this one stood out from all the rest, as I'm sure you will agree." She notes down the details as I explain them to George. "I reviewed all of the applications, and this is the one I have chosen. Her name is Naomi. Let's move quickly on this, Miriam, please. Today if possible. I want to be at my best when she arrives so I will be taking a quiet day today."

George interjects. "You need to eat, sir. I will bring your lunch to your room."

"Yes, thank you, George. I'd like that." I notice that Miriam has pursed her lips. In some ways, Miriam seems to have settled in very comfortably, but I still sense a reticence to come forward. "Miriam, I can sense you have more to say today. Please don't hold back."

"Thank you, Monty..." She opens her mouth to say more, but I want to finish my thought first.

"You have all of my instructions for today, as do you, George. I know that this time everything will go just as it should."

Miriam moves forwards and rests her hands on the polished table.

"I have more of an observation than a question, Monty."

"Please. Go on." I am genuinely keen to hear what she has to say.

"I feel like you are handing over too much to us." She holds up the application as she speaks. "If, as you say, this is a way for you to find a purpose in life. A quest for freedom almost. Why are you standing back so much?" She is analysing me, and she's wrong, that was an observation and a question.

I don't like this level of scrutiny from her, but I can understand why Miriam would need to justify this to herself, to find a positive slant on what we are doing. She is trying to ease her conscience.

I challenge her. "Are you saying I am not in control?"

She shakes her head instantly. "No. That's not what I mean at all. It just seems that you are handing over a lot of control. Separating yourself from it all. This is not our wish, it is yours. If this is your way to seek clarity and truth, I'm surprised you don't want to stay closer to it."

I'm intrigued to hear Miriam being so philosophical. It is not a side of her I have seen before, and I wonder whether the gravity of the ask and the potential consequences are weighing heavily on her shoulders. We are all bad, far worse than we could ever imagine when life demands it of us, but that doesn't make it an easy choice. I remain silent and let her continue.

"You keep talking about preparations and plans," she says, "but avoid using all of the words that describe what you are doing. I wonder whether this is how you actually feel."

I can see where she is going with this. She is hoping that I will change my mind. That, when faced with the cold, hard reality of this, I will realise the error of my ways. She doesn't realise that I choose my words, and omit others, to protect the people around me. Not myself. If she needs to hear it all, then so be it. But she won't like it.

"Miriam, I would like you to meet Naomi and bring her back here. George will make her comfortable in the basement. I want to look after her, but I need to feel loved and wanted too. I want gratitude. I want control. If I don't get the things that I need, then I may have to kill her. As I have said, that isn't my intention, but it may be the only way."

They both watch me intently. My heart is racing with the enormity of saying this out loud and admitting it to the world. I own every word. I mean every word. Shame holds no power over me now. The self-revulsion is no more. This is who I am.

I see Miriam swallow hard and, despite what she already knows, I can see that it shocks her to hear it so coldly.

"I may be charming and friendly, Miriam, but you'd do well to remember exactly who I am and why you are here." She winces and puts down the piece of paper, trying to hide her shaky hands. "Does what I say repulse you? Do you think it is wrong? Am I evil?"

She answers only the questions I have asked. In order. And with a calmness that shows her strength and self-control to be greater than I had given her credit for.

"Yes, it does. Yes, I do think that killing innocent women is wrong. No, I do not think you are evil. I think that in time you will come to see that, too."

I could say more, but I can see that Miriam needs some time. Her lower lip trembles as she breathes out slowly. I know that listening to me today will have been tough for her. The dark reality of her promises will have hit her. Hard.

I wake from my afternoon nap to the sound of a knock at my bedroom door. A note has been pushed under the door. I can see the small square of white paper from across the room. I know what it says before I even pick it up.

She is here.

Butterflies dance inside my tummy. I don't have to wait long. As the note informs me, I will be able to meet Naomi with Miriam in the office in less than an hour.

I take a shower to wake myself up and stare at myself in the cloudy mirror. I make my way to the office with a heady mix of excitement and trepidation coursing through me. I don't know what to expect. What will she be like? How will she react? I try not to think too hard. High expectations of others only ever lead to disappointment.

Miriam and Naomi are sitting on one side of the table. The

lights are on even though it's bright outside. George isn't here. I assume he will be getting Naomi's room ready, but his absence unnerves me. Why isn't he here? It's unusually thoughtless of him. Naomi watches me as I enter the room, her eyes flitting up to mine and then down to her lap. My eyes stay focused on hers, and I pull my shoulders back. It is an intimate level of eye contact for someone you've just met, hence her natural reaction to look away.

Miriam looks focused. Her jaw is clenched, and she is passing a pen between her fingers. She sits up straight. Painfully straight. Naomi's application is on the desk alongside the other paperwork I have given Miriam. Naomi is completely still; the only movements I see are the shallow rise and fall of her chest and the occasional blink of her eyes. The room is quiet and still. Everyone is waiting.

"Hello, Miriam. Hello, Naomi," I say as I approach the table.

Naomi doesn't stand and I wonder whether there has already been a struggle. Whether restraint has been required. Nothing is telling in Miriam's eyes as she says hello to me.

Naomi offers a weak hello; she is timid and unsure of herself. Her hair is pulled back in a sensible, low ponytail and her clothes are functional and nondescript. There is no obvious make-up on her unblemished face. She is slightly younger than I had imagined and almost painfully thin. I sit down, take a deep breath, and begin talking immediately. I cannot let the doubt creep in.

"Naomi, I have quite a lot to say, and I'd like you to listen." She looks to Miriam, as if for instruction or permission. Miriam raises her eyebrows and nods in agreement with me. Miriam turns her head to focus on me and Naomi mirrors her. "I don't know how much you have been told about why you are here." She is about to speak, and I hold my hand out. "At this point, it doesn't matter what you've been told. The most important thing is that you are here and what is going to happen now."

I sit and settle myself into a comfortable position. I have considered this carefully and I have a lot to say. "I'm going to tell you about my life." I glance at Miriam. "Miriam, this is for your benefit, too. This may seem unorthodox, but I feel it is necessary. It's something I have never done, and I'm starting to realise that's where I have been going wrong. It's the very fibres of who I am." I check that they are both paying me the level of attention that this requires, and then I continue my story. "I don't remember much about my mother. As a child, I lived with my father. If I could go back in time, I would ask him what happened to my mother, but I was always too afraid. I think that he killed her, but I don't remember it clearly." Miriam's eyes widen and Naomi's breathing has already quickened. I can feel anxiety welling up inside me at saying this out loud, but I need to get it out. To set it free.

"It's okay," I hear Miriam say to Naomi almost inaudibly. Miriam is clearly shocked by my words but is holding herself together much better than Naomi. I turn my attention to Naomi as I describe the details of my childhood.

"My father used to kidnap women. He would bring them back to our home and kill them."

Naomi puts her hand to her mouth and stifles a whimper. Miriam places a hand gently on Naomi's shoulder.

"Don't worry, my dear, I won't tell you how," I say. I can see Naomi wants to escape, but she doesn't move. Her face is even whiter now. I continue with my story. "At first, I used to hide under my bed and push my fingers deep into my ears until it was done. I used to squeeze my eyes closed so tightly I thought they would pop. I would lie there, thinking of stories, singing the words to songs I loved in my head. Despite my efforts, I couldn't drown it out. I knew what was happening and those images crept their way into my brain, getting more and more vivid each time. I didn't dare come out until the noises stopped. I used to pray for it to be over quickly, but then I realised I was praying for someone's death, and I was horrified. Even at that young age, I felt responsible. I was helpless." I stop and take a moment to steady myself. Nausea is creeping in as my brain conjures up hideous, long-buried images. I haven't said any of these things out loud since my early sessions with Dr Pathirana. They hurt me just as much now as they did then.

The room is silent. I don't think anyone is even breathing. I pause and exhale loudly. Letting the painful memories out into the room. Letting them out of my head where I've trapped them for so long. Neither of the women is looking at me.

"I do appreciate that this may be hard to hear, but certainly not a patch on living through it as an innocent child." I have no sympathy; all they are doing is hearing a story. "I feel terrible that I have no idea how many people my father killed. I feel guilty that I hid and prayed. He never talked about what he was doing, and I never asked. My father was an extremely professional and well-respected man. I couldn't believe what he was doing, but the world kept on turning. Unsuspecting."

Naomi and Miriam are listening intently now. "One day, something changed. I became a part of it all. Father came into my room shortly after the shouting and the banging stopped and forced me to help him clean up. I vomited almost immediately, and he was furious, as now there was even more mess." Naomi raises her hand to her mouth, and she looks nauseated. I ignore her. "I heaved until my stomach was empty, and I cried the whole time. He shouted and screamed. Furious at my weakness."

The broken vision of the room flashes before my eyes and I push down the rising sickening feeling. I only realise that I have stopped talking when Miriam addresses me.

"Go on, Monty. If you can." She sees my pain and she knows I want to do this the right way. Conversely, Naomi's face is a mask of dread and panic. She is trying to quash it but failing entirely.

"I never looked. I saw their blood. I saw their bodies, but I never looked. I heard the noises, but I never listened. He didn't see the difference, but I did, it was my only available act of defiance. But I survived him. I survived. I was taken to live with another family, and I flourished. The horrors I had experienced ebbed away over the years. I packed them away. I had a wonderful doctor who helped me carry it all. You see, you don't get over something like this. It's a part of you, and you must learn to carry it. If you try to put it down or leave it behind, it just finds you and is more unwieldy than ever."

Despite the repulsiveness of my story, I can see they are gripped by what I am telling them. "I learned how to take it with me, but it had dulled me. I was a child with no sparkle. Dead behind the eyes. My new family was perfect. They were selfless and loving people. My feelings overwhelmed me on a daily basis. I decided to try and not feel anything whenever possible. Feeling nothing can be a choice. I chose feeling nothing over feeling everything. I chose strategy and survival, and I became hugely successful. As you can well see."

I close my eyes for a moment. This is a lot for them to hear, and a lot for me to say all at once. It feels very physical, and the words are starting to exhaust me.

"I lived for years doing exactly that. Just living and using other people's reactions and measures of success as my own personal yardstick. I was doing well, and everyone told me so. I was a miracle. But inside, I wasn't any of those things, I was an imposter."

Naomi is starting to look as though she may faint.

"Do you need a break, my dear?" I ask her.

She answers apologetically. "No. No, I'm fine. Thank you."

I could add a lot more, but I stop describing. I think I've said enough about my past.

"You see, Naomi, despite my efforts, nurture has lost the battle. Nature has prevailed. Please don't assume that this is what I want, it is what I have to do. My father's blood runs strong in my veins and his voice lives on through me. I hate what my father did, but I'm simply not strong enough to resist him."

I am aware that I am being somewhat dramatic with my choice of language, but it feels fitting. I look at the picture mounted on the wall directly opposite me. I see my face in the perfectly polished glass and watch my mouth as I say the words. Recognising and owning every word.

"I am a killer."

My heart races as I watch myself. I don't let myself look away.

"I am a murderer."

The words fill the silent room. There is such strength in their truth, that it almost brings me to tears. Naomi draws in a sharp breath. I thank them both for letting me speak freely and then turn my attention to Miriam. Her lips are pressed tightly together.

"Miriam, you know what to do."

Miriam nods. "Thank you, Monty. Is there anything else you need today?"

I point to the papers on the desk. "Just stick to these instructions, please." I turn to Naomi. "Naomi, I'm going to leave you in Miriam's hands now. Please do let her know if there is anything you need during your stay with us. I will see you later this evening."

George is waiting for me outside the office. His face is red, and his cheeks look hollow.

"Good morning, sir. How did that go?"

"Very well, thank you, George. Have you seen her? I think she's perfect. Respectful, but understandably nervous. Miriam seems to have done a fantastic job. No hysterics."

"Is there anything you need, sir?"

"Not just now thank you, George."

I don't want to tell George how my head feels. A panic attack would be most unwelcome at this moment. I won't have to explain how I'm feeling to him if I can keep my words clear. Letting all that out was certainly a relief, but the after-effects will be hard. "I'm going to take today to prepare, and you and I can meet as usual before I visit Naomi this evening." I pause for a moment before adding, "I told them everything."

"What do you mean, sir?"

"I told them about Father. I told them about my life as a boy." I pause and look him deep in the eye. "I told them I have no choice but to kill."

George looks alarmed. I know he'd rather I divulge as little as possible. Keep myself safe. "And how are things now?"

"Good, I think. It's taken it out of me a bit, but I'll be fine by this evening. This is all new to me, George. I need to take it step by step, day by day. But I've made a commitment and I can't go backwards."

"And what about this evening, sir?"

Just as he wants to protect me, I want to protect him, too.

"You let me worry about this evening, George. You and Miriam have done your part and I will take it from here. I know the things you have done for me, but I know that deep down inside you are not a murderer."

He presses his hand to his chest as I say the word. "I see you, George. I can see you have changed. I see your moods fluctuate and I have noticed you struggling to work through different emotions every day." George looks uncomfortable, he doesn't like me talking about his feelings. "The next part is all me. I won't infect other people with my actions as my father did."

He doesn't offer up any of his thoughts. His voice is strangled as he answers me resignedly. "Of course, sir."

"And thank you for everything you have done with Miriam. I know you have been doing an incredible job of taking care of her."

I almost collapse in my room as George leaves. I sit with my back to the door and try to breathe. I am dizzy and my heart is beating out a rhythm I don't recognise. I crawl towards the bed on shaking limbs and lie down. I must hide my breaking self from George and Miriam. Otherwise, they won't trust me. I take slow, deep breaths and place one hand on my chest and the other on my stomach. I watch my hands rise and fall. This technique works well for me if I catch the panic early enough. Slowly, it begins to ebb away, and I drift off to sleep.

Before I know it, George is knocking on my door for our meeting. I take pride in my timekeeping and feel flustered when I'm caught on the back foot.

"I need ten minutes, George. Just attending to something. I'll be out shortly."

I straighten my clothes and squint sleepily at myself in the mirror. I'm relieved to find that I look nowhere near as dishevelled as I feel. I know that George will wait if I ask him to. I don't like leaving my room without putting everything in its place and making the bed perfectly, but I dislike tardiness even more. I can attend to my room later.

When I emerge, George is resting comfortably against the wall outside my room, his legs crossed at the ankles.

"You look great, George. Did you manage some rest this afternoon?"

His cheeks flush at the compliment. "I am well rested, thank you, sir."

We sit and drink tea together in my office. His company steadies and settles me. I am quieter than normal, and, unusually, he breaks the silence.

"Is there anything you want to talk to me about, sir?"

"Actually, please could we just sit? I always feel so comfortable with you and this morning really took it out of me. I didn't say anything to you earlier because I know how you worry, but all of this is really exhausting me, much more than I had thought possible. I constantly need sleep, but even that is disturbed sometimes."

"Are you sure you are okay? You don't need to hide anything from me."

"To be honest, I am struggling a little. But I'm okay. I promise. And I need to save my energy for this evening."

"Can you..."

"Before you ask, George, as I said earlier, you have done enough. Naomi is here because I want her to be. I can't ask you and Miriam to be involved any further. It's not fair and Miriam is right. If I don't own my actions, it will all be for nothing."

We sit quietly, the only sound is the occasional sip of tea or clinking of china cups. George seems uncomfortable with the prolonged silence. Constantly picking at his fingers or at the expensive velvet of the chair arm. I want to tell him to stop it, but even in his fidgety state, the simple act of sitting with George helps me. It fills me up.

George lets out an enormous pent-up breath when our

meeting is over. I must try and help him to embrace silence, rather than treat it as an uncomfortable state.

"Please call if you need anything this evening, or overnight, sir. Don't hesitate."

"Don't worry, George, I know what I am doing, and I appreciate your concerns. Truly I do." He reluctantly accepts my reassurances, and I don't see him again until the following day.

Until Naomi is dead.

Chapter Thirty-Eight

My visit to Naomi is uncomplicated. Everything goes as expected. Naomi is frightened and I put her out of her misery quickly. A clean cut to her throat. She barely struggles. Her blood flows, smooth and thick. She whimpers and gurgles as the life drains from her. I don't listen. It is over so quickly, her life extinguished in mere seconds. The heady smell of her blood takes me back and I choke down tears and push my fear away. I am not a child anymore. I am a man.

I don't look Naomi in the eyes. I look past the reality of the body and concentrate on the feeling. It's the act that is important, not the identity of the person.

Her body is heavy, surprisingly so, and I buckle under her weight as I try to move her. My hands are red and the sight of them makes me want to vomit. But I won't. There is no room in my life for weakness anymore.

I feel every movement as I clean her and wrap her body. I do it with respect. My mind knows exactly what to do, my body willingly follows commands. I am kind to her.

I clean the room ferociously. It is part of the ritual, a mark of respect.

I had always known that my father was a despicable monster, who chose to carry out heinous crimes. I can see now that this is not entirely true. This life is not a choice. It is something that lives within you. Something that you are. The entirety of a person cannot be judged by their worst parts alone.

———

Finally, I take Naomi to be with Penny. They are both in a better place. No longer haunted by the horrors of life.

They are safe now. They are at peace.

Chapter Thirty-Nine

I wake up too early the next morning. I have slept with the curtains open, and I have a thumping headache. My body aches and lifting my limbs is a mammoth task. I need to pull myself together.

I have arranged to meet Miriam this morning. I need to provide her with instructions for our next visitor, and make sure that she remains committed to me. I don't know how the death of Naomi will affect her. I hope the reality of her complicity in murder won't become a problem.

Before our morning meeting, I watch the news. There is nothing about Naomi. I wasn't expecting there to be. Nobody will notice that Naomi is missing for some time, Miriam has seen to that.

My meeting with Miriam this morning does not go well. I am upset to find that George is absent, and that sets the tone for the rest of the discussion. I can't understand why he would choose not to be here this morning. What else could be more important?

"Is he in the basement? He doesn't need to be! I sorted

everything. Doesn't he trust me?" I pace aimlessly around the office, smouldering with resentment.

Miriam is immediately back-pedalling, watching me curiously and trying to defuse the situation.

"I'm sorry, Monty. I think there's just been some confusion. I know he'll see you later." She trips over her words, a forced smile on her face. It is obvious that she is not being entirely truthful with me. Something is going on.

"I can't believe he wouldn't be here after last night. Doesn't he care?"

She tries to distract me. "How was last night, Monty?"

I ignore her blatant attempt to get me talking. I want to know where George is.

"Just get to work on the next one, would you? I got rid of the list you gave me; I need another copy. There will be other perfectly good options on that list. I will get back to you later today for my next choice."

Her mouth sets into a hard line. The reluctance is obvious. Without George by my side, anger begins to stir inside me.

"Are you questioning me, Miriam?" I dig my nails into my palms as I speak, trying to keep some semblance of control over my growing resentment.

She watches me carefully but says nothing.

I lean towards her, breathless with simmering anger. "I let you live, Miriam. Don't forget that. You are here to work, to deliver the promises you made. You are not here to sit and judge. Maybe it's time you went back downstairs? Maybe you need to remember your gratitude?"

Rage churns my insides. Anger ripples through me like intense heat. I can't control it and I have no desire to. Her silence and indifference to my behaviour are fuelling the fire even more. I want to scream, throw something. Instead, I stand, a swirling vortex of fury, and point my finger, jabbing it menacingly towards her face.

"Just do your fucking job, Miriam."

There is a knock on the door, and I know it is George. I lower my head and crash through the door before he can enter.

"Sir?" he says weakly as I storm away from him. I can't bear to look at him right now.

I march back to my room, anger propelling me.

George follows me but I ignore him. "Leave me alone, George!" I shout without turning.

I slam my door closed. I can barely breathe. Tight pains course across my chest and I pull hard on my hair until they begin to subside.

I lie on my bed, and I cry. I cry until I am empty. I scream and I punch the pillows. I don't recognise myself in any of this, but I do what feels right.

Just as I risk tipping over into a full-blown attack, I grasp at the fine threads of reality and manage to restrain myself. I force myself to be calm. I breathe and I lie still. Letting the anger subside, letting my thoughts go. Letting them all go.

I can't trust these people. They can't possibly know what it feels like to live with this wickedness eating away inside you. It is me against the world. It pains me to think of George betraying me, but I know he will in the end.

I don't meet George this evening. I refuse and stay in my room when I know he is around.

"Sir, please? I really think you need to come out and talk."

His words may sound caring, but they are riddled with insincerity. It's well hidden, but it's there.

"That's not your call anyway, George."

"Sir, please? I won't come in."

The nerve of him. I can't actually believe it.

"Too fucking right, you won't." I go to the door, press my nose against it and imagine him on the other side of the door. Things change so quickly. When faced with reality, they have turned on me. I am sure they are just biding their time before turning me in to save their skins. They may think they can outmanoeuvre me, but they will regret it if they turn on me.

"Sir?"

I try to remain calm and think about what I need to do next. I need to play this very carefully. If they get any hint that I am onto them, then they will have the upper hand. I have trusted them and as such, I have taught them everything they need to know to get away with killing me. I can understand their thinking, I am a very rich man, with little to no connections with the outside world. Nobody would ever miss me.

"Sir?" I shake myself out of my thoughts.

"George, please. Just leave me be for tonight. I'm not myself and I need some rest. I will see you and Miriam tomorrow morning. As always."

"Sir, I really think..."

I shake my fist and snarl my teeth behind the door but manage to force my voice to reply politely.

"Please, George, I'm exhausted. I just want to sleep." There is silence. Anger burns inside me. George somehow has me feeling like a prisoner in my own home. It began subtly, but he is trying to control my movements and behaviour. He has placed himself in the centre of my life, constantly tugging at my emotions and making me dependent on him.

No more.

"Okay, sir. Call if you need anything."

I will do no such thing. I will not rest either. They may think they have me trapped and vulnerable, but they could not be more wrong. I have something in this room that they know nothing about. Something that should make them think twice before turning on me. I reach far into the back of my wardrobe with trembling fingers and find the box. It was my father's and I usually avoid looking inside.

I close my eyes and blow the considerable layer of dust from the top of the box and wipe my finger across the carved wooden surface. I open it cautiously, breathing in the musky odour, and cast my eyes carefully over the contents. I may have trusted George completely, but life has taught me to always be prepared.

Chapter Forty

S taying awake is harder than I thought. Sometimes I think I hear feet in the corridor but it's probably my imagination. George seemed to be placated by my pleas for sleep and solitude, but I don't trust him. It infuriates me that I have no idea what is going on out there.

Perhaps they are planning, just as I am. I may never make it out of this room again. There are two of them and an ambush is a very real risk.

The hours pass painfully slowly. I change position regularly and avoid the bed. Sleep has been arriving unannounced recently and I can't have that tonight.

I have been so blind. I wanted to believe in George so badly that I ignored all of the warning signs. How could I have been so naive? With me out of the way, he can take all of my money and my beautiful home. I have no heir to my fortune. No partner or children. I only have George.

George might think he has an accomplice in Miriam, but she will turn on him, too. And he will deserve it.

Time jumps. It is morning suddenly. I don't remember falling asleep, but I clearly have. My eyes are crusted together, and my mouth is bone-dry, but my resolve is absolute.

I look at myself in the mirror. I take in the lines on my face and the white hairs that have started to appear around my temples. I will not let these people take what is mine. I have not fought this hard to have everything ripped away from me.

I will fight. To the death, if necessary.

I decide to catch them off-guard and head to my office early. I have my father's box with me. My concern is that George may recognise it, but that is a risk I am willing to take.

I am beyond enraged to find my office door locked. I want to put my fist through it. I did not lock it; I am certain of that. Who knows what they have done, what they have taken? My money may already be making its way into one of their bank accounts. I ball my fists tightly and feel the rage flowing through my veins. I will make them suffer.

I don't want to give them the upper hand, so I return to my room for ten minutes to wait. I sit on the bed and clench my fists again. Digging my fingernails into my palms. I squeeze so hard that I draw blood. I can hear my heart pounding in my ears. Soon this will all be over.

If I have to give my life, I will.

George is standing outside my open office door when I return. He gives me a warm smile.

"Good morning, sir. Beautiful morning, isn't it?" He motions to the window. There is not a cloud in the sky. I don't know this man anymore. He is nothing like the George I knew. Nothing like the George I loved. I'd love to wipe that stupid smile off his face.

I stand uncomfortably close to him, making sure my breath touches his face. I want him to feel all of the hate that lives inside of me. I know, George. I know everything.

"Good morning, George. Yes, it is a beautiful day. Perfect even."

He shrugs and pats me on the back.

He has changed his hair again, only slightly, but it looks ridiculous. Perhaps this is Miriam's doing. Maybe they are together now. Partners in every sense of the word.

"What's with the box?" he asks and points and furrows his brow. He may have fooled me before, but I can tell that question is genuine. My father must have kept it hidden from him.

"Why don't you come in and I can show you?"

Miriam is sitting at the desk. My desk. She is leaning over it, her hands clasped in front of her, and she has shifted her usual sitting position slightly. She looks powerful. In charge. Another wave of anger crashes through me.

"Good morning, Monty. Please sit down."

I answer her before my brain engages.

"I don't need an invitation to take a seat in my own office. If anything, you should be the one standing. Where are your fucking manners?" I stare at her, rage pounding within, and I stay standing. Defiant.

"Very well, Monty." She shuffles her papers and writes something down. I feel as if my head is going to explode. George closes the door as he steps inside the room.

I listen carefully to hear if he locks it. They may think that they have the upper hand. Two to one. But they are wrong.

He takes a seat close to me. A fake show of solidarity. I stay standing. My fists rest on the table in front of me. Miriam attempts to break the tension.

"How are you today, Monty? Did you sleep well?"

She is smiling at me. I cannot believe the nerve of this woman.

"I don't know what you think you are doing, Miriam. I am

not here to answer your questions. And why are you always so obsessed with my sleep? It's all you ever bloody say."

And then I wonder. Perhaps she is planning to drug me or kill me in my sleep. Perhaps they have already attempted to. My sleep has been more disturbed than usual and I've woken feeling confused and often later than normal. I seethe at the thought that she might have been in my room. I should never have trusted her. Ruthless bitch.

"You misunderstand me, Monty. Of course, you are not here to answer my questions. We are here to work together."

Not a hint of irony in what she says. The grandiosity is sickening.

My voice is loud but shaky. "No. No! We are not here to work together. You are here to do exactly as I say. You are here to follow orders."

I suspect I know why she is so comfortable and calm. She thinks my only source of strength is George. That without him, I am nothing and she has everything.

George interjects.

"Why don't we all calm down? Things seem a little more tense than usual this morning."

He is right. But I don't like him taking control of the situation, exerting power that isn't rightfully his.

He then looks at Miriam and raises his eyebrows before asking her, "Or we could postpone?"

I bang my fists on the table so hard that it sends painful shocks up both of my arms, and I bellow directly at George's face.

"Why are you asking her? She is nobody, she has no say here. I do. Me." I point at my chest. Poking hard at my breastbone. "Not her!" I throw my arm and point at her with all of the hatred and loathing that I feel inside.

I am delighted to see Miriam jump back. A flicker of anxiety in her eyes is quickly followed by a look of pure determination. I smirk and sit down slowly.

"Sorry if that made you jump, Miriam." I pull the box towards me. "I don't know what is going on with you two. What you are planning. But you will regret underestimating me."

Miriam answers coldly. "I don't underestimate you at all, Monty."

"Very well then. Have you done what I asked with regards to a replacement for Naomi?" I ask the question, knowing full well that the answer is no. She looks at George and back to me.

"Monty, I think we need to talk about that. You see–"

"No, we don't need to talk about that. I only let you live because of the agreement that we made. How do you not see that? It's been days, Miriam. Days! Do as I fucking say. Or..." I leave it there. Much better to show than to tell.

I open the box and let them see my father's gun. It is more beautiful than I remember. I run my fingers across it, caressing it. My actions get exactly the reaction I was hoping for. Stunned silence.

The flippant disrespect is gone. They are speechless.

We sit quietly for a while. The silence in the room is only broken by the sound of shallow, fearful breathing. They both stare at the box and the gun.

Eventually, Miriam speaks, her voice quieter and softer this time.

"Monty, why did you bring that in here?"

"Why do you think?"

She looks alarmed, but genuinely at a loss. "I don't know. Please tell me."

I turn to George. "And you? Uncle George. My flesh and

blood. You, who always professed to be there for me and give me everything I deserve in the world. What do you think?"

He answers quietly. He is looking at the gun, his forehead puckered and angling his body away. "I don't know."

"You don't know what?" I hiss.

"I don't know why you..."

Inside my head is a hideous screeching sound. Anger is swarming around my head and heating my blood.

"Sir! Address me properly. You don't know, *sir!* Your fucking manners are a disgrace."

George looks at his hands and says nothing. I point to George and then to Miriam. Drunk with rage. It feels good.

"You two have been working together. I can tell. Do you think I am stupid? Did you think you would get away with it?"

George doesn't look up, but Miriam answers immediately.

"No, of course, we don't think you are stupid. But the way you say it suggests that we are somehow working against you. Of course, that could never be true. We are here for you. I am sorry if you feel that way, but it's simply not true."

The gun has clearly spooked her. She is backtracking. I continue with my questions.

"Then what have you both been doing? Why have you not been following my orders?"

She speaks very calmly and carefully. "Monty, please just listen to me for a second. I want to show you something. I think it may change the way you feel about things. I think it could really help you."

George gets up and leaves the room without a word. I want to grab him and yank him back down onto the chair. If I was physically capable of overpowering George, then I would.

Intrigue has been my weakness before. I know I shouldn't allow this, but I want to see what she has to say for herself. I am not in any danger here. I am the one with the gun.

"You can have five minutes. Five minutes, not a second longer. Do you remember the last time I said that to you, Miriam? Well, please think of this in the same way."

I tap the box in front of me.

Then, I hear voices outside the door. They are muffled, but they are certainly the voices of a man and a woman. The man sounds a little like George, but I can't be sure.

Miriam holds her hand out to me as she speaks, pleading with me to wait and listen.

"Now, Monty, I want you to remain calm. Please stay seated and let's all just talk."

I jump to my feet immediately and feel the blood drain from my face.

"Who is that?" I demand.

"Monty, please. Don't upset yourself. It really won't help at all. Try to stay calm. Please, Monty, it is time."

Time for what? I wipe my palms on my trousers and force myself to sit still. The voices continue and, just before the door opens, I realise what they have done. They've done what George said he would never do.

They've called the police.

I sit back down in my chair, throw my head back and laugh heartily.

"The police? You are joking. Bring them in. I have got nothing to hide." I shout playfully at the door, "Come on in, officers."

I look at Miriam, shake my head, and whisper so only she can hear me.

"I am going to kill you, Miriam. Slowly." She flinches and shrinks back slowly into her chair. I repeat the word again. "Slowly."

Two people enter the room together. The man sits on one side of me, and the woman sits on the other.

I recognise her immediately, and my whole body goes numb. She is not a police officer. I look at her closely, unable to collect any thoughts that make sense.

There is no doubt about who I am looking at. But it's simply not possible. It cannot be true.

I look to Miriam. A tremor makes its way up my spine, and I feel bile rising in my throat. I can't hide my disbelief and I cannot stop myself from shaking. I expect Miriam to be revelling in my discomfort, but she isn't. I open my mouth, but nothing emerges. My heart begins to beat wildly, and I take a sharp, painful breath in. My brain tries to find reasons but there aren't any.

Miriam speaks.

"Monty, this is Bethany."

Chapter Forty-One

I stumble backwards away from the woman that Miriam called Bethany. My useless legs get caught in the metal legs of the chair. I fall onto the floor, struggling and fighting with the chair as it topples. My heart hammering at the back of my throat.

The woman sits calmly and watches me with confusion. George, who I now realise entered the room with her, tries to come to my aid. He grabs my arm and places his other hand on my back, lifting me to my feet. I let him. I don't know what else to do. I look at George, pleading with him silently to help me understand. He rights the upturned chair and offers me the seat. I stay standing and back towards the door until I am leaning against it. Miriam stands.

"Monty, I know this must be very difficult for you, but please sit down and we will explain everything."

How could they have done this? My head swims with pieces of thoughts that make no sense at all. There must be some mistake. They couldn't. But they must have. I look at her again, checking to see if I have been mistaken. My heart seizes and dread fills every inch of me. There is no escaping what is in front of me. The room begins to distort. Everything is tilting at a nauseating angle. George puts his hand on my shoulder, and it's only then that I realise I am swaying. His face looks distorted, too. His voice is slow and unrecognisable as I grab the door handle behind me and stumble out of the room.

The corridor is too bright. I try to run, but my legs are bloodless. I am slow and unsteady, wading through quicksand. My room seems to be getting further and further away as I run towards it. George helps me to my bedroom. It may be a foolish mistake, but I let him. I need to get away from that room. From her.

I collapse on the floor as I enter the room, crawling on my hands and knees towards my bed. I use every ounce of strength to climb up and under the covers. I close my eyes tightly and beg my mind to make sense of it all.

Nothing comes.

I lie there, a tangled mass of fear.

Terrified, just as though I had quite literally seen a ghost.

Chapter Forty-Two

I lie motionless on my bed. My mind racing with possibilities that make no sense at all.

There are too many voices in the corridor. These people are not welcome in my home, whoever they are. I don't want to hear Miriam's explanation. I never thought they'd stoop so low as to mess with my mind like this. Making me question my own perceptions and judgements. Trying to make me think I have lost my grip on reality. Manipulation at its finest.

My certainty at what I saw begins to fall away. I didn't look at her for more than five seconds.

"But you didn't need to. You know it was her."

I ignore the voice in my head. It was not her. It could not have been. She is dead. I killed her myself.

I will regain control of my house and I will rid them from my life. But first, I need to get out of here. I need to get to safety.

I look inside my bedside table drawer, but my phone is not there. I creep out from under the covers and look around the room. It's not anywhere. My spirits sink as I realise that I have made another huge mistake. In my haste to leave my office, I left my father's gun on the table. That is a mistake that may cost me.

I should have grabbed it right away. In fact, I should have shot her.

They will have taken the gun, I am sure. I stand with my ear to the door, my nerves on fire, waiting for it to go quiet. They won't be expecting me to run.

Eventually, there is silence. I wait longer than I want to. Unease unfurling inside me. I want to go now but being reckless will not get me out of this.

I take nothing with me. Anything of use is in my office and I can't risk it. Everything else here is disposable. I sneak out of my room and tiptoe down the corridor towards the back stairs, anxiety weighing me down. The stairs lead directly to one of the kitchen doors.

I enter the kitchen quietly, grateful that the door opens silently. My stomach flips as I peer into the room but thankfully, the kitchen is empty. I consider grabbing a knife, but I'm worried I will make a noise. I take a coat I don't recognise from the back of one of the chairs. It's a horribly scratchy material and far too big. But it's waterproof, and my only available option of any kind of disguise. I fasten the zip up to my chin and pull the hood down over my head. There's something wrong with this room. Something I can't quite place. Everything looks as though it has been wiped down, and a dizzying smell of bleach and chemicals hangs in the air. I don't have time for any distractions now. I banish all thoughts to the back of my mind. Getting out of here is all that matters at this moment.

The next part won't be quiet, and I know they will come running as soon as they hear the glass break. I lift one of the stools from the breakfast bar and smash the legs against the window. The glass shatters on my first effort, leaving a hole large enough for me to climb out of the window without struggling or hurting myself.

My own window.

I am breaking out of my own home.

I have to move quickly now. Out in the open, I am vulnerable. I have no weapons and no means of transportation. The car is not an option and, even if it was, I don't have the keys. If I exit down the drive, they will see me.

I stay close to the house until I am out of view of the windows and then I make a run for the hedge at the side of the house. I am fuelled by adrenaline, and I am as sure as I can be that they haven't seen me. I don't know the garden well, I never come out here. The hedges are thick and well looked after. I find a weak spot and I push through it into the woods. It is cold and wet, and I am grateful for the large water-resistant coat.

I look back at the building before I disappear into the woods. Rain splatters my face and drips into my mouth. A lump forms in my throat. I never look at my home properly from the outside and I am amazed at how vast and grand it looks. It doesn't feel like my home. But it is, and I will be back for everything that is mine, and this time I will take no prisoners.

I will be back when they least expect it. They won't see me coming.

I run through the woods. The ground is slippery and uneven and I misstep and roll my ankle more than once. I am not used to running and my chest aches after only a few minutes. I am panting heavily and sweat begins to break out everywhere. My mind is racing with possibilities. So much has happened and I can't piece it all together. I need to stop thinking. There will be plenty of time for thinking. I need to act.

I exit the woods after running for less than ten minutes and I am grateful to find I am exactly where I hoped I would be. I tuck in behind a tree and suck in some much-needed oxygen. My lungs are burning. I watch the road. The traffic is light, and the rain is heavier here without the protection of the tree canopy. This is a road I know well. If I keep a good pace, in less than fifteen minutes, I will be at Miles and Susannah's house.

I don't know where else to go. I'm hoping that, despite my selfish behaviour, she will still help me. Susannah is the closest thing I have to family now. If she won't help me, at the very least, I can get a car or money.

I walk facing traffic, with the hood pulled low over my head. If I run dressed like this, I will draw attention to myself. My shoes have puddles in them, and I can feel blisters developing. I will be off this main road soon, but I don't want to be caught off-guard. The rain becomes heavier, bouncing off the ground and distorting the headlights of the cars coming towards me. I need to keep going. One foot in front of the other.

I am soaked to the skin by the time I arrive at Miles and Susannah's house. Despite the time of day, the rain and heavy cloud mean that there are lights on inside. Someone is home.

I consider walking in. After all, I am family. Isn't that what families do? Instead, I check over my shoulder and knock. I hear footsteps inside, and I take down my hood, letting the rain soak my hair and drip down my face. It mingles with the sweat and cools me down. I lick my salty lips and pray Susannah doesn't turn me away.

She opens the door. An inviting cooking smell flows out of the house and I can hear the hubbub of family life indoors. As I look over her shoulder into the warmth, she crosses her arms and blocks the door with her body.

"Monty. I wasn't expecting you here. I thought you didn't want anything to do with us anymore. I thought we weren't worth your time, weren't good enough." She is being flippant and sarcastic. She may be irritating, but I know she is a good person inside. She won't leave me here on the doorstep.

"Susannah, I am so sorry. Can you please let me in? There's been a bit of trouble at the office, and I need to sort a few things out. Can I come in, please?" I am pleading uncharacteristically, and she seems to be warming to me, but not enough to stand aside quite yet. I continue, appealing to her good nature. "I know I was selfish and rude, and I am so very sorry. It's just been a very difficult time."

She still doesn't move. One last chance and I'll have no choice but to take the decision out of her hands. I don't have any other options. Before I can try to persuade her further, she pulls me roughly inside the house and closes the door.

"You are wet through. Give me that coat and I'll get you a towel."

She looks at the coat and stifles a laugh. It's quite clearly not mine and I can imagine how ridiculous I look.

"I grabbed the wrong coat on the way out. I wasn't thinking."

She's not convinced but lets it go. I stand, drops of rain continuing to fall from the coat and onto the monochrome tiled floor.

"Go through to the kitchen, Monty, and I'll get you some tea."

The doorway is crammed with discarded shoes, boots, bicycle helmets and other miscellaneous items. Quite frankly, it's a mess. I manoeuvre my way through the various obstacles towards the kitchen. Susannah comes back with a fluffy, pale pink towel and closes the door to the noisy front room.

"So we can talk in private," she explains.

I sit at the solid wooden table. It is covered in circular water stains and pen marks. It looks well loved. As I rub my hair dry, I notice some scratches on my arms. They aren't deep and only sting a little, but they leave a few telltale red streaks on the towel, and I hide it under the table.

"So, what's going on, Monty? It must be bad if you decided to grace us with your presence."

She's not going to let this go quickly.

"Oh, come on, Susannah, I'm sure you haven't missed me in the slightest. You've got your family here."

Her eyes fill up. "But I don't have Miles, do I? You were the only person who knew him as I did. Who cared about him as I did."

Her lower lip quivers. I didn't mean to upset her.

"The kids miss him terribly, but I can't talk to them. I'm their mother, I have to be strong for them. It's exhausting, Monty, I needed you."

Tears continue to threaten, but she sniffs loudly and holds them back. I can imagine she's become very good at that lately.

"I'm sorry, Susannah. But I'm here now. I hope it's not too late?"

My words sound feeble, but I can see that she doesn't have it in her to stay mad at me for long.

"No, of course not. You are family and you always will be. Nobody behaves well after something like that. We all struggle, and we all cope in different ways. Who am I to tell you how to grieve?"

I am amazed at her level of forgiveness. If it were the other way around, I wouldn't have let her in the house.

A mobile phone rings. Susannah wipes her eyes. "Sorry, I need to take this. I think it's the hospital about my mother. She's had surgery today. That's why everyone is here, waiting to hear how she is."

She turns away and takes the call and I take the time to think. I know I am safe here. Susannah knows nothing and, as far as I know, George doesn't know where she lives, even if he did suspect I would be here. I can take stock for a few days and plan my next move.

I'm surprised to find that I enjoy speaking with Susannah. There's something about her that makes you feel cared for. There's no hidden agenda, no holding back or protecting herself. She is genuine. I know there must be a lot of people out there like this. Most people are not damaged and broken.

Miles dying is the worst thing that has ever happened to her and there is a part of me that hates her for living such a charmed and ordinary life. It's so easy for her to be good. All the good parts of me have been broken or switched off.

"I'm more than happy for you to stay here, Monty, but will you tell me what's happened? I don't need detail. But my family is here. I don't want any trouble or anything."

She loves her family; I can see it with such certainty in her eyes.

"Thank you, Susannah. It means a lot after I was so terrible to you. I promise you I haven't done anything wrong. I have a problem with an employee. I will have it sorted sharpish. You have my word."

She smiles at me and places her soft hands over mine. I am still holding my cup of tea which is going cold.

"Why don't you go upstairs and have a shower? Your hands are freezing. I'll get you some fresh clothes if you don't mind some of Miles's and then you can come and meet everyone."

Her eyes glisten and I can see that she is pleased I am here.

"I know life hasn't been easy for you, Monty." I offer a weak smile but say nothing, I don't know how much she knows. "I hope you know that Miles always thought of you as his brother, that he couldn't have loved you more if you were his flesh and blood. You do know that, don't you?"

I don't know what to say. I didn't expect her words to hit me so deeply, but they do.

"I'm not sure. I guess we never really talked like that. Not as adults anyway."

"He loved you so much, Monty. He would always talk about how brave you were and how clever you were."

"Did he? He never said." I'm both surprised and pleased by her words.

"That just wasn't his way, Monty. He kept his feelings to himself. But he always opened up with me."

I see her face crumple at that last sentence. The loss for her is enormous, much bigger than I had anticipated, and likely bigger than I can appreciate at all. I want to say something back, something fitting. I want to be able to tell her that I admired him, too, that he was the most wonderful brother anyone could ever wish for, and that I am as devastated as she is that he is gone. But I find I can't say the words out loud.

Perhaps if Miles were still here now, we could work on a better relationship. I wish that I had made the effort to continue the special relationship we had as children. But it was easier for me to distance myself. As an adult, he was only on my periphery. A secondary character. I didn't see him for who he was, and I am beginning to wish that I had. I thought we had all the time in the world.

Susannah startles as my seat scrapes across the floor. I walk and stand behind her chair, placing my hand on her shoulder, and comforting her the best I can.

"Thank you for saying those things, Susannah, and thank you for letting me be here." I tell her something I know to be true. "Miles loved you very much and he was lucky to have you."

Both Miles and Susannah have shown me a level of respect and care that I have not earned. I can only imagine how they felt about each other. I let her cry it out and I stand with my hand on her shoulder. I feel awkward and uncomfortable with the intimacy. But I stay standing exactly where I am. Susannah wipes her eyes and turns to look up at me, her face etched with sadness, and I realise I am crying, too.

Chapter Forty-Three

Susannah eventually stands and throws her arms around me.

"Oh, Monty. I am so glad you are here."

I stroke her hair and hug her earnestly. Allowing myself to be in the moment.

"I am glad I am here, too." I know that a big part of me means it. I ignore the rest of the parts that are shouting in my ears.

Susannah shows me to the bathroom and leaves to be with her family. The bathroom is tiny and musty. I can't imagine how so many people manage to share this room. I stand in the shower and let the scalding water bounce off my back. It feels amazing, like millions of needles waking me up. I feel warm to the core and a little light-headed. The bathroom is as chaotic as the rest of the house. Bottles of various shapes and sizes and discarded toys everywhere.

I wonder how the rest of the family will react to me being here. If Susannah has told them how I behaved towards her, I can't blame them if they don't want me here. The whole family is gathering to support each other, waiting on the results of a loved one's surgery.

The water is starting to drop in temperature. Telling me I've outstayed my welcome. I dry myself with the gigantic towel given to me by Susannah. A sudden knock on the door startles me.

"There's clothes outside the door when you're done, Monty," Susannah shouts through the door.

"Okay, thank you. I'll be down shortly."

"No rush. I'll be in the kitchen when you're ready, or you can take a nap up here if you prefer?"

A nap sounds tempting, but it will have to wait.

"No, I'll come down when I'm dressed. Thanks again."

I wipe the condensation from the bathroom mirror and catch a glimpse of my exhausted face before it disappears again. I open the door just enough to get my arm through and drag the clothes into the bathroom. I push the clothes to my face and inhale deeply. They smell too clean. Overuse of floral washing powder.

Surprisingly, they fit rather well and are unlike anything I'd ever normally wear. I towel-dry my hair and make my way downstairs.

Susannah chuckles to herself as I enter the kitchen.

"I have never seen you in jeans, Monty."

"To my recollection, I have never worn jeans. Maybe I should start."

We both laugh.

"Would you like to come and see everyone?" she asks, taking my arm gently.

"Uh, yes. I mean if you think that would be okay with everyone?"

She answers without hesitation. "Yes, of course! Everyone will be delighted to see you. It's only my dad, my sister, and the boys. There's nothing to worry about. Plus, Mum is out of surgery and doing well by all accounts, so the atmosphere is much improved from when you arrived."

I consider asking what surgery, but I'm not sure it would be appropriate, so I simply offer up, "That's great news. You must all be so relieved."

"Yes." She beams. "Dad especially. She's not out of the woods yet, but it certainly looks promising."

I'm still apprehensive about meeting them.

"Did you tell them that..."

"That when my husband died you decided to ignore me?" I scrunch up my face. I'm shocked at how upfront she is. "I'm kidding!" Her whole face lights up and she whacks me on the back playfully. "No, of course, I didn't. You must stop worrying about that, you know. I don't know why you are giving yourself such a hard time. I've been through days where I hate everyone, including Miles. There's no right way to feel, you know. At least that's what my counsellor says."

"Counsellor?"

"Yes, absolutely. You should think about seeing one." Clearly, from the innocence of that remark, she doesn't know too much about me or my past. "She told me that there is no right or wrong way to experience grief, that anyone who tries to keep me to some kind of timetable is wrong, and that I will go through it in my own time."

I nod in agreement. "That sounds sensible."

"Doesn't it! And did you notice I said, 'go through it' and not 'get over it'?" She mimes quotation marks as she speaks. I hadn't noticed, but she continues before I answer. "It's because you don't get over it. And if you try to go back to how things were, you'll just fail. You have to learn how to live with how things are now and not waste your efforts trying to get back to where things were. This is what I am trying to tell the boys. It's early days, but we are getting there."

I don't know what to say. She's evidently put so much time and effort into recovering from what has happened. I can't help but be impressed by her strength.

She opens the door to the front room; everyone is silent and staring at the TV. There is a log burner roaring away in the corner, and there is barely an inch of the wall that isn't covered by a framed photograph or print. The boys are a tangle of arms and legs on one extra-large sofa and the adults are sitting together on the other. There is an air of ease and comfort in the room. It looks lived-in.

"Harry, Joseph, Uncle Monty has come to visit, isn't that lovely?"

The bigger one gives me a nod and his younger brother manages a "Hi" before they both turn back to the television. Thankfully, Susannah used their names, but I have no idea which one is which.

Susannah's father stands and holds out his hand. I know I have met him before. He looks much older and thinner today and I can see from the bags under his eyes that he hasn't slept well, the concern for his wife imprinted on his face.

"You remember my dad, Steven?"

"Yes, of course. It's good to see you again, Steven."

"And you, Monty. How have you been?" He looks sympathetic and I know he's offering condolences without being obvious about it.

"Okay, I mean, it's been hard obviously. But I'm doing okay. Thanks for asking. And how are you? I'm pleased to hear that Jean is out of surgery. You must be so relieved." I'm rambling and not giving him time to answer my questions.

"I am, Monty, she's my absolute world, you know. I don't know what I'd do without her."

I watch the moment unfurl before me with curiosity. I see Steven's face fall with the guilt of what he's just said. Assuming that his care for his wife is somehow insensitive towards his daughter and her recent loss. He pulls Susannah towards him fiercely.

"I'm so sorry, my love, that was a stupid thing to say."

Susannah is tearing up now, too. Squeezing her father back just as tightly.

"Don't be silly, Dad, of course, it's not. None of us would know what to do without Mum."

They hug and they cry. Steven gently strokes Susannah's face and I watch them with amazement and awe. Everything is raw and untouched but has a level of sensitivity about it that I am not used to. I wish I had spent more time watching and understanding people.

The kids haven't turned their heads. Susannah's sister, who I don't remember being introduced to, comes and joins in the family hug. I feel out of place. A weird, emotionless observer. They don't seem to care that I'm witnessing it all. They are at ease with the world, at ease with themselves. I can tell that they don't think about every action before they do it, weighing up the options and wondering which would provide the best outcome. They just do what they feel in the moment. It seems so natural, but the thought terrifies me.

Susannah shakes herself out of their intimate family moment and wipes her eyes on the sleeve of her cardigan.

"Sorry about that, Monty, it's been an emotional few days for us."

"Don't apologise, there's no need."

She squeezes my arm warmly and turns to her sister. You can see that they are related yet they look different in almost every way. I think the family resemblance comes from the way they carry themselves and the kindness in their eyes.

"Do you remember Fran?"

Fran flashes me a beaming smile that reaches all the way to her large, brown eyes. I have seen her before. I remember her as the shorter, darker-haired bridesmaid that looked out of place against the willowy bride and her fellow bridesmaids.

She puts her warm palms against my cheeks. "It's lovely to see you again, Monty." And then she wraps her arms around my shoulders and presses her body against me. Hugging me like I'm the most important person in the world to her. She is on her tiptoes and her eyes are wetting my chest. I hug her back and wait for her to step back. It feels far too long.

The four of us stop and look at each other for a moment. I am the only one who isn't crying. I think that's okay. I think it would be weird if I were crying. I don't really know Jean.

It surprises me to say it, but we have the most wonderful afternoon. We drag the boys away from the TV for a few hours and play games at the table. We play cards and there is light-hearted competition, cheering, and jeering. We drink tea and eat cake. Everyone moves freely and easily, it's almost as though they are a single animal. I wonder if this is what a family really is.

I say very little, but I laugh and smile a lot. I have to force it at first, but soon it comes naturally, and I find myself blending into the room, doing without thinking, and genuinely enjoying myself.

We play another game where one person draws, and the other person has to guess what they have drawn. We are in teams, and I am partnered with Fran. She is a terrible drawer, and I am an equally terrible guesser. I am horribly embarrassed at first, but it's so obvious that there is no need. This is a room where positivity thrives. This is a room where nobody is out to get you, hurt you, or make a fool of you. This is a place of love and compassion. These people are living. Really living. By this standard, I haven't lived a single day in my adult life.

We roar with laughter until our eyes stream and our sides ache. Susannah and the younger boy, who I now know to be Joseph, win and they are warmly congratulated by everyone. It's obvious they cheated, but nobody feels the need to point it out.

Susannah stands and addresses her boys.

"Right, you two, out from under our feet for a couple of hours. The grown-ups need to get started on dinner."

The boys slope off gratefully. More than happy to spend a couple of hours in the digital world. We clear the table.

"What can I do to help?" I ask.

Susannah embraces me warmly and bundles me towards the door.

"I won't hear of it, Monty. Come and I'll show you to the spare bedroom and you can take a nap. I'll call you in plenty of time for dinner. I'm going to make a shepherd's pie; I hope that's okay?"

It's more than okay. "Yes, that sounds wonderful. But I feel awful. Surely, I can help somehow? You've all had such a difficult time. Shouldn't you be the ones taking some rest?"

She dismisses my suggestion with a wave of her hand and a smile.

"Not at all. You are our guest. Please, let us look after you."

I relent and Susannah shows me to the spare room. It's small with chunky wooden furniture and at least a dozen pillows on the bed. It has an intimate and cosy atmosphere. I close the curtains and lie on the bed.

The room is dull, but not dark, and tiredness washes over me. I feel like I am living a double life. What happened only hours ago doesn't seem possible and I'm afraid of letting any of that horrible reality back in.

I want to stay here. I want to learn how to do this. I want to be a part of a proper family again. Be around people who think of the needs of others, and not just in relation to their own. I don't need the big house or the money. I don't need to hurt people.

What I need is simple. But as I lie alone, listening to the friendly chatter and family noises coming from downstairs, I realise it isn't possible. I have come too far. I have been a monster and monsters have to pay. I don't get to have the simple beauty of a normal existence.

But I can enjoy it for tonight.

Chapter Forty-Four

Before

"Well done, son, you're really getting the hang of this now." He seems proud of me. I hate it, but I know it's the only way to stay alive.

I squeeze my eyes together so tightly it hurts. He will be mad if I cry. I feel the tears pulsating behind my eyes and I can't stop them from falling onto my cheeks. I turn my head and hide my face. I can't remember when I realised my family life wasn't normal, but I know it now.

It is a horrible thing. You are supposed to love your dad, but I wish mine was dead. I'm not just saying that. I don't mean it in the pretend way that you might shout downstairs at your parents when you don't get what you want. I mean it in the way where he wouldn't be living anymore. It makes me feel all twisted up inside, but I think if he was dead it would fix everything. I could be normal again. I'd like that.

I've often wondered if I'd be able to kill him myself. I know that makes me a monster too. I'd be no better than him. I've decided that if I could be sure it would work, then I would probably do it. But I think I'd be the one who would end up dead. Or worse.

"Chin up, son."

He is in a good mood. I don't know how that is possible, but he radiates happiness. I think this one went well. It's always better for me when it goes well. I push down the nausea that rises at this thought. I despise feeling this way. I don't turn round, and I wipe my tears away. My hand is clammy and shaking uncontrollably. I try to block out his bright tone and hideous words.

"They deserve it."

I'm not sure if he's still talking to me or just speaking out loud. I always get it wrong. My heart starts to race. If I speak when he's not expecting an answer, he'll punish me. The punishments are always worse when he is in a happy mood. All the moisture has disappeared from my mouth. I don't think I could speak if I wanted to. I nod, hedging my bets. I am wrong and he slaps me. My head whips to the side violently but I stay standing. My face prickles with heat, but I've had worse. Much worse.

"Manners, boy! Respect. Have I taught you nothing?"

You've taught me plenty, I think. But if I say it he'll do that choking thing again and my throat only just feels normal again after the last time. I imagine that's how I'll probably die. He simply won't let go one day, and then I'll be buried with the others. Perhaps that is what I deserve. I try not to think. If I think, I end up feeling things and then my brain starts crumbling.

"Sorry, Father." I force my words into the respectful tone he likes. There's moisture in my mouth again, but I think it is blood. I must have bitten my tongue. He smiles and ruffles my hair. I try not to look horrified. I'm worried there might be some of her blood in my hair, but I can't check.

"Now go and clean up like a good boy. I need to get to work."

He laughs and I feel physically sick. I think I might actually be sick. If I am, I'll have to swallow it. I've done that before. It's much better than the alternative.

I watch him getting ready and I stand still. Taking it all in. He is so normal. There is nothing in his behaviour that reflects what has just happened here. That's what scares me the most. I've tried to stop it over the years, but my brain continually tries to piece everything together. I can never manage it. The pieces don't fit together.

"Yes, sir." My voice sounds far away. I am on autopilot. I'm going to need it for the next few hours. It's become my best friend in moments like this.

"That's better, boy." I watch his mouth form the words. It's a normal mouth, just like mine. He laughs again. "It's rather a mess. This one misbehaved somewhat." He chuckles and an icy chill runs down my back. My whole life feels like one long nightmare. I'm not asleep though. I was sure I must be the first time it happened. But I am not, this is real.

I'm terrified of what awaits me in the room. I used to wait and psych myself up before going in. I don't have to do that anymore. I try not to think about what that says about me.

I am relieved to find mostly smashed glass and little blood. Father pokes his head into the room.

"Not too much for you to do in here, but don't go in the bathroom until I get back." He puffs out his cheeks and then exhales and shakes his head, as though replaying a fond memory, before laughing for the third time. It's like screaming to me. I force the sounds out of the way and into a different part of my brain. I have to do as he says. I've learned that the best way is to just do it, but not live it. That sounds impossible but it's not.

I start to pick up the glass with trembling fingers and terrifying images of what must have happened begin to flood my ten-year-old brain. I push away my thoughts, but they come anyway. I want them to leave me alone to do my job, but they keep coming. Panic is rising within me and when I look down, I can see my heart hammering in my chest. I need him to leave before he sees it.

Something is happening. Something new. Whatever it is, I'm not doing it. My body isn't listening anymore. My self-control is failing, I am trying to step away from the fear, but it is taking over me. My autopilot isn't working, and everything has rushed forward. I can hear a hideous, high-pitched noise. It hurts my brain, but I think that's where the noise is coming from. I am crashing, I am going to break. This is it.

I take a large, knife-shaped piece of the glass and turn to face Father. The glass has some blood on it already, but I don't care anymore. I close my hand around the glass, and it cuts through the skin of my palm with ease. I don't feel the pain, and the tremor in my hands stops suddenly. I poke the sharpest part of the glass into my neck and a small trickle of blood appears. I watch his evil eyes widen with fear. He is not laughing now. I don't hide my smile and I let the happy tears fall freely onto my cheeks. This feels good. He is afraid and I am happy.

"Son. What...? Don't even..." I watch him and I continue to smile. There are butterflies in my tummy, but I am not afraid. I am excited. Even at ten years old, I can see that there is no way out of this for me. There will be no happy life one way or another. Fighting it is pointless. At least this way I have some control. All of this will go away. It's a wonderful feeling. Perhaps this is the perfect end.

His lips curl and the devil returns to his eyes. There is no way he is going to let me have this moment. He lunges suddenly and I fall backwards. I hit the ground hard and feel my head bounce off the floor. Stars explode in my eyes and shards of glass scatter beneath me. He is on top of me in an instant. His hot, sour breath on my face. He spits and snarls as he speaks.

"You useless, worthless excuse of..."

I can imagine the rest, but I never get to hear it. He can't finish the sentence with glass sticking out of his neck. The blood spurts out. It gushes onto me, soaking my clothes. I focus on his eyes. The anger has disappeared, now there is only fear. Just before the light is distinguished from his eyes, I think I see something else. It's not a look I have ever seen in my father's eyes. I think it is regret.

He bleeds and I lie underneath. He doesn't struggle and neither do I. The warm, thick blood pools around us. I close my eyes and breathe in the familiar metallic tang. I could probably push him off, but I don't. I lie still. I feel calm and a smile appears on my face again.

I was wrong. This is the perfect end.

Chapter Forty-Five

I sleep and the nightmares don't come. There is nothing in these walls. It is calm and quiet. None of that can reach me here. I am safe and I am happy.

I hear a gentle knocking on the door.

"Monty, it's Susannah."

I sit up, clear my throat, and answer her. "Hi, Susannah."

"Dinner will be twenty minutes. Take your time."

She leaves before I can answer. There is little for me to do. I slept in my clothes, and I know there will be no ceremony surrounding dinner. I am fine just as I am. I splash my face in the bathroom, I have a hint of stubble growing and it makes me smile. I look nothing like myself. It feels fantastic.

The dinner table looks like something out of a Christmas movie. There are steaming, bowls of food placed in no particular order all down the table. All different colours and sizes. Lots of different vegetables and a huge shepherd's pie in the centre. They have gone to a lot of effort. I know it's not specifically for me, but I can't help feeling humbled anyway. It makes me realise that I don't eat enough and certainly not properly. I eat purely for function and sustenance. This food has been made for enjoyment, to be shared.

Steve pulls out a chair and gestures for me to sit. The three adults are a little glassy-eyed. There is an open bottle of red wine on the table, but I suspect there is at least one empty bottle somewhere else. Fran pours generous glasses of wine for us all without asking and we sit down for dinner.

"Can I have one?" asks Harry cheekily.

"Of course you can," answers Steve, and Harry's eyes shine brightly.

"Amazing, Grandad!" And he holds out his glass. "No problem, son, as soon as you're eighteen." Everyone roars with laughter, except Harry who rolls his eyes.

"Very funny, Grandad."

Steve pats him on the back and ruffles his hair playfully. "I'm only messing with you. Tell you what, later I'll let you beat me on that fighting game you're always on to make up for it. Deal?"

Harry smiles at his grandfather with such love. "Sure, Grandad. You know I'd beat you anyway, right?"

"We'll see about that."

Everyone laughs again. The food is seamlessly passed and dished out around the table. No rules, no stress, and no complaints. Completely harmonious. The meal is hearty and tasty, the kind of food that sticks to your insides. It warms me like a giant hug.

"This is fantastic, Susannah, thank you so much," I say.

She waves away my compliment.

"It's nothing special, Monty. We are all glad you are here."

Everyone smiles at me, and I know they are telling the truth.

"Well, thank you, anyway. It means a lot."

Steve takes the opportunity to stand and raise his glass.

"I hope you will all indulge me for a moment."

There is a friendly groan from around the table.

"Keep it short this time, Grandad," says Joseph. "The food went cold after your last speech."

Steve taps him lightly on the back of the head.

"Oi, mind your manners, kid." And they both laugh.

My face feels cold as I am reminded of how different words can sound.

"Mind your manners, son."

I force the memory away and focus on Steve as he addresses his family.

"I just wanted to say how grateful I am for my two beautiful daughters and my wonderful grandchildren. I wish Jean could be here with us, and I know with all my heart that she will be home and bossing me around again before we know it."

A low-level chuckle reverberates around the table. I feel again like I've stepped into a private moment. I don't know if Steve notices, but he turns to me.

"I'd like to raise a toast to Jean, but also to Monty. I hope you know you are welcome anytime. You are our family, and we are here for you."

I am touched. His wife is in hospital, and he is still able to find space in his heart for someone he barely knows.

"So, if everyone could be upstanding and raise your glasses." Everyone stands clumsily, bumping chair legs and knocking elbows as they find a space to stand and raise their glass. "To family. Life's greatest blessing."

In unison, everybody shouts, "To family."

I don't find the words in time, but nobody notices. Everyone settles back down and continues with their meal, chatting easily. I watch everyone carefully. Trying not to appear odd but taking in every inch of them as they speak.

I am mesmerised by the ordinariness of it all, by the people. I don't feel real in comparison. I'm just a collection of bits and pieces that functions like one of these people. I have shielded my broken self away from any semblance of real life. My body may have survived my horrible childhood years, but my inner self, my soul, and anything that truly mattered was blown to pieces.

Today has given me a small hope that these pieces are still there and, if circumstances were different, I could be one of them. But outside of this front door, my world is different. Evil still lurks and deeds have been done. I cannot invite that evil into this house. These people have suffered tragedy and turned it into love. I have turned tragedy into a bitter, self-serving sense of survival.

Susannah spots me across the table and mouths, "Are you okay?" She does it kindly and carefully, not alerting others.

I flash her a smile and a look that says, "Sorry, I was miles away."

She smiles back and mouths, "Good."

"I think someone's at the door," interjects Steve.

I hadn't heard the knocking. We've been laughing and chatting so loudly.

Fran stands. "It's Wes. I told him to come straight here after work. I didn't know what time he'd be back. He's having a rotten time of it at the moment. So bloody busy."

With absolutely no hint of annoyance at a late arrival, Susannah stands and grabs a plate from the cupboard.

"Oh, brilliant. I'll make him a plate. Dad, can you clear all the junk off that chair at the end? Uncle Wes is here, boys. You can ask him about that thing with your computer."

Susannah turns to me. "I don't know anything about computers, and I have no desire to learn. It's funny, there are so many things I didn't even notice that Miles did." She looks pensive but carries on dishing out the food. "I guess it's true what they say, you don't know what you've got until it's gone."

Fran re-enters the room quietly and her face is ashen. She looks nervous and her voice is barely audible.

"Susannah?"

Susannah doesn't look up; she's putting the finishing touches on Wes's dinner. Fran raises her voice as she repeats herself, high-pitched and urgent.

"Susannah!"

Susannah looks up and rushes to her sister as soon as she sees her grave expression.

"Fran, what's wrong? Where's Wes? He's... He's not..."

Fran turns and walks towards the hallway, beckoning Susannah to follow her. Susannah is with her in an instant, her arm around her shoulder, closing the kitchen door behind her. Steve looks terrified. I can see him praying that his daughters are going to be okay.

We wait for what can only be minutes. The silence is tense and broken only briefly by Steve telling the boys to head upstairs and play. I can see they are worried, but they disappear off together without argument.

The kitchen door opens slowly, and Susannah stands there alone. She looks traumatised; it's obvious something terrible and unexpected has happened. I don't know where to put myself and I somehow feel guilty, even though I haven't done anything.

Steve gets up, but Susannah quickly turns her head.

"It's okay, Dad, just sit down. Please." She gives him a serious look and he follows her instructions.

She's looking at me with an expression I have never seen before. I can see fear, confusion, and pity all at once. Her voice cracks as she speaks.

"Monty, there's a doctor here to see you."

"A doctor?" I answer instantly. That was not what I was expecting to hear.

"Yes, she's waiting in the hallway." She looks over her shoulder.

I can't see anything from where I am sitting. I don't understand. I don't say this out loud. Dr Pathirana doesn't know where Miles and Susannah live, and even if she did, why would she be here? I stand and position myself so I can see the doorway and beyond it into the hallway. Fran is nowhere to be seen.

Susannah steps to the side and Miriam steps forward. A bolt of shock hits me and I feel a sudden surge of energy. The most powerful and instinctive fight-or-flight feelings flood my brain. There is too much to say and nowhere near enough time to say it.

Susannah is standing far too close to Miriam, and I know that heartless bitch would have no hesitation in hurting her. My heart clenches with pure dread. I need to make Susannah safe.

"Susannah, move away from her. Come here. Come and stand next to me. Now. Do it now. Do not trust her. She is not who she says she is." My chest constricts and I swallow hard. I point at Miriam and curl my lips back, snarling. "She is dangerous."

Steve is watching helplessly. His eyes darken with concern. He doesn't move but watches Susannah's every movement. Susannah looks at Miriam and back to me. She doesn't know what to do. I try again, pleading with Susannah to move away.

"Susannah, get over here. Trust me, please. You know me, you don't know her. She'll hurt you, or worse. I am so sorry, and I don't know how she has managed to find us, but I can tell you with absolute certainty that she is lying to you." Panic crawls over my body and the words keep tumbling out. "I can't begin to explain any of it to you now. She has been conspiring against me and you need to get away from her. Now!"

I shout the last word and it makes Susannah physically

jump. Steve stands instantly and beckons his daughter towards him. She goes into her father's arms willingly and this allows me to see into the hallway.

There are two male police officers, here to arrest me, no doubt. I knew they would betray me. I don't care that they called the police. What bothers me is that she called them here, to this house.

"You called the police. You bitch. You deceitful, horrible bitch."

I look at Susannah with pleading eyes. She is horrified by the way I am speaking to Miriam. "She is lying to you, Susannah, you have to believe me."

Miriam finally speaks. She fixes me with an icy stare. Her tone is emotionless and calm, with no hint of guilt at her betrayal.

"Monty, I'm sorry."

I hadn't counted on how ruthless she could be.

"I've spoken to your sister and told her that you're going to be coming back to Park Hall with us."

Susannah is nodding gently, indicating that what Miriam says is the truth.

"She isn't my sister, she's my dead brother's wife." I spit the words out with venom, and I regret it as soon as I see the words wound Susannah. "I don't know what lies you've told her, Miriam, but I am not going anywhere with you."

I look over her shoulder and address the two statue-like officers standing behind her. "I don't know what she's told you, but you'll have to arrest me if you want me to leave here." I look to Miriam and scoff. "And why are you pretending to be a doctor? Who on earth would believe that you are a doctor? You are a disgrace."

Miriam doesn't react to my insults; she's maintaining a sense of calm. To everyone else in the room, she looks like the one telling the truth. My reactions are showing me up, but I'm struggling to control myself.

Miriam throws me a warning glance and addresses me again, still calm, but firmer this time.

"Monty, I don't think this is the place, do you? Wouldn't it be better for everyone if you just came away and we can talk?" She looks over to Susannah and Steve, their faces are stricken. "We want to make sure everyone stays safe."

Anger burns inside my chest. Her threat is subtle enough that they don't see it. They don't know what she's capable of.

"Don't you dare threaten them!" I scream at Miriam, before shouting to Steve and Susannah. "Get out of here, both of you." They look to Miriam who nods her approval. I don't know who she thinks she is.

They leave us and I focus all of my hatred and stare directly into Miriam's eyes. I hate her. I hate her with everything I have, everything I am. She has ruined my perfect evening. The one last chance I had at a glimpse of happiness. Miriam sits at Susannah's table and motions for me to do the same. I stay standing.

"I thought we could sit and talk now that they have gone," she says.

Barely minutes earlier, I was sitting at this table having the most wonderful time, feeling the warmth and care of everyone around it. I will not ruin that memory by sitting here with her.

"Very well, Monty. If that's the way it has to be. I'd much prefer you came back willingly and I'm sure that's what you would prefer, too. But if you won't comply, then I will have to insist that we leave here immediately."

I want to scream and shout. I want to turn the tables and chairs over. I want to smash her face into the kitchen counter. How could things have gone so wrong? How can she be here, holding me to ransom? None of it makes any sense and I am furious at myself for letting it happen.

There is no sign of George. I hope he is hanging his head in shame somewhere. Most likely he is preparing for my return.

The master becomes the prisoner. How ironic.

"Monty, we'd like to leave now." Miriam stands and the police adjust their position, making it abundantly clear that I don't have a choice.

"What has she told you?" I shout at them. "Everything she has told you is a lie. I haven't done anything wrong. You have no right to make me leave here."

Miriam feigns a concerned and regretful look. She is a fantastic actress; I have to give her credit for that.

"I am so sorry, Monty, but we will be leaving now, and you will be coming with us." She nods to the police officers, and they walk purposefully towards me.

A wave of fury crashes through me. I can't let them take me. If I do, I'm done for. Miriam clearly had this all planned out. I have nothing.

I turn away from them and run for the kitchen door and slam it behind me. It jars as it hits one of the officers in the shoulder, and barely slows them as they chase me up the stairs. Harry and Joseph poke their heads out of their room at the commotion. I can't look at them. What must they think? I make it to the top of the stairs before I feel one of the police officers grab me. Then I feel the weight of the other one on me and I can't run anymore.

I try to twist my arms and legs free, but they have me. I am panting and my pulse has skyrocketed. I can't see what's happening. I can taste blood. It feels like I'm rolling down a hill, my vision changing so quickly that I never really see anything.

I hear their words; they sound something like the words you hear on TV when someone is arrested. I hear Miriam's voice mixed in. I sink into it and let it happen. There will be a moment when I can have my say, but this isn't going to be it.

They are going to take me.

I switch off and replay the evening in my head instead. I remember Susannah's warm embrace, I remember Fran's wide, bright smile. I remember Steve's kindness and acceptance. I inhale deeply and savour the memory of the food, the drinks, and the games. The laughter. I live all of these memories as I am carried out of the house.

They can take me away, but they can't have those memories.

I close my eyes and I replay them time after time as we travel along the bumpy and winding roads.

They will pay dearly for this. I will have them begging for their lives. Begging for forgiveness. Forgiveness that will not come.

Chapter Forty-Six

I feel like I am dreaming. I don't know if I am asleep, and I don't care. I can't remember my last waking moment.

Maybe they killed me.

I picture my father standing in front of me with open arms. He is smiling. He looks alive and dead at the same time. He frightens me, but I want him.

I walk into his arms, and they close around me. It is not the comforting embrace that I felt with Susannah; his arms are hard like the branches of a tree. They splinter and crack and lock into place around me. Pieces of him start to flake away and fall off and they gather at my feet like fallen leaves. They continue to break off and tumble, cascading down my shoulders and back. Pooling at my feet and trapping them.

I am stuck. It is like quicksand, and I can't walk away. I am locked in his cold, sharp embrace. I try to look up. What remains of his arms are heavy on my neck and shoulders. I see his face, blackened and coming away, only emptiness inside. The pieces of his face are falling onto mine. His body is falling away around me. Surrounding me.

My hands are trapped now, pinned to my side. The last pieces of him fall.

I can't move air in and out of my lungs anymore. My face is covered, and I don't see. I breathe in the pieces of him. I feel them fill my insides.

Chapter Forty-Seven

The first thing I notice when I wake is the taste in my mouth. It is disgusting and my tongue is completely bone-dry. I am lying down on my back, and I know that I have been drugged. My head is heavy, and my thoughts are trapped under layers of drug-induced fog. I suspect I have been unconscious for days. I turn my head to the side and my neck hurts. I'm not injured, it's just stiffness.

My eyes are crusted shut. I blink to try and clear them, but it's as though I'm looking through water when I finally manage to force them open.

All I know is that it is daylight and that I am lying on something soft and reasonably comfortable. I take a few long breaths and fight off the nausea that is creeping up on me. I motion to rub my eyes and my hands won't move. I try my feet and it is the same. I try to sit and feel a tightness across my middle forcing me back down.

My eyes start to clear. I am lying on a bed, and I know immediately that it is not my bed. I look around the room as much as I am able. I can't make out anything clearly, but it is obvious even through the haze that this is not my room. This is not even a room in my house.

I am completely strapped to the bed. I laugh, I laugh loudly and heartily. The world has gone to shit, so why not? The stiffness in my neck eases and I turn my head further. I am able to see almost all of the room from where I am lying.

I have never seen a prison cell before. It is remarkably clean and brighter than I would have thought. I inhale deeply. There's a recognisable smell. I can't place it, but it's something I have smelled before. A clean scent with chemical undertones. I blink and my eyes begin to moisten. Some of my eyelashes are stuck together and it feels as though they will rip out if I force my eyes open too quickly.

There is a source of brightness to my right. As my vision adjusts, I realise it is a window. From my angle on the bed, all I can see are clouds and a grey sky. It's a gloomy-looking day out there.

My head feels strangely empty. I feel like I should be panicking or thinking of a plan, weighing up options. But there aren't any. I wonder how Susannah and everyone else are. That must have been terribly frightening for them. I'll explain everything, well, not everything, to them as soon as I can.

It is remarkably quiet. If I strain, I can hear faint footsteps. There is a small, frosted window in the door to my room. I watch for shadows, but nobody comes. I bet they leave you alone for hours in here. Only just enough human contact to keep you alive. I wriggle my wrists and ankles. There is no chance I'm getting out of here.

I think I've been awake for about an hour. There is nothing to confirm that and I am starting to need the toilet. I consider shouting but decide that's probably not the best plan. I need to show compliance and build their trust. Be a model prisoner.

They can't keep me here long-term anyway. They'll soon realise there's nothing to back up Miriam's claims.

I don't want to think about George or Miriam anymore. They don't deserve any of my time. I hear a door closing and muted voices. I think there is a group of people in the room next door. I can't make out any of the voices, not even if they are male or female, but it all sounds very amicable.

I hear the door open and close again and brace myself. It makes sense that I am next. The brightness coming through the small window in the door is blocked by bodies. There must be four or five people standing outside. They are speaking in hushed tones. Clearly, I am not meant to hear them. I might feign sleep, just lie here, and listen to what they say about me. Find out what they know and what kind of trouble I am in. They stop talking and there is a light knock on the door. There's no point hiding or pretending, I am strapped to the bed with no hope of freedom.

"Do come in," I shout jovially. I strain my neck to watch the door open.

Miriam walks in and sits down on the chair next to my bed. I turn my head the other way in mock disgust. I can't bear to look at her. But then it dawns on me. Why is she here? Why is she allowed to be here? She can't just waltz into a prison.

Then where am I? My mind begins to race. My memories of what happened at Susannah's house are unclear. I remember the look on Susannah and Steve's faces. Shame washes over me.

Miriam continues to watch me. She hasn't spoken yet. Thoughts are still rushing through my mind. I don't know where I am, and I am sure that means nobody else knows where I am. Miriam is going to make me disappear.

I look around the four plain white walls, praying that these are not the last four walls I ever see.

"Where am I, Miriam?" I keep my voice as calm as I can. I do not want her to know that I am upset or afraid.

"What do you remember, Monty?"

"Don't fuck with me, Miriam. I have had quite enough of your shit. Whatever you want to do to me, just get it over with. I'm done." I turn my head and look straight up at the ceiling to signal that my contribution to the conversation is over. A pitiful act of defiance, but I have little else available to me.

"Monty, I know you are upset and confused. I understand. Believe me."

"Believe you? Are you fucking kidding me?"

She was right to restrain me. My muscles are straining against the straps that bind me. I know there is no hope, but the anger inside me is much greater than that knowledge and I can't contain it. If I weren't trapped, I would have put her head straight through the window.

I breathe in through my nose and out through my mouth, trying to distance myself from the rage.

"Monty, I want to try something." She sounds apprehensive. "I am going to start talking in a moment and I am not going to stop until I have told you everything I need to say."

I turn to look at her and scrunch my face. "What?"

"I need you to listen, Monty," she says, much more firmly this time.

"Why should I listen to you?"

"I know you don't trust me, Monty."

I snort and return my gaze to the ceiling. "That's the fucking understatement of the century."

"But I think if you knew and understood who I was, that might be different."

I look into her eyes. She appears deeply uneasy.

"I am not who you think I am, Monty."

That I am certain of. I have no idea who this woman is, but one thing is evident: I have massively underestimated her.

"You do know me, Monty. You have known me for some time now."

I had been led to believe that Miriam came into my life through my choices. That I picked her name from a list and could easily have chosen someone else instead. But I have realised that was never true. I have been manipulated all along.

Who is she?

She stops and looks at me with a curious expression on her face, searching for something in my face.

"Please listen, Monty. Please listen and try to understand that everything I tell you is true."

She takes a deep breath and speaks very purposefully, enunciating clearly as though I were hard of hearing.

"My name is Dr Miriam Shaw."

I laugh. This is completely absurd. What does she take me for?

She repeats herself. "You know this, Monty. My name is Dr Miriam Shaw. I am a doctor here at Park Hall psychiatric hospital and I oversee your care."

I look at her. There is not a hint of insincerity in her words or movements. She waits for my reaction and seems relieved when there is none.

She looks at the restraints apologetically.

"We avoid anything physical wherever possible, but you've been extremely violent since you returned."

I shake my head and wait for the punchline, but it doesn't come. A coldness creeps over my skin, making my hair stand on end and my cheeks ripple with goosebumps.

She continues. "Monty, I know you don't see it, but you are my patient. You have been unresponsive for several days, partly due to necessary sedation, but also due to your mental state."

Her voice feels far away, but I can hear it clearly. I take in every word. I want to turn it off, but I force myself to listen. I don't want to hear any of what she is saying, but I can't stop. It's like staring at a car crash. Only in this case, it's the car crash of my life. I can't look away.

"I really am sorry about these restraints, but the last time we tried to tell you that you were in a hospital, tried to explain what was happening, you smashed a window and escaped. Thankfully, nobody was hurt, but we can't take that chance again. I am so sorry, but for now, you've lost the freedoms you had before your escape. We can't have you walking around freely until you're a lot better. I hope you understand."

I try to sit up, but my chest hits the strap anchoring me to the bed. I curse inwardly and the bed wobbles a little. I want to get off this bed and I want her to stop talking. I need to be far away from here, far away from her and everything else. All the lies. I need to get free.

My lungs feel small and there are black spots in front of my eyes. I can't make my breathing keep up; it's getting away from me.

I can't fill my lungs.

I close my eyes tightly and try to concentrate on moving the air in and out, but it won't listen. I can't breathe. My body won't breathe.

Miriam stands and opens the door and I feel two people enter and stand one on each side of the bed. I hear a familiar voice and I look to my right.

"George," I gasp.

He looks concerned. "Monty, I need you to breathe. If you can't do it on your own, we'll have to sedate you again and we don't want that."

I look deep into George's face; he looks thin and more

serious than usual. I hate him. But I also love him, and more importantly, he is here.

"Breathe, Monty. Come on. Stay with us." I hear another voice and I look to my left. It's just George again. He looks more relaxed now. I look at both men standing above me, their faces blur and mix in with the tears forming in my eyes.

I shout and I bang my head violently from side to side, one last attempt to get out of here. I know I am not safe. I cry and I shake, but the bed will not move, and the restraints do not loosen. I am trapped.

"Big breaths, sir. In. Out." I try to follow their instructions, but I feel myself fading away, the black spots swarming together to form a deep hole. I start to fall into it. I hear them discussing my breathing and what they are going to do with me next. It seems I have disappointed them. This did not go according to plan.

I am glad to be free of the restraints at least.

Free.

Now

Dear Doctor Alonge,

I am writing to update you on Mr Montague Barclay.
As you are Mr Barclay's General Practitioner, it is
important that you understand the extent of his condition
and our efforts to manage him here at Park Hall psychiatric
hospital.

As you will be aware, Mr Barclay has a complicated
and extensive history of contact with psychiatric services,
beginning when he was a child.

Approximately two years ago, Mr Barclay felt that his
mental well-being had begun to deteriorate. He had stopped
leaving the house and had begun to experience troubling
thoughts. For many years, Mr Barclay had been under the
care of a community psychiatrist, Dr Pathirana. However,
he did not contact her initially, deciding instead to contact a
private provider. He arranged for a mental health nurse to
visit him daily in his home.

Mr Barclay lives alone in a large, remote country house.
He inherited a substantial amount of money from his
adoptive parents and does not work. Instead, he manages a

portfolio of investments. Until recently, he had maintained the property to a high standard.

The nurse he hired was named George Glover. George worked for Mr Barclay for slightly over twelve months. For the first eleven months, George describes mostly driving Mr Barclay to appointments, some administrative tasks, and conversations. He described Mr Barclay's mental state as unremarkable, although noting that he did not like to discuss the nature of their arrangement and would become avoidant when questioned.

Mr Barclay also had a personal assistant who helped him manage his stocks and shares. She was removed from her role when he was admitted to us.

Although it would have been preferable if Mr Barclay had taken a more traditional route when he felt his mental health was suffering, hiring a private carer does show a level of insight.

After twelve months of this arrangement, Mr Barclay's brother died unexpectedly. Immediately after the funeral, he contacted Dr Pathirana. Again, I feel this shows a good degree of insight and a desire to stay mentally well.

Mr Barclay had not visited Dr Pathirana for several years, and she will provide you with a detailed account of her sessions with Mr Barclay separately. When I discussed their sessions with her, Dr Pathirana described Mr Barclay presenting initially with a normal grief reaction. She did comment that he did not mention his brother's death immediately, choosing instead to focus the session on a friendship he was developing with a man named George. Dr Pathirana suspected he was beginning to develop some delusional beliefs about his relationship with George.

Mr Barclay's mental state deteriorated quickly from this point. Dr Pathirana believes that the catalyst for the behaviour change was the death of his brother. Mr Barclay's adopted family had played a major role in his recovery as a child and the stability of his mental well-being as a man.

The following day, Mr Barclay began exhibiting florid delusions and hallucinations regarding a prisoner supposedly living in his house. George described the episode as "like watching someone acting out their nightmares", and that it was clear that Mr Barclay believed that a prisoner was being held in the basement room of the house. He was able to deduce that the supposed prisoner was named Penny.

Following the episode, Mr Barclay proceeded to wander around the basement moving furniture and tidying up haphazardly for many hours. After tidying, Mr Barclay asked to be taken for a drive. He exhibited unusual behaviour during the drive, including becoming unresponsive briefly. At this point, George drove Mr Barclay home.

Mr Barclay improved significantly in the following days; however, things began to deteriorate further after his second appointment with Dr Pathirana. Mr Barclay had indicated that he may not attend future appointments.

George describes being handed notes or lists that made no sense and instructions that he didn't understand. Mr Barclay began to address George as though he was a member of the family, specifically his uncle on his birth father's side.

At this point, and following an alarming phone call with Mr Barclay, George decided to call Dr Pathirana.

Dr Pathirana subsequently contacted me and asked me to assess Mr Barclay for an inpatient stay and inform me that he was refusing to attend any future community appointments. I arranged to see Mr Barclay at his home the following day, ensuring that Mr Glover understood the procedures, should this become an emergency in the meantime.

Mr Barclay was exhibiting increasingly chaotic behaviour, describing receiving applications for a new assistant to keep captive in his basement. The night before my assessment, George arranged to stay overnight as a precautionary step, after Mr Barclay described a presence at his door. He named the intruder a "she", and whilst he used no names, George suspected that he imagined it was either his doctor or his sister-in-law.

Mr Barclay's final days at home were filled with hallucinations, delusions, bouts of anxiety and paranoia, and periods of both high and low mood. Despite the range and severity of symptoms, he was not considered to be a danger to himself or others.

I attended Mr Barclay's home the following day. Mr Barclay was in a continuous delusional state. He had created a situation where our consultation was an interview, including a pre-meeting that I had arranged with George as a kind of selection process. I view this mostly as a way to protect himself from the truth of his deteriorating mental state.

There were possibly some rare moments of insight. Initially, I was unsure about admission to hospital. I was concerned that any further changes to his life may be detrimental, rather than improve his mental state. However, as the assessment progressed, it became clear that even high-level care in the community would not be suitable.

A moment of particular concern was a direct request from Mr Barclay that he wanted me to stay and live with him. I tested his thinking by asking him how he would react if I were to refuse. I didn't push him too far, as his mood appeared volatile, and his home doesn't offer me the same level of personal protection as my professional environment. I did allow him to show me to "my room". This was partly to assess his delusional thinking and also George accompanied us for safety.

This gave me further opportunity to assess his surroundings. Mr Barclay's house was mostly clean and well-ordered. The basement was crowded and disorganised and filled with expensive, ornate furniture. Some pieces were broken, and they were not arranged as you would expect. He did seem to be enormously proud of this room and certainly visualising something different from what was there.

Towards the end of my assessment, I felt an increasing level of threat. I began to feel that he may not let me leave voluntarily. I allowed him to deliver a long monologue convincing me to stay. This enabled me to see the extent of his delusional thinking. He had created an extensive false reality and was becoming more unwell. Significant changes to his medication were required as well as close monitoring. After becoming angry and highly aggressive, Mr Barclay had to be heavily sedated. Further assessment continued as an inpatient at Park Hall psychiatric hospital.

I thought that a change of environment may help with his delusional behaviour. A challenge to his insight as such. On admission, he had to be routinely sedated for several weeks. When he was not sedated, he would simply shout and scream. I began a new regime of medication for Mr Barclay.

All medication changes, dates, and doses as an inpatient are listed separately at the end of this report.

After the first month, Mr Barclay began to settle into a routine. The medication began to take effect and he became *more responsive and less volatile. Most days he would wake and come to the communal room. He was allowed to walk freely from his room to the communal area. These areas of the hospital are always supervised. He would routinely sit in the same chair, in front of a desk with a computer monitor. This became a part of his ongoing delusions. His thoughts regarding holding a prisoner continued as an inpatient. This time, with me as the subject. He believed me to be his prisoner. He ignored anything I said to contradict this or prove it to be false.*

Mr Barclay often had conversations with the nurses. Only the male nurses and he always referred to them as George. We have a lot of male nursing staff and Mr Barclay didn't acknowledge the changeover of staff. I think this comforted him and allowed him a connection to his life outside of Park Hall hospital. I encouraged the staff to respond and to encourage him to speak, but not to directly lie. He likes to be addressed as "sir" and I encouraged this, too. I feel it allows him to explore both his old and new identities and could help build trust.

Initially, our consultations were short. He would speak and I would listen. He was grandiose during these times and would give me instructions, ignoring any attempts to steer the conversation in a different way. He would often leave the room before I could ask any questions. Any efforts to encourage him to speak or confront reality at this stage would have been futile.

I have discovered that it is important to him to maintain a sense of professionalism and purpose, with a particular fixation on papers and contracts. He refers to communal areas as his office and spends most of his time writing and drawing. He is well supervised but not disturbed during these times.

Mr Barclay is regularly unresponsive. He offers no
insight into these unresponsive moments. I believe they
make up a large part of his inner world and thinking. This
is what makes him particularly difficult to understand and
treat effectively. On assessment, he was calm and detached
and kept asking me questions about hospitality and food.

I reached out to Dr Pathirana to try and get Mr Barclay
to understand that he is now an inpatient. This was largely
unsuccessful, but a useful handover, nonetheless. I suspect
he feels let down and abandoned by her in some way, but he
is simply too unwell for community care.

Following a medication change, Mr Barclay was mostly
unresponsive for ten days. He returned to his usual routine
rather suddenly. I assume this is related to the medication
taking effect, but I can't be sure. This was followed by a
period of increased anger, volatility, and paranoia. These
are unwanted side effects, but worth persevering to see if
they improve the symptoms of psychosis. Mr Barclay's
behaviour started to become more extreme and it became
clear that he believed that he had committed terrible acts.
Murder and mutilation.

I suspect the following events will have been reported
to you directly, but I enclose them for completeness and the
flow of this report.

Mr Barclay subsequently called the police with a report
of the supposed disappearance of Dr Pathirana. Although
access to telephones is not allowed, we discovered that he
used the telephone in one of the consultation rooms. The
telephones do not make external calls, except to the
emergency services. As mentioned, his movements were
restricted, but not completely. He refused to acknowledge
this act and was evasive when the police arrived. The police
were accommodating and only asked the questions they

needed to close the report. No charges were brought, despite their time being wasted, and we explained the situation in detail after they had spoken to Mr Barclay. This was a difficult situation for us to manage as an organisation and we have taken steps to ensure it can't happen again.

Mr Barclay is tortured by visions of physical traumas he has inflicted on others, up to and including their murder. He imagines himself as a ruthless sociopath. As you know, this is not his diagnosis. He occasionally cleans his room using whatever he can find. Often simply moving items or tidying things away. Sometimes he speaks as he moves. He will sometimes engage if disturbed but not always.

Mr Barclay refused consultations for a short period after believing that I had attacked "George" during a consultation. He began by asking me if I wanted to hurt George and became paranoid and anxious while hearing voices.

I believe that Mr Barclay's delusions about being a murderer are fuelled primarily by a feeling of guilt over his father's death, accompanied by a wish to be loved. Something he has lost following his brother's recent death. Mr Barclay's adopted family were very loving towards him and now he has lost that. He doesn't believe that he is grieving, and he has developed coping mechanisms that mostly involve him closing himself off.

I decided to attempt to make Mr Barclay confront the reality of his situation. To do this, I invited a student doctor into one of our consultations. Disappointingly, he treated her as though she were another of his captives. This was a very difficult situation for her, but I feel he was using it subconsciously as a tool to begin to tell his story. He revealed a lot of harrowing detail and described his feelings and remembered experiences as a child. Despite the subject matter, I feel this was a definite step forwards as he talked more honestly and shared his experiences more than in any previous session.

Shortly before his escape, I thought that he was beginning to acknowledge the existence of other staff at the hospital, describing hearing the voices of staff members in the corridor during a conversation with a male nurse. His concentration and energy levels began to improve at this point.

The precursor to his escape was a loss of trust in "George". He became irritated and suspicious of George for not attending a routine consultation. He wouldn't share the details of what was worrying him, but he became acutely paranoid, experiencing auditory hallucinations, and withdrew to his room.

At the final consultation before his escape, he brought a box from his belongings and placed it on the table in the consultation room. The box appeared to contain ashes. We cannot be sure they were human ashes, but the appearance of the box suggests it. We knew that he had the box in his room, it was checked in with various other personal possessions on arrival. I don't know why he brought the box to the consultation but his actions towards us suggested that we should feel threatened by it.

The escape itself was certainly preventable. I openly admit that I pushed him too far. I brought the junior doctor that he had previously met back into the room. I had hoped it would help him understand that he is not a murderer. Her name is Dr Bethany Wagner, and I introduced her to him. He had imagined her as Naomi, a captive he had imprisoned and murdered. His escape was not predicted, and lessons have been learned. Sadly, he will no longer be allowed free rein in the corridor and communal room.

Mr Barclay escaped to his sister-in-law's house. It took us several hours to locate him. Thankfully, nobody was harmed. The family described him as charming and were shocked to hear he was a psychiatric inpatient. They didn't seem to know anything about his history. Mr Barclay had to be detained under the Mental Health Act after refusing to return to Park Hall hospital.

Mr Barclay's biological father was a serial killer. He was never convicted as he died before he could be charged. Mr Barclay killed his father when he was a ten-year-old child in an act of self-defence. The body of a murdered woman was found in the house at the time of Mr Barclay's father's death and Mr Barclay was able to help the police recover multiple buried bodies. As a child, Mr Barclay was forced to be involved with the disposal and burial of his father's victims. One of the victims was Mr Barclay's mother.

He remains an inpatient with us and is currently heavily sedated most of the time. I will write again in six months with a further update report.

I expect him to be with us for some considerable time.
Regards,
Dr Miriam Shaw

THE END

Acknowledgements

Writing and publishing a book is a dream come true, and I can't thank Bloodhound Books enough for turning my dreams into reality. Thank you to Betsy for believing in my story and to Shirley, Tara, and Vicky for your help and expertise. Working with you is a pleasure.

Thank you to my husband, Allen, for being there every step of the way on this journey. I am beyond grateful to have you in my life. Without your constant support, this book wouldn't exist. And to our three remarkable children who make me smile every day and are so excited and proud that Mammy wrote an actual book!

Thank you to my Mam who has always encouraged and shared my love for books, and to Dad, who loved a twisty, dark thriller just as much as I do, even though he always guessed the twist. To my brother, Chris and his wonderful family - your strength is inspiring.

I am so grateful for my friends who have all been incredibly positive and excited about this book. You know who you are, and I can't thank you enough. Special mentions to Lindsay, Jaybird, Lisa, and Anne for always believing in me.

Thank you to Sherryl Clark for being an excellent mentor at the conception of this story and to Matthew Cash – your work is a constant source of inspiration.

A final thank you to Monty, who has lived in my brain for so long that, to me, he is real. The best is yet to come for Monty. Mountains cannot rise without earthquakes.

A note from the publisher

Thank you for reading this book. If you enjoyed it please do consider leaving a review on Amazon to help others find it too.

We hate typos. All of our books have been rigorously edited and proofread, but sometimes mistakes do slip through. If you have spotted a typo, please do let us know and we can get it amended within hours.

info@bloodhoundbooks.com

Printed in Great Britain
by Amazon

34150229R00169